Cover design by Maggie Toussaint

Copyright © 2017 by Maggie Toussaint

Print Book ISBN: 9780983361428

Really Truly Dead, copyright 2016 Maggie Toussaint, Happy Homicides 2 Anthology, Spot On Publishing; copyright 2017, Author's Edition, Muddle House Publishing.

Turtle Tribbles, copyright 2016 Maggie Toussaint, Happy Homicides 3, Spot On Publishing; copyright 2017, Author's Edition, Muddle House Publishing.

Dead Men Tell No Tales, copyright Maggie Toussaint, 2016, Happy Homicides 4, Spot On Publishing; copyright 2017, Author's Edition, Muddle House Publishing

Published in 2017 by Muddle House Publishing

Muddle House Publishing
1146 Tolomato Drive SE
Darien, GA 31305

Acknowledgements

This collection was a long time coming. "Really, Truly Dead" was the first mystery I tried after deciding I wanted to branch out from romantic suspense. The original full-length story got several makeovers before I shelved it. Years went by, and I responded to a call for a romantic mystery for a novella anthology. Since this story was a romantic mystery, I decided to delete 50,000 words, thinking that would be easy. Ha ha on me! It wasn't easy, but I'm very pleased with the result. I'm also thankful to Joanna Campbell Slan and Linda Hengerer for including the Lindsey & Ike Romantic Mystery Novella Series in three successive editions of their Happy Homicides anthology series.

No book is written in a vacuum, and this one took some hand holding. An especially big thank you goes to Kathleen Russell, the editor of *The Darien News*. She walked me through all phases of putting a newspaper together and later gave me the opportunity to write feature articles for the same paper. Atwood the News Hound and Bailey in this story have a lot in common, so thank you, Atwood for being such a stellar role model.

Thanks also to the U.S. Coast Guard Station in Brunswick for their time and expertise in explaining how they search and rescue people lost at sea. Georg Trexler of the McIntosh County Sheriff Office helped with general police details. Beta readers Terry Odell and Nancy J Cohen gave me the fresh eyes I needed for a final read. Any errors in this series are mine and mine alone.

Lindsey & Ike Mysteries

The Complete Novella Series

MAGGIE TOUSSAINT

In recent years, turtle egg poaching became big news in my Coastal Georgia hometown. A man was arrested for stealing turtle eggs. With loggerhead turtles being a protected species, it's a federal crime to steal eggs from their nests. The penalty for violating the Endangered Species Act carries a maximum penalty of one year in prison and $100,000 fine for an individual and a $200,000 fine for an organization.

That got me to thinking about a fictional scenario involving turtle eggs, which is nothing like our real-life incident other than the missing eggs. Writing a second novella in this mystery series helped me to flesh out the developing story of Lindsey & Ike, which I continue in the next installation of this series, "Dead Men Tell No Tales."

I thank the staff at the Georgia Sea Turtle Center on Jekyll Island, GA, for their thorough knowledge of turtles.

The final novella in this series began with a near tragedy in my hometown, a hunting accident, only that accident turned out to be just that. I pushed the envelope by extrapolating the incident into something more for a fictional presentation. Thank you to a certain restaurant for inspiring another scene where Lindsey is to meet a source.

None of the characters in this collection are real, of course, but I am inspired by everyone I meet. Kindnesses and rudenesses alike seem to stick in my head and tumble onto the page.

None of my books would see the light of day without my critique partner Polly Iyer and the encouragement of my husband Craig Toussaint. It truly takes a village to grow a book. All errors in this book are mine and mine alone.

Really, Truly Dead

A Lindsey & Ike Mystery, book 1 of 3

Maggie Toussaint

Chapter 1

The two a.m. call from my aunt got my blood pumping. Daddy's drinking had the family newspaper on the rocks, and now he'd totaled his car. By the time I emailed my boss to let him know I was going home, packed, and hit the road, it was nearly three. The miles between Atlanta and Danville rolled by with me alternating between being thankful Daddy survived and being worried about his mental health.

My first stop in town was the Morrison County Sheriff's Office. My family was a tad off-beat, but we were law-abiding citizens. Until now. I'd never been inside the jailhouse before. For courage, I clipped the leash on my black lab so she could accompany me.

An attractive blonde deputy rose from the reception desk when we entered. Her crisp uniform and bright smile contrasted with the worn-out lobby. "We don't allow dogs in here," she said. "Hey, I know you. You're Lindsey McKay."

I smiled, aware my carrot top had given me away. "Guilty as charged." I squinted discreetly at the shiny name plate on her pocket flap and startled at the familiar name. Sister or wife, I wondered. "Sorry, Deputy Harper. I drove through the night, and I wasn't thinking. Excuse me, while I return Bailey to my car."

"Never mind. It won't take two shakes to out-process your Dad. Bailey can stay." The woman smiled. "I'm Alice Ann Harper. You were in my brother's class."

My jaw dropped. Ike's sister had grown into a beauty. "I didn't know you were a cop."

3

Alice Ann reached under the counter and withdrew papers and a brown paper bag with Daddy's name on it. "The employment opportunities are somewhat limited in Danville."

I nodded. An office door banged open, and a brawny male in a close-fitting white polo shirt navy slacks, and a holstered gun swaggered my way. Age had been kind to Ike Harper. He'd filled out through the shoulders and chest, but his waist was as trim as ever.

"How've you been, hon?" Sheriff Ike Harper crushed me in arms of steel.

Masculine warmth made my cheeks burn. Uh-oh. He still had it, and I didn't want it.

"I'm good. Nice to see you, Ike." I gently pushed against his chest until he released me. "I'm here for my dad. What can you tell me about his wreck?"

Ike squatted and gave my dog the same effusive welcome I'd received. I noticed he wasn't wearing a wedding ring.

"Mr. McKay clipped an oak and rolled his car on Oldham Road at one a.m.," Ike said.

How odd. "What was he doing out so late?"

"He kept muttering about a deer in the road. EMTs checked him out, and he refused transport. My guys brought him here. He has a court appearance for the DUI and a fine. Shouldn't be too bad for his first offense."

My thoughts whirled at the news. "This feels . . . surreal. I mean I knew his drinking increased over the years, but he always drank at home. I'm stunned. Thank you for getting him checked out. That's one thing off my mind."

"He'll come him around now that you're here. On another note, want to get a cup of coffee while you're home? We missed you at the ten-year class reunion last month."

With those lady killer eyelashes and luminous brown eyes, Ike had been a player in high school. That wasn't for me. "I had a conflict with reunion weekend, and no thanks on the coffee. Between tending to Daddy and salvaging the newspaper, my time won't be my own."

Alice Ann slid papers my way. "Sign these forms."

Ike leaned against the counter as I signed. "You still working for that science magazine in Atlanta?"

"Yes. *The Georgia Journal of Science.* I like it there."

4

"They're lucky to have you. If you need anything while you're home, just ask. I'm swamped today coordinating the search teams looking for Judge Sterling, but I should be free soon."

"The judge is missing?"

"His wife reported his disappearance at dawn." Ike waved and headed to his office. "Good to see you, Linds."

I collected the bag of Daddy's things and trailed Alice Ann down a long corridor, Bailey padding silently beside me.

My plan was to be stern, but I caved when I saw my father behind bars. In the seven hours since his accident, the cuts on his face and arms had scabbed over. Both eyes were blackened. Alcohol fumes permeated the air. "Daddy?"

He perched on the narrow bottom bunk. "Lindsey? That you?"

Alice Ann waved me inside the unlocked cell. "Take your time."

Bailey trotted in and licked my father's toes. "Who's this fine retriever?" my father asked, as he patted my dog.

"That's Bailey. I told you I'd rescued her from the shelter when we talked in March. On your birthday." I knelt and pulled his shoes from the brown bag. He'd lost more weight since I'd seen him at Christmas. With Mama overseas, was he even eating regularly? My heart sunk. Why didn't Aunt Fay call me earlier?

"Where's your brother?" he asked.

The question caught me off-guard. "Colin's dead, Daddy."

His brow furrowed, and then he nodded. "Forgot."

Oh, dear. My father was worse off than I thought. I helped him with his shoes. "How do you feel?"

"Sore. And hungover." He met my gaze. "You going to yell at me?"

"You're making bad choices. That wreck. You could've died. We'll discuss this later, when you have a clear head. Let's get you home. Can you stand?"

Together we walked down the corridor. Why was he thinking about Colin now? After my brother was lost at sea ten years ago, my family fractured. At least I'd gotten counseling in college and started over. For years, my father had refused to talk about Colin.

A young boy burst in the sheriff's lobby. He looked to be about eight and he had Ike's eyes and hair.

"Dad, hurry," the boy shouted. "There's something dead under the bridge. Can I have it?"

5

The blood drained from my face. I froze in mid-step. What father allowed his kid to collect dead animals?

Ike ruffled the boy's hair. "Easy, Trent. You've shocked Miss McKay. She doesn't know the animal refuge needs road kill for their injured hawks."

My heart started beating again. "Thanks for the explanation."

Trent tugged on Ike's arm. "Come on. Someone else might get it. I wanna feed the hawks."

Reassured all was well, I waved goodbye, loaded my father in my car, and headed home.

We took Dock Road to River Road, passing the bronze historical marker outside St. Paul's. My crazy ancestor, Beulah Lindsey McKay, had saved the church from fire-wielding Yankees over a hundred and fifty years ago. Other towns had bats in the belfry. We had Beulah in the bell tower.

"What's going on with the newspaper?" I'd helped with the family paper in high school so I knew the routine. This was Tuesday. The *Gazette* should be already made up. If not, I'd need a miracle to launch this week's edition by tomorrow.

He hung his head. A lot of gray silvered his hair. Seemed like he'd aged twenty years in the nine months since I'd last seen him.

"A fellow writes a few editorials, and everyone's a critic," Daddy said. "Cut me some slack here. I've got one heckuva hangover."

I made a mental note to read those columns as I parked in front of our two-story Victorian home. "That reporter still with you?"

"Robert quit months ago."

Swallowing a bitter retort, I helped my father up the porch steps. I should've been reading the online edition to follow the news from home, but I stayed so busy, I'd deleted the latest links unread.

White paint curls furred the plank siding and the gingerbread trim. "The house needs work."

"So it does." Dad grunted and continued to his bed, nudging his shoes off with his toes. "Ellen's at the paper."

My dad's assistant had been two years ahead of me in school. According to Aunt Fay's emails, Ellen's divorce had been finalized six months ago.

"I'll check in with her next. Get some rest. We'll talk later."

I lugged my suitcase in and then drove up River Road to the brick newspaper building. The shoulder of the road by the *Gazette* was jammed with cars. What now?

Bailey and I hurried into the *Gazette*. "Ellen?" My voice echoed through the building. How odd. Maybe Ellen was out back. With growing unease, I clipped on Bailey's leash and trotted out the side door to the waterfront. A murmur from the crowd reached me just before the Danville River Bridge. A pungent odor brought tears to my eyes, and a dark stain marred the embankment. Summer flies buzzed.

I threaded my way through the throng, my dog at my side until Ellen Mattingly snagged my arm. Despite the August heat, my father's assistant looked cucumber-cool in her khaki pants and white blouse. Long hair hung down her back.

"Lindsey," Ellen said. "Hold up. This is a crime scene."

"Hey. Good to see you." I hugged her. "What's the story here?"

Moisture brimmed in her blue eyes. "Judge Alan Sterling is dead."

News reporting ran in my veins, but I wasn't prepared for this. "Oh, no. What happened?"

"Leroy Brown over at the shrimp docks saw him before all the cops arrived." Tears rolled down her face. "Judge Sterling was stabbed to death."

My thoughts hit turbocharge. The judge was dead. Really, truly dead. Stabbed. Not an accident.

I patted Ellen's back. "It's going to be all right."

My gaze traveled to the concrete pillars supporting the Danville Bridge. Overhead traffic thumped by in a blur. I understood their haste. Ten years ago I felt the same need to hurry out of town.

Bailey tugged the leash out of my palm and bolted inside the forbidden zone. My stomach knotted as she headed straight for the dead man.

Chapter 2

Judge Sterling. I knew him, his wife, his kids. His son, Alan Jr., had been in my grade. Thoughts whirling, I chased my dog.

I stumbled to a halt near Bailey and tried not to inhale. If I didn't look down, I could pretend I wasn't standing over a corpse.

"Your dog." Sheriff Ike Harper had a tight grip on Bailey's leash.

"Sorry about that. She jerked the leash out of my hand."

The sheriff's glittering gaze pinned me like a laser. "I can't have animals running loose in my crime scene."

Judge Sterling could've been sleeping if not for the darkly stained grass. He wore black wingtips and a conservative dark suit, though his white dress shirt was crimson. A knife handle protruded from his belly.

"Sorry." Bile rose in my throat, and I closed my eyes and willed my nausea to pass. Where were my journalistic instincts? I summoned a question from the goo of my mind. "How long has he been dead?"

"Don't know yet. We're still securing the scene."

"What did you find so far?"

"His watch is missing." The sheriff waved his deputies farther out with the crime scene tape.

"This was a robbery?"

The sheriff handed me Bailey's leash. "I don't know yet." He swore under his breath. "There goes your dog again. Get her out of here."

A river of sweat coursed down my back as I chased Bailey. She darted here and there, nose to the ground, just out of reach. I accidentally saw the judge's fly-covered face and lost my fast-food breakfast.

Bailey stopped twenty feet from the body and barked. I wiped my mouth, hurried over to her, and wrapped the leash twice around my hand. On the ground was a photograph of a flower.

A vivid pink rose. Maybe even Inverness Pink, named after our local river, a variety of rose the judge had developed. Sheriff Harper appeared at my shoulder. "Don't touch that." He waved Alice Ann over to bag the photo.

Ike marched us to the newly erected tape barrier. "Keep Bailey under control. If you mention the photo to anyone, I'll impound your dog."

Mortified, I scurried through the crowd, up the riverbank, and into the newspaper office. I took a few minutes in the bathroom to freshen up. Ellen waylaid me afterward. "You saw Judge Sterling?"

"I did, but I forgot to be a reporter."

"I snapped a few pictures, but I'm not sure they're relevant," Ellen admitted. "You're here to run the paper?"

I nodded. "Temporarily. What's the deal?"

Ellen composed herself as we strolled to the break room. "We've lost some big accounts. It's been rough."

I grabbed two Cokes from the fridge. "Make a list of the accounts. I'll call them before I leave town."

Ellen opened her drink. "You always could talk the hide off an alligator."

"I wish it were that easy." I sipped my Coke greedily. "What about the articles? Who writes them?"

"Mostly me. George has good intentions, but . . ."

No wonder Aunt Fay was worried. "How long has this been going on?"

Ellen frowned. "Pretty much all year."

My emotions seesawed into the anger realm again. "I'm surprised. Everything was fine at Christmas."

Ellen sighed. "We were making it work, until the advertisers pulled out."

"Thanks for all you've done to keep it going. Is this week's edition ready to go to press?"

"No. We run a few days behind now. Can't catch up, but this week's stories are written. You want to see them?"

9

You couldn't run a successful paper if you couldn't deliver the news on schedule. "Yes. And arrange for someone to watch your kids tonight. We're working late."

~*~

At eight that night, I drove home with a stiff neck and the dream of crawling into bed. I had done what I could, reworking all the stories for this edition, calling folks for article quotes, and writing a feature on the alleged murder of Judge Sterling. Ellen's crowd pictures were great. I used a large color photo of shocked faces above the fold on page one.

"Everything under control?" Daddy asked from the deep shadows of the porch.

I nodded, yawning and flipping on the lights. I could sleep for the next seven years. "Why didn't you join us at the office?"

Daddy exhaled slowly. "Can't do it."

Everything in me went still at his announcement. "Why? Don't you care about the paper anymore?"

"I've been going through the motions of life for a long time, and I didn't want you to know. With your mother. With the newspaper. I started changing after Colin went missing."

His melancholy mindset surprised me. "Colin drowned, Daddy."

He didn't answer. Ice tinkled as he raised an amber-filled glass to his lips.

Anger flashed like heat lightning through my tongue. "Will drinking solve anything?"

Daddy studied his empty glass. Minutes ticked off my life clock as I waited. I didn't expect him to quit on anything. He'd never done it before.

"I'm trying to forget my failures."

"It isn't working. Why were you drinking and driving the other night?"

"I had an errand to run." Daddy stared into his glass. "Thought I could handle it."

"What if you'd hit someone? What if you killed someone?"

He lifted his gaze to the distant river, even though it was now too dark to see it. "You're making too much of this."

"You're making too little of this. Have you talked to anyone about your problem?"

He didn't answer. Heat flamed my face. Didn't he care about anything besides his next drink? Disgusted, I headed for my room. I couldn't stay in Danville for long, but how could I leave when my father was a mess?

I felt a sudden gust of anger at my mother. She'd chosen to run away to a Third World country where no one could contact her.

Leaving me to deal with Daddy on my own.

~*~

Dark circles ringed newly widowed Trish Sterling's eyes, but her jaunty nautical scarf, pressed slacks, silky blouse, and gold shoes gave her a polished appearance. She managed to get one step from the newspaper's front desk where I sat, when a clutch of papers slid out of her hand and littered the floor. She burst into tears.

I walked her to a chair. "It's okay. You'll get through this."

Trish pawed through her purse. Grateful for something to do, I plucked tissues from Ellen's desk.

"Thanks," Trish managed between sniffles. "It's been three days, I should be cried out by now."

I sat down next to her. "Grieving is an individual process."

"I'm glad you're here, Lindsey." Trish dabbed her eyes. "It would've been awkward talking about Alan's obituary with George."

"Why?" Daddy and the judge grew up together.

She wrung her hands in her lap. "Because of those editorials George wrote."

I exhaled slowly. "What did he say?"

Trish closed her eyes for a moment. "Alan wanted a saw mill here, and George got it sidelined. Then they had an ugly shouting match at Shorty's Market."

This woman was a gentle soul who painted watercolor landscapes. She must've been horrified at two grown men hurling insults over cans of creamed corn and Vienna sausages. "I had no idea. How embarrassing."

Trish nodded, but the silence felt prickly to me. I scrambled from my seat, collected her papers, and handed the sheaf to her. "I assume you brought Alan's obituary."

She pushed the papers at me. "I couldn't write it. Will you? I couldn't deal with the funeral parlor man either. Too grim for me. Everything you need to write it is here. The graveside service is Monday at McKay Cemetery."

11

I understood the pain of losing a loved one, but her request was unusual. "I can draft something, but you should proof it."

Trish collected her golden purse and rose. "Whatever you write is fine."

I blinked at her sudden composure.

She paused at the door. "It's a shame about Alan's Rolex. He loved that watch. It was the only one he'd found that was truly salt water resistant."

Trish climbed in her Lincoln Town car. A Jack Russell terrier patrolled the top of her seat. How had shy Trish Sterling handled marriage to the extroverted judge? She must've been uncomfortable with his very public life.

Was there a reason why she refused to write her husband's obituary?

It bothered me that I was even thinking such thoughts about a longtime family friend. I watched as Trish drove away.

A familiar silver Jeep pulled up, and Ike Harper strode in. "I saw Trish leaving."

Ike's belt carried enough police equipment to outfit a SWAT team. Hand cuffs, a riot baton, a spray canister, a handgun, and a cell phone dangled like ornaments around his trim hips. The sheriff was on the case.

I edged behind the reception counter to minimize the testosterone poisoning. "She brought me Alan's personal records for his obituary."

"I need copies for my investigation."

"No problem." I ran the papers through the copy machine behind me. "Any progress in your investigation?"

"For starters, we're looking into people who lost cases tried in his courtroom. Any of them might've had a grudge."

That would be a lot of people to check out.

"Do you need any tech assistance? I'm good with databases, and I'd like to do something to help. Alan Sterling helped me get my job in Atlanta by recommending me to my boss."

Ike's gaze turned icy. "I got this. Civilians shouldn't nose around in police business."

My temper flared. "I didn't say you couldn't handle it. I was trying to be helpful. Data review is one of my strengths."

He leaned heavily across the counter, entering my air space. His wintergreen-scented breath caressed my face, making my pulse spike.

"I'm good at what I do. Stay out of it, Linds, or I'll lock you in the bell tower."

My hand shot up to smack him. I came to my senses just in time. "I'm not crazy or naked." My ancestress who'd saved the church was a noted eccentric. Her state of undress had been omitted on the church's historical marker.

His dark eyes burned into me. "But you're a McKay."

"Always."

"I'm planning on catching that killer. Mark my words."

But that forty-eight-hour golden window for catching the bad guy had already passed. I bit my tongue rather than remind him. However, I couldn't control my expression. Ike must have read my mind, because he stomped out of the newspaper.

As I watched his retreating back, I thought, *Serve him right if I solve the murder before he does. Then I'll lock him in the bell tower. Naked.*

Chapter 3

The sweltering cemetery teemed with mourners. I accompanied Daddy, Aunt Fay, Uncle Henry, and Cousin Janey and hoped the Presbyterian minister kept his remarks brief. My sleeveless black sheath was soaked. Nothing like August in coastal Georgia.

The judge's children were here. Alan Jr. stood beside the mahogany casket with his pregnant wife and four children. Beside him was his sister Emily and brother Stephen. Emily's marriage had been a one-month miracle. Rumor had it, Stephen had a male life partner in Jacksonville.

As the eldest son of a rich man, Alan Jr. had everything he'd ever wanted, as long as he heeded his father's wishes. The judge cut Alan off when he married during his first year of college and chose teaching instead of a law career.

Alan no longer had that glow of affluence. A dryer sheet hung out of his pants leg. His narrow tie was framed by a dingy white shirt that had never seen an iron, and his wife looked like she was roasting in her dark tent dress. Poor woman.

After the ceremony, folks visited in the cemetery because there wasn't a place in the county big enough to hold all of us. Daddy, Aunt Fay, and Uncle Henry strolled over to Trish. Cousin Janey left to retrieve her daughter from her ex, and I decided to extend my condolences to Alan Jr.

As I approached, a tot scampered across the graves, climbing over the headstones in her way. Alan shoved his son's hand in mine and bolted after the escapee.

I squatted beside the child. "Hello, I'm Lindsey. What's your name?"

He pulled his thumb out of his mouth long enough to say "Gene." Success. "How old are you, Gene?" He held up four fingers. Smart kid.

Alan returned with the wandering child in his arms and kissed my cheek. "Sorry. This is Sally. We should've named her Greased Lightning. How've you been?"

"Fine. Sorry about your father." Sally's legs pumped a mile a minute, and a distinctive odor emanated from her diaper. If I had kids, they'd arrive potty trained.

His eyes looked sad. "The old man was a tyrant, but he was my dad. I'll miss him."

Alan's wife waddled up to us, two kids in tow. If you lined up their children sequentially, they would resemble stair steps.

"Hi, I'm Daisy, and I'm roasting."

I immediately liked her for her plain speaking. "I'm Lindsey. I attended school with Alan."

"Nice to meet you." Daisy turned to Alan. "The diaper bag's at your mother's, and it's needed. Let's go." They made their goodbyes and left.

Alone, I stood in the shade and studied faces. I'd been too busy to give this any thought, but who killed the judge? Brodie from the hardware store? Alice Ann from the sheriff's department? Shorty from the market? Misty from the beauty shop? Everyone looked innocent.

"You seem troubled," the sheriff said.

Ike Harper heated my patch of shade to boiling. His thick eyelashes swept my length, and my hormones rioted. Mercy.

"I saw you with Alan's boy," Ike said. "You're good with kids."

Even the air was Ike-scented. Ocean fresh with a hint of musk. "Kids are okay."

He edged closer and whispered. "I saw you observing everyone, Linds. Stay out of my investigation."

A threat. "How do you know what I'm doing?"

His expression warmed. "Sweetheart, you're an open book. Besides, I'm a highly skilled investigator, remember?"

Foiled, I cleared my throat. "Any luck narrowing down the suspects?"

"I've talked to everyone on my suspect list. I know who has an alibi for the time of death, which the medical examiner has set at eleven

15

p.m. I'll know more when I get the fingerprint analysis of the murder weapon from the state crime lab."

"What about that photo my dog found?"

"Don't know if it ties in."

"Bailey was certain it was important."

He braced one arm against the tree and leaned close enough for his breath to tickle my ear. "Forget the case. How about lunch tomorrow? Say yes, Linds."

His voice resonated deliciously through me. Lunch with the sheriff would go down easy, but I didn't need another tie to the community. "Thanks, but no thanks."

"It would be good between us," he whispered.

A flash of molten heat shot down my spine. I slipped out from under his arm. "That's exactly what I'm afraid of."

Chapter 4

When I came downstairs for breakfast the next day, Daddy was sipping coffee. I let Bailey out and poured myself some. "You working today?" I asked.

"Nope."

My jaw clenched. "Daddy, my job's in Atlanta. I have to return soon."

"The Colonel and I are birding today. There are interesting birds at the county's north end just now."

He probably hadn't had a day off in ten years.

"How will you approve my decisions? What enticements should I offer advertisers?"

"Whatever you do is fine."

What if Daddy didn't snap out of it in two weeks? I needed him to accept his responsibilities. "We'll talk more about this at dinner."

"How about breakfast?"

I glared at him over my cup. "I don't eat breakfast. For a detail-oriented man, you have a selective memory."

"I eat breakfast."

Something inside me snapped. My cup hit the counter hard, and coffee sloshed over the rim. "Do you want a caretaker? A pretend wife?"

"I have a wife," he shot back, "though she wants nothing to do with me."

17

Mama was off on her third international mission trip, but they hadn't been close in a while. "Forgive me. I'm under a lot of pressure to do your job and mine too. Time is precious."

"Let me rephrase. If you'll join me for breakfast tomorrow, I'll cook," he said.

It was all he'd asked for since I'd been home. I caved. "It's a date."

As I walked to the door dressed in heels and a suit, I glanced at him, sprawled in his easy chair as if he didn't have a care in the world. But I knew better. Moreover, I knew something was up. What was he hiding?

~*~

My coworker had the door unlocked and the lights on by the time I arrived. Ellen and I exchanged greetings and got to work finishing the paper. After it went to the printers, I posted the judge's obit on our website, and began crunching numbers. A courier picked up my work for the *Georgia Journal of Science*.

I was wondering about lunch when the front door opened. Ellen's mother had already picked her up for an early lunch twenty minutes ago, so I hurried to greet our customer. Bailey trotted after me.

Thomas Mattingly, Ellen's ex, still looked lean and lanky. What was he doing with a potted plant? "Thomas. How's the shrimp business these days?"

"Doing good." He glanced around the office. "Is Ellen here? I brought her flowers."

He wore clean jeans and an Oxford shirt, but his shoes were tar speckled. His grocery store cologne made my eyes water. I accepted the hyacinths. "She's out of the office, but I'll make sure she gets them. Is there a message?"

"The flowers are from Thomas. That's the message."

"Got it."

Thomas leered at me. "You shouldn't have dogs in a place of business. It's unprofessional."

Why was he picking on Bailey, who sat straight and tall by my side? The ringing phone saved me from spouting off. "Anything else I can do for you?"

"Nah." He left.

"*Gazette*."

"Lindsey?"

I sank into Ellen's chair. "Hello, Aunt Fay."

"I saw Thomas Mattingly pass by here with hyacinths."

"He left them for Ellen."

Aunt Fay snorted. "He's tired of frozen dinners and wants her back. Is she reconciling with him?"

"She hasn't mentioned it, but I'm famished. Have you eaten?" We agreed to meet at Kingfishers in fifteen minutes.

When Ellen returned from lunch, her smile faded. "What's this?"

"Thomas brought you flowers."

Ellen hurled the pot in the trash and swore under her breath.

Nope, not reconciling. "You want to talk about it?"

Her long hair shimmered as she paced the office. "He owes me months of child support, and he buys flowers? If I didn't have this job, we'd starve."

"What a jerk. I'm sorry for accepting them."

"I should've left him years ago."

"Aunt Fay invited me to lunch at Kingfishers, but I can cancel."

"I'm fine." A slow smile tugged at Ellen's lips. "I'm surprised Fay will go there. She swore she'd never return after they banned her raccoon from the premises."

"Aunt Fay takes Scarlet everywhere. I want Bailey with me, but she's not invited to lunch." I shouldered my purse and drove to Kingfishers.

Aunt Fay had a table on the far side of the packed restaurant, so I threaded my way through the gauntlet of tables. Alice Ann Harper paused while buttering a roll to wave at me. I waved back, noticing that she was dining with a young man. Cousin Janey lunched with an elderly couple I didn't recognize. Real estate clients, I guessed.

Brodie Dwyer from the hardware store rose to shake my hand. "Great paper last week, little McKay. Keep up the good work, and I'll advertise again."

"Thanks."

Sarah Tidewater from the phone company captured my attention next. "Great mullet wrapper. Welcome home, dear."

I blushed. "Thanks."

Finally, I reached our table. "Did they run out of the special yet?"

"I ordered it for both of us," Aunt Fay said.

"Good. I'm starved."

"Everyone's talking about last week's paper, so you're on the right track there, but what about George? I haven't seen him in days."

My good mood fizzled. I sipped my sweet tea. "Daddy's in denial."

The overhead light glinted off my aunt's glasses. She patted my wrist. "Don't leave. He needs you."

Dishes clinked. Conversations pulsed around us. "I live and work in Atlanta."

"So you do. Is George talking about the accident?"

The food came. Heavenly smelling fried shrimp, French fries, coleslaw, and green beans heaped on platters. If I ate like this every day, I wouldn't fit in my Atlanta power suits. "We don't talk much."

"Pity."

~*~

By closing time, I had a handle on the paper's outstanding debt. The newspaper was fixable. Deep in thought, I almost didn't hear the front door open.

"Where are my flowers?" Thomas Mattingly demanded.

Ellen's chair squeaked. "All I want from you are child support checks."

My hand on my dog's neckerchief, I hovered in the hallway, out of sight but ready to help Ellen if needed me.

"You'll be fixed for money once you come home."

"We're divorced. I'm never coming home to you."

"If you don't, I'm taking the kids."

"Your threats don't work anymore. Grow up and pay your bills."

I'd had enough. I motioned Bailey toward the lobby. "Get 'em."

Bailey started barking. I followed her and stood beside Ellen. Bailey backed Thomas up to the door. "Time to go, Thomas," I said over the barking dog.

Ellen echoed my words. "Get out of here."

Thomas turned red in the face and stomped away.

"He's a bully, but I stand up to him now." Ellen gripped her arms across the front of her chest so tightly her knuckles turned white.

His anger concerned me. "Ask the sheriff for a restraining order."

"I can't. Then Thomas wouldn't make the effort to see the girls."

Ellen leaned down and hugged Bailey. "But you, dear heart, are the best. You can have my entire box of breath mints. Good dog."

~*~

Daddy's big talk about breakfast together the next morning turned out to be a fairytale. I even tried to wake him, but he rolled over. So much for getting him to realize he had a problem. At least, I was making headway at the paper. As I wrestled with the ad log, my boss called.

"Ready for civilization yet?" Ted Townsend asked.

His deep voice reminded me of Starbucks coffee, of Metro buses, and Atlanta gridlock. The six hours between us seemed infinite. "I'm needed here. Did my work package arrive?"

"Yes. I was shocked about Alan Sterling. Did they catch his killer?"

"The sheriff's working on it."

"Is he qualified? I've got connections with the GBI."

Ike would hate Georgia Bureau of Investigation intrusion. "The sheriff's no dummy."

"Let me know. We can't have killers on the loose."

No joke. "Agreed."

"You sound different. Are you quitting, Lindsey?"

His question surprised me. "Not planning on it, sir. Aren't you satisfied with my work?"

"Yes, but I need a favor. Bob Harvey in ecology missed his deadline because of his wife's heart attack. Would you finish his assignment?"

The old me would've said, *sure.* The new me sent my sympathy to Bob and asked, "What's in it for me?"

"I can't pay overtime, but I won't bill your time as leave until you turn in Bob's piece. You'll still have two weeks of leave if you need them. I think that's overly generous on my part."

It was surprisingly generous. "Deal. I'll watch for the package."

A few pleasantries later, I ended the call. Just when I thought I was caught up, more work came my way. But at least I had made headway. Ted had recognized my worth to him and my obligations to my family. Speaking of family, I needed to touch bases with my father.

It was half past ten. He should be awake by now. His head should be clear. My to-do list could wait an hour. I wouldn't mind working late if Daddy was on the right track.

I strode briskly into the reception area with Bailey at my heels. "I need to go and talk with my father. Everything okay here?"

"Peachy, boss." My coworker grinned. "Ten new subscriptions today. You're amazing."

Heat scorched my cheeks. "Thanks, but I'm a short-term fix. How's that archive search for past crimes coming along?"

Ellen grimaced. "It would be easy if everything was computerized. Searching old records manually is the pits."

"Yes, but this retrospective will sell papers."

"How do you know?"

I shrugged. "I just know. People are interested in the past."

"I'm interested in paying bills. I'm headed to the Thrift Shop at lunchtime to look for kid shoes."

And I thought I had problems! Poor Ellen had larger issues than a father on the skids.

There was no traffic on River Road, but the oak canopy provided nice shade. At home, I dropped my purse on the hutch in the foyer. "Daddy?" The house was silent. I knocked on his bedroom door, called him again, and peeked in.

He was still in bed. "Wake up."

His eyes opened slowly. "Lindsey."

At least he knew my name. "Get dressed. I'll make coffee."

"Sleepy." He nestled deeper into his pillow.

I pulled down the covers. "We need to talk."

"No talking."

"Get up. You missed breakfast. You're missing life."

He stared at me dully. "Why don't you leave? Everyone leaves. Why should today be any different?"

His words stung. "I'm here now."

I found his robe, put it on him, and gave him coffee in the kitchen. Daddy shielded his eyes against the bright sunlight streaming in through the windows.

"I'm worried about you." I started his breakfast. "Aunt Fay and Uncle Henry are worried about you. You're making bad choices."

"A man's life is his own to do with as he sees fit."

"You could've hurt someone the other night."

"I didn't hurt anyone."

Sirens wailed in the distance. Had the sheriff's son discovered another dead animal? "Make me understand. I want to help."

"I'm tired. I drink so I can sleep. When I don't drink, I can't sleep."

I held his gaze. "Have you seen a doctor?"

"I'm not sick."

The sirens were much louder now. Bailey's ears cocked to listen.

"There's all kinds of sick."

Daddy slapped his palm on the table. "I'm not seeing a shrink. Just because I'm a McKay doesn't mean I'm crazy."

Good old Beulah. We had her to thank for our crazy McKay label. "You need help."

"I'm fine."

The sirens were too loud to speak over. Bailey howled until the sirens stopped outside. Ears ringing, heart pounding, I opened the door. Sheriff Ike Harper and three deputies stood on the front porch.

"Step aside, Lindsey," Ike said.

His aura of violence electrified the air and iced my thoughts. "What's going on?"

A deputy flashed a paper at me. "Arrest warrant for George McKay."

The sheriff breezed inside and walked over to Daddy. "Mr. McKay, you're under arrest."

As the sheriff Mirandized my father, I fought back tears. Did Ike see a loving father? Or did he see an angry old man?

"What's the charge?" I asked.

"The murder of Judge Sterling," the deputy said.

Murder? The ringing in my ears intensified. After allowing my father to dress, the deputies led him out to a squad car.

"You've made a mistake," I told Ike. "Daddy didn't kill anyone."

The sheriff smoothed a stray hair from my brow. "The evidence says otherwise. Your father's fingerprints are on the murder weapon."

"You've got the wrong man. He was in your jail when it happened."

"George didn't wreck his car until one. The judge died two hours prior. George had means, motive, and opportunity."

"I don't believe you." My insides felt squishy.

The hard glint in his eyes softened. "Should I call your aunt to come over?"

I didn't want sympathy. "No. My father's innocent. I'm calling Billy Mertz, and we're getting Daddy out on bail."

"These things take time, and we've got the right man. Between those fingerprints, the scathing editorials your father ran, the shouting match they had last week at Shorty's, and the public threat to kill the judge at the County Commissioners meeting, George McKay is the only suspect."

A public threat? Okay, maybe those editorials were stronger than they should've been. But murder? My entire world was unraveling. "What about Judge Sterling's court cases? What about his personal life? Did you look into that?"

Ike shook his head. "George has been our prime suspect all along."

"What about known felons?" My collar felt too tight. "What about, um, that druggie guy, Jerome Stewart? Maybe he killed the judge for his watch."

"Jerome's dope dealing days are long over. He's a drug rehab counselor over in Brunswick. He was never a suspect. Take a deep breath."

"Have you questioned Daddy?"

"I interviewed him the day after the murder, same as I talked to everyone else. Based on the time of death, your father is the only suspect who doesn't have a solid alibi."

Why had Ike and Daddy kept that questioning secret until now? "My father isn't a murderer. And he doesn't have the missing Rolex."

"Someone else could have stolen the watch after the judge was killed. We may never find it. Your father's changed, Lindsey. He's not the man he used to be."

The sheriff's parting words hit a nerve. Hadn't I been fussing at Daddy about his bad choices? A whisper of doubt lodged in my thoughts.

Chapter 5

The lawyer assured us he'd work on getting Daddy out of jail. After our visit with the attorney, I suggested we hold a strategy session, so we gathered at Aunt Fay's for lunch.

"This is ridiculous." Aunt Fay tore iceberg lettuce into huge chunks. "A McKay arrested for murder."

Uncle Henry eased his bulk into the chair. "The charges against George are serious. We'll get him released on bail, but we should nose around."

"Why don't we hire a detective?" I asked.

"No one talks to outsiders," Aunt Fay said, handing tea all around. "Henry can make inquiries at the bank and with his friends. I'll shake the grapevine at the Post Office, the bridge club, and the DAR. You and Janey can poke around in the judge's personal life. We'll compare notes."

My gut hurt as Judge Sterling's corpse surfaced in my thoughts. I'd never forget that blood-soaked shirt. And whoever killed him was still walking around Danville.

"He married Trish, and they raised three kids who grew up and moved away," I said. "Besides his professional career, what else is there to know about Judge Alan Sterling?"

Aunt Fay and Uncle Henry exchanged glances.

"What?" I asked.

Uncle Henry stared into his tea. "Alan led a double life. For starters, he owns The Oaks Motel."

I shrugged. "So?"

"So," Aunt Fay pushed her eyeglasses up her nose. "Alan got around. His car is often at the motel. Angie Johnson—she's the manager there—and Trish can't stand each other."

I blinked, too stunned to move more than my eyelids. "The judge and Angie were involved?"

"And then some." Uncle Henry tugged at his necktie. "Some say her youngest is Alan's son."

Nothing seemed quite right. I fingered the ridges of my glass. "I thought roses were his passion, not Angie. Did he give you roses, Aunt Fay?"

Aunt Fay turned tomato red. "Yes, but the man gave away hundreds of his Inverness Pinks."

"I always thought Alan was odd," Uncle Henry said. "Rubbing roses on women's cheeks is peculiar. The way he'd corner them and insist on stroking their faces with his flowers."

I blinked at Uncle Henry's strong tone. "Was he a pervert?"

"There are degrees of perversion." Uncle Henry shook his head. "I prefer to think the judge was merely too friendly with the fairer sex."

"He talked to us ladies about gardening. Can't blame us for humoring him." Aunt Fay dealt out salad bowls and sandwich plates with card-shark ease.

"Hold the bus," Cousin Janey said. "What about his court associates? Did the sheriff look at those?"

Aunt Fay beamed. "That's the spirit. Go to the courthouse and root around. His clerk knows everything."

"Dixie Lou? She can talk for hours." Janey's face fell. "Who's gonna rescue me?"

~*~

After lunch, I returned to the *Gazette*. Ellen rushed out to meet me in the parking lot. "Is it true? They arrested George?"

"Yes."

Ellen clutched her hands to her chest. "Oh, my! Why?"

I outlined the circumstantial case as I strode to my office. "Plus Daddy has no alibi for the time of death."

Her mouth gaped. "What does George say?"

"Daddy says he's innocent, and I believe him. Our attorney, Billy Mertz, is handling bail. After that, it's a waiting game until the trial."

"How awful. What will you do?"

"Find out who killed the judge. Tell me about Angie Johnson."

"You know about the judge and Angie?" Ellen asked.

I sighed and sat. "I didn't know anything until thirty minutes ago. Being in Atlanta has put me out of the gossip loop. Tell me about them."

She went very still. "The judge has been seeing Angie forever, maybe even before he was married."

Angie had managed The Oaks Motel my entire life. Two of her children were older than me. Her youngest was my age. "What about Boony?"

Ellen shrugged. "Boony is the elementary school custodian. Zero ambition and no personality. People whisper he's the judge's son, but he's nothing like Alan."

I'd question Angie first and see if she had motive to kill the judge, and then I might talk to her kids. "The idea of secret children and double lives has me spooked. Is anyone in Danville who they claim to be?"

"Probably not."

Chapter 6

A faded sign marked the entrance to The Oaks Motel. The deserted parking lot hinted at vacant units. "Business looks bad," I observed.

Cousin Janey snickered. "Business is booming. Come back tonight, and you'll see plenty of vehicles here. This place is the Love Shack Motel."

"People come here to hook up?"

"Yep."

Good grief. "I had no idea. I feel like I've had blinders on my whole life. I always thought this was a sleepy little town."

"Don't feel bad. I didn't figure it out until three years ago when I caught my ex here." Janey jingled her keys in my face. "Move it or Angie will call Junior Curtis to bust our chops."

I opened my door. "The bail bondsman? Why?"

Janey locked her VW bug and nodded. "He's also her bouncer. The rule is: no pay, no play."

"Jeez."

Janey bustled in the motel lobby. "Angie?"

Dark paneling wrapped the reception counter that dominated the tight quarters. Tourism brochures littered the countertop. Country music blared. A petite bleached blonde in a flowery top looked up from a collection of paint strips she was studying. "Janey Dupree. What brings you here?"

"Family. Angie, you remember my cousin Lindsey?"

Angie focused on my red hair. "You were in Boony's class. Aren't you in Macon now?"

Her strained welcome piqued my curiosity. "Atlanta. I write for the *Georgia Journal of Science*."

"Lindsey's helping at the paper right now," Janey continued with the cover story we'd worked out. "She wants to interview local businesses for their take on the economy, and I suggested you."

Angie shuffled the paint strips together. "The economy is good. Real good."

She had yet to look me in the eye. I pulled out a reporter's pad and a pen. "Wonderful. Please, continue. I'd love to have quotes for the article."

"We've always turned a profit. Recently, I began renting by the month. Two units have efficiency kitchens, and I'm adding more kitchens."

"Sounds good."

"If I turn this place into apartments, I'll have more time with my kids and grands."

"Looks like you're already in fix-up mode," Janey observed.

"Considering the possibilities."

I pressed on to fill the awkward silence. "Would you say Danville is a good place to raise a family?"

Angie made a strangling sound. *Uh-oh.* I hastened to explain. "Because of the low crime rate, low student-to-teacher ratios, fresh seafood, that sort of thing."

"You want my opinion about this community?"

Her shrill voice made me squirm. "Whatever you want to tell me."

"This community is full of backstabbing, lying, no-good cheaters, and I'm sorry I ever landed here." Her eyes bore into mine. "I'm doubling my rates, effective immediately. They want to play house out here, they can pay for the privilege. Put that in your newspaper and smoke it."

Janey's jaw flapped mutely.

I grabbed my cousin and eased toward the exit. "Thanks for your time. We'll be on our way."

Janey raced me to the car. A few miles down the road, she pulled in the trailer park.

"Look." She held out her trembling hand. "Holy cow, Cuz. I bet Angie killed Judge Sterling. She's mad at the whole town. Think of the dirt she knows. Think of the affairs she's seen."

Janey was right. Angie knew secrets, but adultery was good for her business. "Angie talked like the motel was hers."

"No way. Back in my waitress days, the judge barely tipped. I'm guessing he only paid Angie minimal wages."

I shook my head. "Following your logic, she's mad about thirty years of low pay? And she's taking it out on the community? I don't think so."

Janey fingered the ridges on her steering wheel. "Well, one of the Sterlings must own this place. Otherwise how'd that gossip get started? If it's Trish, can you see her employing the judge's mistress? I can't. So who owns the hotel? And why would Angie be renovating if she's not the owner?"

"We need answers to those questions."

Janey shuddered. "The deed room in the courthouse is a mess. It could take years to figure this out."

"We don't have years." I pinched the bridge of my nose. "Daddy needs our help now."

"Let's see if Uncle George's bail bond went through." Janey headed the car into town.

"Are you coming in with me?" I asked my cousin.

"Nope. Junior Curtis played with guns as a kid. He has this way of looking straight through you, and he's got a mean streak. Plus, he gets Florida visitors in black limos with tinted windows. Rumor is he's connected."

"Connected?" I had that dumb-as-a-rock feeling again. "He's related to us?"

"It's a family all right, only not ours. You cross Junior, and you cross the people he represents, you catch my drift?"

Had the script of my life been hacked? What happened to my hometown? "You're telling me that Junior's got mob ties, he's Angie's friend, and she hates us."

"Good recap."

"You think Angie or Curtis did it?"

"Anyone could've done it, including Uncle George. Imagine the judge cheating on Trish for so long. My husband cheated on me once, and I kicked him out. I wouldn't stand for that. Trish has the most motive."

The spurned wife angle. Worked for me. "I should interview Trish Sterling next."

"Yeah. She's due."

Janey stopped in front of the bail bond office. The bottom two-thirds of Junior's windows were blocked so I couldn't see inside. No black limos on the street. The coast was clear. Janey kept the motor running.

"Should I wait for you?" she asked.

We were across the street from the jail, two blocks from the *Gazette*. "I'll be fine."

The bail bond office looked ordinary enough. A metal desk, wooden chairs, a computer, a phone, and a filing cabinet occupied the room. Plants lined the walls and filled the window. It smelled like a greenhouse, hot and humid and earthy.

Junior Curtis rose and extended his hand towards me. "Ms. McKay."

His handshake was firm and business-like. Junior wore dark green slacks, black boots, and a khaki shirt with rolled sleeves. His head was shaved, and his biceps bulged. Sunglasses peeked out of his shirt pocket.

"You know me?"

A half-smile crossed his lips. "Sooner or later everyone walks through my door."

I sat in the seat he indicated. "I'm here about Daddy's bond."

Junior raised his hands skyward. "Out of my hands. George insisted that Henry sell some of George's investments to cover the bond. He'll be out once the money transfers. I check the account hourly. Where's your dog, Red?"

My brother used to call me Red. This guy had no right. "My name is Lindsey, and my dog's at home today."

Junior steepled his fingers together. "Keep the dog with you. We've got a murderer running loose in this town."

Blood rushed in my ears. "Do you know who killed Judge Sterling?"

His dark eyes bored into me. "I know enough to carry a gun. A pretty gal like you needs protection."

Protection? Or what? I'd be wearing concrete boots? Cars zipped by on the street. I didn't care for this man. He was too familiar, too much in the know, and too smug. I wished I didn't have to deal with him. I could easily envision him killing a man.

Junior nodded toward the jail. "This time of day, Ike allows his prisoners a walk in the fenced exercise yard behind the jail. If you go over there right now, you'll probably be able to see your dad."

I did a double-take. In my mind, I'd convicted him of being a bad guy, and he was being nice to me? "Thanks for the tip."

Confused about Junior's true nature, I dashed across the street.

Daddy saw me, came over, and placed his hand on the inner chain link fence. The concertina wire atop the outer fence hovered over us like a bad dream.

"You didn't have to come," Daddy said.

"Yes, I did. I can't believe you're here."

"My lawyer says their case is circumstantial."

"You didn't do it." I said.

"I've covered many trials." He frowned. "All that matters is I look guilty."

Not in my book. "Don't worry. We'll figure this out."

"No. I want you back in Atlanta as soon as possible."

Daddy was protecting me? "I can take care of myself."

"I need you to be safe."

My fingers gripped the wire. "I'll be careful. Everyone in the family is helping."

Daddy shoved his hands in his pockets and studied the grass. "What've you got so far?"

"Secrets. Adultery. Resentment towards the judge."

"Alan ticked people off. Me included."

"Which brings me full circle. Why was he murdered?"

"That saw mill. He wanted to put it mid-county."

"Near the shrimp dock?"

"Exactly."

My family owned land out there, but the Sterlings owned more. After my father and I talked a few more minutes, the sheriff waved Daddy inside. Ike caught my eye. "Don't leave, Linds. You and I need to talk."

I waited in the parking lot. Ike emerged and escorted me to the shade. "You'll overheat out here."

The sun wasn't heating my blood as much as the man beside me. "I'm acclimatizing."

"I heard you've been asking people about the judge."

32

I blinked in surprise. *Dang.* So much for the family's stealth investigation.

He must have guessed the direction of my thoughts. "Small town. Look. The evidence points to your father. Leave the town's dirty laundry hidden where it belongs."

My hands balled into fists. "Daddy didn't kill anyone."

He loomed over me. "He threatened to kill the judge, and now Alan Sterling's dead. That's motive. He can't account for his time that night, that's opportunity. The weapon belonged to him, and it had his fingerprints on it. That's means. I did my job."

I had things to do. Ice cream to buy. "I'm aware of your opinion. Later."

He snagged my arm, gently holding me in place. "I wasn't finished."

"I am."

He sighed. "I want to take you out to dinner."

As long as he thought Daddy was guilty, Ike was the enemy. "Not happening."

His gaze softened. "It took you a few moments. I'm making progress."

My heart fluttered, and I couldn't make it stop. "I took a moment because you think my father is a murderer."

His finger skimmed the scooped neckline of my lace top. "You had nothing to do with the murder."

Yowsers. My whole system went haywire at his caress. I yanked my sunglasses out of my hair and shoved them on. "Neither did my father. Goodbye, Sheriff."

~*~

I laid my mail on the Post Office counter. The lobby was blissfully free of patrons. Aunt Fay sidled up to her postal clerk stool and leaned toward me so we could talk.

"The motel manager hates the whole town," I said. "And the bail bondsman confuses me. Both of them seem wound too tight."

"No news there. Janey says you're planning to talk to Trish Sterling soon."

"Given Janey's experience as a spurned woman, she believes the widow had motive to kill her husband."

"Trish should be questioned." Aunt Fay patted my hand. "Will we get the knife back? It was my father's before he gave it to George."

"I doubt it, but good thing Grandpop's prints wore off, or else Ike would've charged him with murder."

"Don't tease me, Lindsey." With a groan, Aunt Fay clutched her heart. "What about that Harper boy?"

Back to matchmaking were we? I worked my back teeth apart. "Ike believes he's irresistible. I assure you he is very resistible."

"Too bad. The two of you would be a nice match."

This wasn't productive. I switched conversational gears. "What about your inquiries? What about the bridge club?"

"We meet tonight. You should come."

Aunt Fay's bridge club started and ended most local rumors. I'd rather eat worms. "No, thanks."

Chapter 7

As I left work late that evening, the sky glowed like molten fire. The bail money had cleared in late afternoon, and Daddy's lawyer drove him home. That suited me just fine. Ellen and I had worked late to finish another edition of the paper, and I needed some time without Daddy to decompress.

But when I pulled into the drive at dusk, I saw we had company. A black sedan.

Trish Sterling's car. The scorned woman herself. What was she doing here?

With my lab in tow, I slunk around the house, stood in the azaleas, and peeked in the family room window. Daddy sat in his plaid recliner with Trish's terrier in his lap, while Trish sat on the sofa. Two half empty cocktail glasses rested on the coffee table.

The nerve of that woman. Daddy didn't need a drinking buddy. Anger fueled my steps into the house. Bailey pranced along at my side. "Trish, what a surprise."

The dark circles were gone from Trish's eyes. Her polished appearance reminded me of someone on a date, from the coastal casual attire, to the cloying perfume, and the bright red toenails peeking out of her beaded sandals. What were her intentions toward my dad?

Trish rose abruptly. "Lindsey, how are you?"

"Fine." Bailey jerked her leash out of my hand and raced over to greet our company. Trish foiled a crotch sniff and collected her dog in one fell swoop.

Daddy glared at me. "Trish knows I didn't kill her husband."

Air huffed out my nostrils. Frankly, I was surprised flames weren't also shooting out.

Trish edged toward the door, looking guilty as sin. "Your business advice is excellent, George. Look at the time. I should be going."

After Trish hit the road, Daddy lit into me. "You embarrassed me. Trish is my friend."

Between the horror of Daddy's arrest, meeting with two potential killers, and birthing another paper, I had exhausted my patience. "Drinking got you into this mess."

He drained his glass and hers. "I don't have a drinking problem."

I grabbed the empty glasses, trying to get my voice and feelings under control. "You're charged with murder. You can't drink that reality away."

"Wasn't planning on drinking very much. Only drank enough to be sociable."

"It looked quite cozy in here. How friendly are you and Trish?"

"I don't like your tone, young lady."

"Daddy, what if Trish killed her husband and framed you?"

"Trish wouldn't do that. We're friends."

"What do you two do together?"

He shot me a searing look. The truth hit me like a bushel of oysters. "You're having an affair with Trish?"

"It's not like that."

"Are you sleeping with her?"

"We're friends."

My father was involved with the dead man's widow? "What were you thinking? What would Mama say?"

"Lottie and I are overdue for a long talk when she gets home. Trish lived in hell for thirty years. Alan told her if she left he'd make sure she never got custody of their kids or any of the money." He sighed. "We're lonely. And adults. We enjoy each other's company."

"You are having an affair with her. For how long? Thirty years?"

Daddy blanched. "My friendship with Trish was platonic until recently."

No wonder the sheriff thought Daddy was guilty. "What if she set you up?"

"Trish wouldn't do that," Daddy repeated. But this time, he didn't sound as sure.

"Someone murdered the judge in cold blood with your knife. In my mind, everyone outside our family is guilty until proven innocent."

"That's harsh."

"Whoever did this knows things." I glared at him. "They knew about your argument with the judge."

He barked out a mangled laugh. "The meeting was televised."

Didn't he get it? We were trying to save him. "Stay away from Trish until we know who did this."

"Are you sure you're my sweet daughter? Because you sound like your Aunt Fay."

He was smiling at me. He was trying. The least I could do was believe in him. I wanted to believe in him. But Daddy's affair with Trish gave him yet another motive to kill the judge.

~*~

Unable to be civil to Trish just yet, I decided to check out the saw mill angle with Cousin Janey and my dog. The familiar dock aromas of brine, tar, and diesel fuel insinuated themselves in my lungs as we stepped out of my car. Bailey sniffed along the bluff and barked happily at sea gulls wheeling overhead.

"Let me see if I understand," I said. "The judge owns this property, and the Fishing Association leases it. If the saw mill is allowed to operate here, the judge would evict these shrimpers?"

Janey nodded. "The saw mill people need the dock."

The three boats tied at the dock were a small portion of the fishing fleet. From growing up in Morrison County, I knew six to eight boats typically docked here, depending on the season. "Where would the fishermen go?"

Janey shrugged. "To other docks. To other states. The judge didn't care."

"I bet the shrimpers were hot. Didn't they speak out against the saw mill?"

"Jeb Turner from the Fishing Association had glossy brochures printed to explain why this was a bad idea. I was impressed at his impassioned plea to the County Commissioners."

"These fishermen had a stronger motive for murder than Daddy. They were fighting for their livelihood, whereas Daddy protested the action on principle."

Janey peered over her sunglasses at me. "You know that's not true. Uncle George went after the judge because of you. The adjacent land is yours. Uncle George fell on his sword for you."

I'd forgotten. A breath hissed between my clenched teeth. Daddy wanted to keep that parcel of land in a quiet neighborhood because of me. Because he wanted me to settle out here.

"Now I feel awful." I stared at the oyster-lined mud bank and listened to the gulls overhead. "Maybe Jeb can update us on the saw mill status."

Janey nodded to the house-like portion of the dock. "Jeb is inside, unloading the boats as they return."

I whistled to Bailey, and we walked toward the dock. Janey entered the factory house first. "Jeb, you remember my cousin, Lindsey?"

Jeb looked up from shoveling crushed ice into wooden crates of headed shrimp. "Sure do. Good to see you both."

I babysat for Jeb's kids during my teens. His warm smile filled my heart. "Hey, Mr. Turner. How're the kids?"

"Call me Jeb." He leaned on his shovel and bragged about his daughters. When he wound down, I said, "I heard the dock lease might not get renewed."

"Alan Sterling tried to destroy a hundred-year-old industry. No way." He looked me square in the eye. "Sterling was a boil on the county's butt. I'm sorry George got caught. He shouldn't be punished for his public service."

"The sheriff had it wrong. Daddy was framed, and we're gonna get that straightened out. Meanwhile, I'm following up on potential stories for the next paper. Is the saw mill issue resolved?"

Jeb nodded at me as if I wasn't here poking around in his business looking for motives. "We got another notice from the group's lawyers yesterday. They intend to file against us in court."

He spoke as forthrightly and naturally as he usually did. If he was the killer, he'd fooled me. I had no choice but to follow up on my cover story. "You're addressing the concerns through legal channels?"

"They came in here threatening us with legal documents. That's the only weapon they respect. We'll fight them with every dime we've got."

A legal battle. Didn't sound the same as a knife fight. The shrimpers had a grievance, but they seemed focused on judicial battles. Granted, someone could've acted individually and stabbed the judge, but it seemed unlikely. Especially since the legal jousting hadn't been resolved by the judge's death.

Dock hands milled around us. I got the distinct feeling we were in the way. "Good to know. Keep me posted on your status with the saw mill battle. It was great seeing you again, Jeb."

"Y'all drop by anytime." Jeb waved goodbye. "Nice dog."

Janey and I piled into my Volvo, Bailey lounged across the whole back seat. "Well?" I asked.

My cousin clipped on her seatbelt. "The commercial fishermen had reason to kill the judge. He was destroying their way of life. You heard Jeb say the judge's killer performed a public service."

"It goes back to property ownership," I added, as I eased down the dirt road. "At the dock and the motel."

"The judge wanted to repurpose the dock, and who knows what he wanted to do at the motel. We need more pieces of this puzzle."

"How will we get them?"

"We keep digging."

Chapter 8

Five-thirty and I was nowhere near done for the day, when Ellen burst into my office with her three blonde-headed kids in tow. "That jerk," she whispered.

"Thomas?" I asked.

"He got a large shipment from Standard Marine yesterday. New nets. How can he afford them?"

Her little girls looked confused. I beamed at the oldest one and handed her my dog's leash. "Wendy, would you take Bailey for a walk out back?"

Wendy glanced at her mom for approval, and Ellen nodded. "Hold hands with your sisters and stay away from the river."

The girls scurried out of the office with Bailey in tow.

"Thanks," Ellen said, when we were alone. "I shouldn't talk about their father like that in front of them."

"What did he say about the nets?" I asked.

"I was so angry I couldn't speak." Fury lit her eyes as she paced the office. "He's a snake."

I'd never seen her this upset before. But she didn't seem beaten down by her anger. She looked energized.

"How can I help?" I asked.

"Maybe you should go down there and ask him where he got the money. You could do it on the pretense of an article. Maybe you could even give him a heart attack by asking him if his boat was docked when the judge died. Serve him right."

Jumping in the middle of a domestic dispute wasn't smart, but maybe it would provide another lead for the murder investigation. "Did Thomas even know the judge?"

"In passing. They weren't friends."

I owed Ellen for keeping the paper going this year. What difference would a few pointed questions make? "I'll interview him about shrimping, see if he sounds truthful."

Ellen stopped pacing. "Thanks."

~*~

"Anybody here?"

Great. Another visitor.

After Ellen and her kids had left an hour ago, I'd thrown myself into accounting mode. I would never get out of here tonight at this rate. My dog trotted to the reception area. I followed her.

Ike Harper squatted by Bailey, stroking her head.

"What can I do for you?" I asked.

He stood and his warm gaze traveled the full length of my dress, all the way down to my strappy red sandals. "You sure are pretty. Why are you working so late?"

"Administrative duties," I said. "I'm still trying to right the ship."

"All work and no play isn't good for anyone." He glanced at his feet and then back at me. "How about you and Bailey join Trent and me for a day of fishing tomorrow?"

"In a boat?" I couldn't catch my breath.

"I've got a little jon boat. Nothing fancy, but we like it." A slow smile filled his face. "Care to join us?"

"No, thanks." Somehow I managed to speak in a normal voice. "I have other plans."

He studied me closely. "You feeling all right?"

"Actually, I'm beat. I should go home right now."

"I'm sorry you can't make it." He rubbed his neck. "My son wants a dog like Bailey."

Trent loved animals, and my dog loved the water. I chewed my lip. "Bailey can go. Why don't you pick her up in the morning?"

"Thanks. Maybe you'll change your mind and come with us?"

I blanched at the thought. "I don't plan to ever get on another boat."

Understanding dawned on his face. The crinkles at the side of his eyes disappeared. "Gosh, Lindsey, I'm sorry to dredge up the past."

41

"I just can't." Drat. My voice was shaking. My eyes were watering. I couldn't fall apart now.

Ike stepped forward. "Don't," I started, but he shushed me, enfolded me in a big hug, and held me close. Tears streamed down my face. It had been so long since someone held me. It felt so good. Maybe I wouldn't be empty forever.

When I finally lifted my head from his shoulder and stepped back, he released me. The caring in his eyes tore at the defenses I'd built around my heart.

I tried to dispel the cloud of intimacy that surrounded us. "How come every time I see you, you end up hugging me?"

"You're overdue a few hugs. I don't mind helping you reach your quota."

I retreated further, and my arm bumped the wall. Ike immediately snagged my hand and checked for damage. "Easy."

My heart missed a beat. So much for keeping him at arm's length. "Thanks. Nothing personal. I can't start up something with you."

"Linds, I hate seeing you hurting. I wanna help."

"Being home is stirring up issues I buried a long time ago, but I'm working through them." My spine stiffened. "Take my dog fishing tomorrow while I get caught up at home."

"That's a start, but I want to take you to dinner."

His sexy grin nearly broke my resolve. "I'm not *that* grateful."

"Just checking."

~*~

The next afternoon, Ike's son stood at my door, dripping wet. Mud boots encased my dog's legs. I'd spent three hours cleaning the house, and wet dog wasn't what I wanted to smell for the next week. "Hold on there, Ace." I stepped outside and closed the door behind me.

The sheriff climbed out of his Jeep. His form-fitting gray tee and blue swim trunks were mud-free. My hand strayed to the messy knot of hair on my head. I wished I'd worn something nicer than this white tee shirt and capris to clean house. "Did Trent and Bailey fall in?"

"I went swimming," Trent crowed. "Then Bailey jumped in the mud. Daddy says I have to bathe her. Can I?"

The sheriff's posture seemed unusually rigid. Did he think I would be mean to this sweet child? "Sure. Bailey needs a bath. I'm glad for the help. Let me get a few things. The hose is on the side of the house."

"Awesome." Trent's face lit up like Christmas morning.

"I'll be right back." I dashed inside for supplies and helped Trent wash the dog. Ike manned the hose. The sun beat down on us in waves of ninety degree heat, so I didn't mind getting soaked. When we finished, Bailey dashed madly around the yard. At last, she slowed, and I handed Trent a towel to use to rub her down.

"You're good with him." The sheriff turned off the hose.

I emptied the wash bucket. "Dealing with little boys is easy. It's the big ones that give me trouble."

Heat flashed in his gaze. "I wouldn't be any trouble."

"That's what they all say."

His grin broadened. "Nice shirt."

My tee shirt clung to me like second skin, and my lace bra had turned transparent. Quickly, I draped a towel over my shoulders. "Don't go getting any ideas."

He laughed and mussed my hair.

~*~

It was noon on Sunday before I connected with Ellen's ex-husband for his "business interview." Thomas Mattingly sat on the stern of his boat with machinery parts spread around him. I wore my darkest sunglasses to help me avoid seeing the water clearly.

Would I ever get over my fear of drowning? As a kid, I could swim rings around people. Once, I even beat Cousin Janey at a hold-your-breath contest, and she was two years older than I. Water sports came naturally to me. Until my brother's death at sea. Now I froze at the sight of water.

The tide was high, so the vertical drop from the dock to the deck of the boat was minimal; thus, I could keep my gaze nearly level and not see the water.

Thomas's fishing nets were uniformly clean of any debris or patches of mending twine. Even to my untrained eye, they appeared brand new. "May I have a word with you?"

He barely glanced my way. "I'm busy."

"I won't take much of your time." I outlined my idea for interviewing local business owners. "I plan to write about commercial fishing next. Are you interested in being featured?"

His chest puffed up like a blowfish. "About time. I'm the best fisherman in these parts."

"Your boat looks so neat and tidy. These nets, for instance, they look pristine."

"That's because they're brand new."

"Can a person still make good money in shrimping?"

"Sure. I'm the model of hard work."

That didn't jive with him stiffing his family. I pushed a little harder. "Where did you make the big catch?"

His face blanked for a moment, and then he settled into an easy grin. "Wasn't just one big haul. I'm having good luck every trip. With newer equipment, I save on fuel and wear and tear on the boat. Fishing smarter and making more."

My skepticism returned. Cousin Janey's ex had relatives that docked here. They'd know the truth about this man's fishing prowess.

"I have a new sonar module in the pilot house." He stood and pointed to the boat's cabin, as if I didn't know what a pilot house was. "Wanna see it?"

"No thanks." I paused, gathering my nerve. "One more question, and I'm asking this of all my business owners. In light of recent events, do you feel safe in our community?"

"Sure." His gaze narrowed. "Why wouldn't I?"

"A homicide occurred near your workplace. Did that event change how you do business?"

"Nah. Three Danville men have been killed during my lifetime. All were personal, same as this matter with your dad and the judge."

"You knew of their dispute?"

"Saw it on the TV, same as everybody else."

"That's all I have. Thanks." Just to be sure I wasn't missing anything, I checked his tanned arms for a watch. Bare. So much for my investigation. I turned to go.

"Send Ellen over to take my picture," Thomas said. "I need to talk to her anyway."

"We'll get a photo if we don't have one in our archive." I hurried through the deserted shrimp factory house. I could write a short feature on Thomas, but I wouldn't. I didn't like his attitude. Besides, he was a deadbeat dad. Definitely. *No feature for him.*

~*~

Daddy and I dined at Captain John's Seafood just over the county line. Thick hemp ropes, net fragments, and plastic fish decorated the walls. Patrons of Captain John's were a mix of Danvillers and folks from nearby Brunswick.

I ordered a crab cake dinner and an iced tea. Daddy had the same. We were actually making small talk, which was progress. I was finishing my salad when Sheriff Harper appeared at our table, breathing dragon fire. He leveled a finger at me. "You. Outside. Now."

What had his shorts in a knot? "Can't this wait? We're eating dinner."

He glared right back. "We can do this one of two ways. Walk out of here with me, or I'll toss you over my shoulder and carry you out."

"You can't talk to my daughter like that," Daddy said, standing.

"Your daughter is interfering with police business. I can arrest her if you like."

Since my lilac blouse and filmy skirt weren't conducive to cave man treatment, I rose. "Excuse me, Daddy. This won't take long."

I marched out of the restaurant and into the humid dusk. I stopped in the parking lot.

Ike's aura pulsed with anger. "I told you to leave well enough alone. You've been all over the county asking questions. You got the judge's women so riled up, I had to pull them off each other. Now you're bothering the shrimpers?"

"I didn't cause Angie and Trish's bad blood. Their dispute has nothing to do with me."

"You also talked to two shrimpers. Why can't you leave it alone?"

I didn't care for his attitude. "I work for a newspaper. I asked questions about the shrimping business, and they answered. Last I checked, this is a free country."

His heated breath warmed my exposed collarbone. I stepped back and bumped into a sedan. I barred my arms across my chest.

"The case against your father is solid," Ike said. "He threatened the judge, his prints are on the murder weapon, and he has no alibi for the time of death. That's motive, means, and opportunity. It doesn't get any clearer cut than that."

But it was all wrong. "Daddy was framed."

He exhaled heavily. "I don't believe that for one second, but—assuming there was a frame job—I'd look for someone who hated your father as much as the judge. The two of them had little in common. And I checked that angle, even though your dad is clearly my guy. Your father wasn't involved in any of the judge's cases, and the judge had nothing to do with the newspaper."

The judge's wife connected them. Much as I hated to admit it, the evidence against Daddy was compelling.

His gaze narrowed in speculation. "You know something. What is it?"

I wasn't blabbing about Trish and Daddy's *friendship*. "It's nothing that will help Daddy's case. If I find any evidence to help Daddy, believe me, you'll be the first to know."

"Police work isn't for amateurs." His voice softened. "I don't want anything to happen to you."

The hunger in his eyes hinted at unfinished business. Something that I needed to avoid entirely. But that something kept weighing on my thoughts.

Chapter 9

My cousin chickened out on questioning Dixie Lou, so the job fell to me. No wanting to have it hanging over my head, I drove to her office and found her.

The clerk of Superior Court wore gray sneakers, baby blue slacks, and a seersucker blouse. Dixie Lou lumbered to her feet and opened her arms. A genuine smile stretched from ear to ear. "As I live and breathe. Look who's here. Lindsey McKay."

I moved forward to hug her.

"Careful," she cautioned. "Still recovering from hip replacement surgery. They thought I'd retire, but there's plenty of life left in this old broad."

Dixie Lou couldn't retire. She was an institution around here. We had a long visit, until finally I wrestled the conversational lead back from her. "I'm trying to help Daddy, and I hope you can help me clear his name. What can you tell me about Judge Sterling's lunch routine? Did he go home for lunch every day?"

She laughed heartily. "Heavens no. He never went home at mealtime. Said it was too far."

Ten miles was too far? "Why didn't he move closer to town?"

Dixie Lou winked at me. "I'm sure the geography suited him fine."

Progress. "Did he have a routine?"

She bit back a smile. "Variety mattered."

Variety. Was I supposed to read between the lines? "Are we talking about a person, place, or thing? Where did he go for lunch?"

"Not where, but who. Sometimes he had business lunches. Mostly he went to the motel. Earlier this summer, he *lunched* with someone else briefly, but no names were ever mentioned."

Interesting.

~*~

After Ellen left for lunch the next day, I realized I'd forgotten to send my work to my boss in Atlanta. Needing a break, I decided to run it to the overnight service myself. I flipped the door sign to the "Closed" side. "Come on, Bailey."

The dog's tongue lolled as we stepped into the heat of midday. River Road ran perpendicular to Main Street. From my position, Ellen's car at the gas station on Main was visible. So was her ex's pickup farther up the street. When Ellen pulled out, the truck followed, several cars back.

The hair on the nape of my neck bristled. My package could wait a minute. I joined the caravan, following at a distance. Ellen stopped at the Post Office, the bank, and her mother's house.

Thomas pulled off three driveways past Ellen's mother's house. I circled back to town, questions simmering in my head. Why was Thomas following Ellen?

Was he stalking her? When Ellen returned from lunch, I'd encourage her talk to the sheriff about her ex's behavior. Meanwhile, I need to learn what else or who else the judge had been involved with.

In his daily life, Alan Sterling kept himself surrounded by women. Dixie Lou had been his court clerk. Trish, his wife. And Angie, his long-time mistress.

A quick glance over at my dog showed that she was enjoying the ride. Not much got past her on the street as she gazed this way and that. "I don't know, Bailey. I keep coming back to The Oaks Motel. Is it significant to the case, or just to me because I had no idea about all the shacking up out there?"

Bailey perked up at her name but then went back to checking out everything outside the car window. Oh, to be as carefree as a dog.

The Oaks was ahead on the left. On impulse, I veered into the parking lot, parked beside a black SUV, left the AC running for Bailey, and hurried into the motel office. "Angie?"

I heard a mechanical sound from the back room, like when Daddy lowered the footrest on his recliner. "Be right out," Angie called.

She appeared a moment later. From her flushed face it seemed she'd been doing something strenuous. Muffled noise continued in the back room. Was someone else in there?

"What can I do for you?" Angie asked.

I cleared my throat, aware that I was fishing for information. "I'm piecing together Judge Sterling's last day. Did he spend the early evening with you?"

She gave a slight nod. "He often came here."

Bingo. "Do you remember what you talked about that night?"

The office door opened, and the bail bondsman swaggered out. Angie touched her hair as if she just realized it was disheveled. Junior nodded to me, before kissing Angie on the lips. "See ya around, Babe."

He roared off in his SUV. Angie flushed sunburn red. "It's not what you're thinking."

Junior Curtis and Angie? Hmm. "What is it?"

Angie squared stacks of brochures on her counter. "Junior helped me move furniture, and we got carried away. A one-time thing."

Until now, I hadn't considered Junior a suspect. He was good with guns, but was he good with knives? Something to consider. "Back to the judge. He visited you the night he died?"

"Alan stopped by to talk to me about the deed. See, he planned to transfer ownership of the motel to me. Been promising it for years. But he said there was a glitch, and he was still working on it." She wrung her hands. "If Trish gets ahold of this place, I'm toast."

"What kind of a glitch?"

"I don't remember, but this place is supposed to be mine. He promised. A long time ago."

The deed. A piece of paper. It should be recorded in the courthouse. Luckily I had a realtor in the family. Cousin Janey had looked up lots of deeds.

As I drove through town, the bail bondsman, Junior Curtis, weighed on my mind. He seemed territorial. He was mob connected. He liked Angie. On the other hand, he didn't tolerate fools and was direct. Shooting someone would be his style. Even so, it didn't feel right to rule him out. He was a definite maybe on my suspect list.

After I overnighted the package, my stomach reminded me I hadn't eaten. I grabbed an ice cream and returned to the paper. Ellen sat at her desk talking to a customer on the phone.

I ambled back to my office and waited. When Ellen ended the call, I joined her in the lobby. My dog followed. "Can we talk?"

A bright smile lit her face. "Sure."

"After you left for lunch, I locked up to run a quick errand. When you headed out of the gas station, a rusty truck followed you everywhere you went. I know because I followed the truck all the way to your mom's."

Ellen's expression darkened. "Why won't Thomas leave me alone?"

"He shouldn't be following you around. That's creepy."

"I don't like it either. I'll talk to the sheriff."

I nodded. "Do it now and take my dog with you. If Thomas follows, Bailey won't let him near you."

Ellen grabbed her keys. "Thanks. We'll be right back."

"Take your time."

Chapter 10

Late that afternoon, Aunt Fay, Cousin Janey, and I met at the courthouse to search for the motel deed. One look at the jumbled stacks of deed books, and I knew why my cousin demanded that we help. "How does anything get found?" I asked.

Janey sank into a wooden chair. "It's best if you walk in here with the deed book number. Otherwise you may have one foot in the grave before you leave."

"Where do we start?" Aunt Fay sat her basket purse on a table. The handkerchief cover parted to show her pet raccoon sleeping inside.

"We have to match the number we have to one in a book," Janey said.

I opened a book and looked for the plat number. The first deed showed the plat number handwritten in large numbers on the first page. On other deeds, I wasn't so lucky. Pages were out of order, and I had to hunt for the one I needed. Realization dawned. Finding the motel deed would take a while.

Ike appeared in the doorway. "Didn't expect to find the entire McKay clan in here."

We all said hello and when he stuck around watching us, I realized it was up to me to divert suspicion. So I headed down the hallway like I was going to the ladies restroom. Except the sheriff took my leaving as an invitation to join

51

That now familiar rush I got in his presence flooded my senses. "Looking for the motel deed."

Ike herded me through a side door toward his Jeep in the lot. "What makes you think the three of you could find a deed that I've had my deputies searching for?"

He was looking for the deed? That was news to me. "I've got a pro on my team. Janey is a real estate agent. She knows how the filing system works. If it's in there, she'll find it."

"You think this has a bearing on the case?"

"Hope so. All I know for sure is that it's a loose end."

Ike opened the passenger door, and I gawked at the high tech instrumentation. "Wow. Look at all this cool gear."

He chuckled softly and waved me inside. "If I'd known you liked high tech gadgets, I would've dragged you to my car the moment you arrived."

Like a sleepwalker, I climbed into the passenger seat. His scent filled me, and I wanted a moment of indulgence, a moment of letting my guard down. Despite my best intentions, I liked Ike. I believed Ike liked me. Too bad it couldn't go anywhere. Not while he wanted to put Daddy away for life. But still, a girl could dream.

Ike came around to the driver's side, cranked the car, and cool air pulsed from the vents. His brown eyes looked troubled.

"What?" I asked.

"I asked if you wanted to get iced coffee or head back to the office. You look dazed."

"Oh, sorry. The office, please." I pushed my sunglasses up on my head. "I've got a lot on my mind. Someone charged my dad with murder."

"You've got to accept that your father did this and move on with your life. It's not doing any good for you to be stirring up trouble."

I was looking for something to point suspicion away from my father, and I was riding in his accuser's car. My ire rose. "My father shies away from his own pain. He'd never inflict physical pain on anyone. How could you believe he did this? He's not a violent man."

Ike reached over and smoothed a stray hair behind my ear. "Hon, I've seen crazy things in this job. Little kids kill each other for a soft drink. Best friends shoot each other over a property line variance. Your father is capable of violence. We all are. It's human nature."

"Daddy didn't do this. You know him. He went on a two-week drunk when my brother drowned because he couldn't face the truth. He stoically endured marriage to my mother all these years, even though she's abandoned him to save the world. He's not a man who takes matters into his own hands. He didn't kill Judge Sterling."

Ike leaned back in his seat, adjusting his body so he faced me. "You've always been hardheaded, but you were rarely foolish. I'm not buying your argument, especially when the evidence points to George McKay, but tell me what you've got."

Here it was. My big chance to change my father's future. "Mostly I've found people with grievances against the judge."

He shrugged. "He's a judge. What did you expect?"

"Alan Sterling had a lot of women in his life. Trish, his wife, who he didn't sleep with; Angie, his mistress, who he did sleep with; and Dixie Lou, his clerk. Dixie Lou claims the judge had an affair with someone else recently. On top of that, the deed to The Oaks Motel is missing. Angie and Trish both think that property should be theirs. My gut says a woman killed him."

"None of them are strong enough to overpower a man that size. Forensic evidence on the judge or at the crime scene area would've alerted us to a struggle. The only forensics we have are your father's fingerprints on the knife."

I rubbed my temples. I didn't like the way Ike had an answer for everything. He didn't believe me. I had to sway him. "That was my dad's knife, which he kept in his unlocked house, so of course his fingerprints were on it. Anyone could've gone in there and taken the knife. Isn't the lack of other evidence a clue in itself?"

The sheriff tapped his fingers on the steering wheel. I got the feeling he was sizing me up for bad news. "Your father has been seeing Trish Sterling lately. Maybe there was a woman involved, and maybe your dad stood up for her against the judge."

My stomach lurched. "You know about Daddy and Trish?"

He nodded. "I didn't want to tell you about their relationship, but I need you to see the big picture. A lonely man who found someone who understood him. Alan Sterling wouldn't divorce Trish, or he would have done so years ago. Alan Sterling was in your father's way."

I could refute his theories too. "Going by that logic, Alan was also in the bail bondsman's way. Junior's sleeping with Angie now. Maybe he wanted her to be exclusive to him."

"That's some wild theory you're spouting."

"Or maybe the clerk finally had enough of his dishonorable behavior," I was on a roll now, "and someone in her family did her a favor by offing the man. Or maybe it's a mystery woman he was seeing. Maybe her boyfriend didn't like competition."

His lips thinned. "Now you're grasping at straws. You're giving upstanding citizens of the community a dirty name because you're desperate to save George."

The steel in his voice irritated me. "I'm not printing this in the *Gazette*. This is speculation, between you and me."

"Speculation won't cut it." The sheriff shifted the Jeep into reverse, drove the three blocks down Main Street to River Road in silence, and parked at the paper. "You have nothing because there's nothing to find."

And he called me hardheaded? He could give lessons in stubbornness. "My father didn't murder the judge."

"The evidence points to him."

"You're wrong, and I'll prove it."

He stroked my hand. "I know a much more pleasant way we could pass the time. Would you have dinner with me and Trent? He'd love to see Bailey again."

I meant to pull my hand away, but his touch felt nice. "Trent can see my dog anytime he wants. But you and I are on opposite sides."

In answer, he reached across the front seat and planted a lingering kiss on my lips, rendering total paralysis of my entire body. "Think about it, sugar. There's unfinished business between us."

I groped for the door handle. "Why do men think sex will cure everything? Don't you think about anything else?"

He smiled. "Rarely."

Ellen and Bailey had their noses pressed against the front window when I walked in. Ellen's eyes were round as sand dollars. "Did Ike kiss you?"

I sailed on past her, hoping Cousin Janey and Aunt Fay had found the motel deed without me. "Don't want to talk about it."

"Wait until I tell the gals at Misty's beauty shop." Ellen followed me into my office. "They were sure he'd date Patsy at the phone company next. I won the pool."

I gasped at the implication. "There's a pool on who the sheriff dates? Does he know about it?"

She shrugged. "Who cares? I won, and I need the money. He's been hanging around you a lot lately."

I wasn't ready for anyone to know about that kiss. I barely knew about it. "He's hanging around because of the murder investigation."

Ellen shook her head. "You're the one who got away. And his son likes you."

I rubbed my temples again. My head ached. I shoved the kiss out of my thoughts and welcomed the buzzing of my phone. It was a call from my boss in Atlanta.

"Lindsey, good work on finishing Bob Harvey's assignment. I like the book proposal ideas," Ted Townsend said. "When can I see a full-blown proposal?"

"Things down here aren't resolving as quickly as I thought," I hedged. "This has a long-term feel to it."

"What?" my boss sputtered. "You're not coming back?"

Now that he'd asked, the idea of staying seemed plausible. Working at the paper was fun. I had autonomy here. The people I came in contact with genuinely cared about me. Other than a job I enjoyed in Atlanta, I had no one waiting for me in the big city. The facts lined up in a decision matrix, and I realized what I'd been denying all along. I belonged in Danville. "My family needs me, and I can't leave until this is finished. I can't predict how long that will take. It isn't fair to leave you hanging indefinitely. You'll have my letter of resignation today."

"I won't accept it. How long do you need? One week? Two?"

"I'm so busy with the paper and working for you that I can't concentrate on my father's case." I exhaled slowly. "Straddling two jobs isn't working."

"Do me a favor, and take another week to decide. Bob Harvey will cover for you since you helped him last week. See if you can finish a proper book proposal, and we'll talk later."

I hung up the phone. I had tried to quit, but Ted had stopped me. I wouldn't change my mind in a week, a month, or a year. I'd finally come home, physically and mentally.

Now if I could just get the facts surrounding the judge's murder to line up in the correct sequence, I could clear Daddy's name. Seemed like Trish Sterling was overdue for my visit.

Chapter 11

The judge's widow answered her door in faded jeans, a yellow blouse, and a speckled paint smock. Her little Jack Russell terrier, Sparky, nipped at my heels. Fortunately, I'd left my dog in the car with the AC on so I could focus on Trish's reaction to my questions.

"Lindsey, what a surprise," Trish said. "Pardon my appearance. I'm painting. What can I do for you?"

"I'd like to talk, if you have a minute."

"Come in." Trish directed me to the sun porch. Sparky scampered up on the sofa and patrolled its length and finally lay down. I chose a wicker chair. "Can I offer you something to drink?" Trish asked.

"No thanks. I'm here about my dad. My married dad. Where is your friendship headed?"

Trish sank into a padded rocker. "George and I are friends. We have mutual interests. Ask him."

I knew he would say nothing more than he already had. "Mama's mission trip ends in six weeks, if not sooner. What happens then?"

Trish laughed harshly. "Sorry. I've never been the Other Woman before. I've always been the one cheated upon. Regardless, George and I take each day as it comes."

Understanding dawned. All the time Daddy said he was elsewhere, he was with her. "But he's here every day."

"Again, you need to ask your father about this." Trish paused before speaking again. "I know it's messy, but that's been my life lately. Alan was a self-centered jerk who couldn't get enough sex, if you'll pardon my frank language."

Ah. Another subject I wanted to pursue. "Did your husband change after marriage?"

"He was always self-centered. I ignored his adultery for the first twenty years. Raising the kids kept me pretty busy, but after the youngest left last year, I've been restless and lonely. I didn't know what to do with myself, only that I was trapped in this loveless marriage."

I scowled. "You could've divorced him."

"Why? I love this house, this view," she said, as she rocked in her chair. "Alan would've taken that away out of spite. I stuck it out, and now I'm free. I won."

"Did y'all talk about divorce?"

"It never came up. Alan wouldn't have been a judge without my family's money. Once he had what he wanted, he left me alone. Divorce would've cost him half his wealth."

I pushed a little more. "Still, it must have been hard, knowing that he sought other women all these years."

She stopped rocking for a minute. "You have no idea."

My last conversation with Ike had given me an idea. "Sheriff Harper said he had a deputy following Daddy. Your affair is one of the reasons my daddy was arrested."

"The world is against us. Why blame George? He'd never hurt a fly." Her concern seemed genuine.

"That's why I'm trying to clear his name. Tell me about Alan's last day."

Her lower lip trembled. "I didn't see him in the morning because we have separate bedrooms. I'd been up late the night before and slept in. I went into town just before lunch to see if he would loan our oldest son the money to add another room on his house. Alan was furious. Said his son should have married money like he did. Then he left for an appointment."

"Do you know who he met?"

Trish's face froze into a mask of hatred. "Maybe Angie, maybe another woman. I don't know."

I cleared my throat delicately. "Was he seeing someone whose husband would take offense? I wouldn't ask except I'm desperate to clear Daddy's name."

"I want to help George, but I always looked the other way at Alan's shenanigans. I don't know who my husband was sleeping with, but I'm glad it wasn't me."

"I see." I considered that for a minute. "I know I'm from the wrong generation and all, but, what was the judge's appeal? How did he get women to sleep with him?"

"Alan could be charming when it suited him, and he was insatiable in the bedroom. Some women like that much physicality, but it exhausted me." Sparky sensed her distress. He jumped off the back of the sofa and hopped into her lap. Trish hugged her little dog.

Insatiable. I never thought of the older generation in that way. "But still, you must've known if he was seeing someone. Did he behave differently? Were there variations in his routine?"

"Alan and I lived separate lives. He kept to his study and his rose garden when he was here."

Another dead end. "Again, forgive me for prying, but is any money missing?"

"Our joint checking account hasn't had any major transactions go through in the last few months. I can account for every expenditure in that account. I already told Sheriff Harper."

What had I missed? "What about money markets or stocks? Did you check them?"

"Those documents go directly to our accountant. I don't know where our retirement money is invested."

"Can you find out?"

"The sheriff didn't ask about our investments. I'll look into it."

"Thank you." I nodded. Maybe we'd find something the sheriff missed. "May I look in Alan's study and garden? The smallest thing could be a lead."

"Be my guest. It's my fault George's involved in this mess." She stood, walked over to the study door, and opened it. "I wanted to move my studio in here because the lighting is better, but frankly, this room is depressing."

I could see what she meant. The room felt oppressive. Built-in bookcases lined three walls. I thumbed through several books, but they pertained to the law and weren't easy reading.

The maroon leather chair behind the massive desk looked comfortable. A cigar box and a green lamp rested atop his desk. There were no personal photos, no home computer, and no phones in here.

His desk drawers held everyday rubble. Pencils, pens, rusty paper clips, rubber bands, extra staples, legal pads, tape, and household files. In the drawer of manila folders, I found a stack of girlie magazines.

I flipped through a few of the well-worn volumes, but they yielded no murder clues. The room smelled stale, with a trace of cigar and a masculine aroma.

The fourth wall led to a patio garden. I opened the French doors and walked outdoors. The brick patio was bordered by rose bushes, Inverness Pinks to be exact. The roses were in various states of bloom, displaying everything from new buds to heads past their prime.

Trish appeared in the doorway with my dog. "I heard Bailey barking in your car and let her out."

"Thanks." Bailey trotted towards me and then veered off to sniff the rose bed. She favored the stems with spent flower heads. Curious.

Trish sneezed from the doorway. "Forgive me if I don't join you. I'm allergic to roses. I swear Alan cultivated them to spite me."

"Would you mind if I cut some?"

"Help yourself. I plan to have those bushes removed anyway. The garden club is taking them, when the heat breaks. I'll grab some clippers."

Bailey sniffed every bush. Certain ones got watered doggie-style. She usually watered everything. Very odd.

Trish returned with the clippers. I cut three nearly-spent roses from the bushes Bailey marked. My plan was to give these flowers to the sheriff and have them tested.

"You're getting yucky ones. Take some buds so you can enjoy them longer," Trish encouraged from the doorway. "You should put Alan's tonic on them too."

"What tonic?"

"Something he keeps in the potting shed. An old Mason jar. Help yourself."

I walked over and opened the shed. There I found some fertilizer. More clippers. And an empty Mason jar, but no liquid. "He must have run out of the tonic," I said, as I closed the shed door.

"That's odd. Alan swore by his tonic. Said it made the roses extra special. Kept the blossoms fresh an extra-long time." Trish disappeared and came back with some newspapers to wrap the flowers. "While I was in the kitchen, I remembered something. A few months ago, Alan came home smelling of oranges. It struck me as peculiar because I'd never seen him eat an orange."

As I drove away, I reviewed what I'd learned. Trish didn't know the orange-scented woman who Alan had been seeing, and no money was missing. There was also Bailey's curious behavior. My dog had only marked certain flowers. I still had nothing solid. But it felt like I was on the verge of something.

I stopped at the jail and carried in the three spent roses. "Is the sheriff here?"

His sister winked at me. "Let me get him for you." She turned around and hollered his name.

Heck, I could have done that. Probably not as loud, though.

Ike strolled into the reception area, a wide grin pasted on his face. "You brought me roses?"

"They're evidence. I want them tested."

"Inverness Pinks?" He looked skeptical.

"Bailey couldn't stop sniffing these bushes. She only watered the bushes these three roses grew on and no others. There's something unusual about them."

"Tests cost money. I can't test everything that comes in here."

Daddy's life was on the line. "I'll pay for the tests if I have to, but I thought since it might be related to the murder investigation you'd be interested."

"How could it be related? The judge was murdered in town, not at his place."

I leveled my gaze at him. "Bailey has a great nose. I trust her implicitly."

"I've seen the places Bailey puts that nose," he said, as his eyes glittered, "and I'm not so sure. But I tell you what. I'll have these flowers tested under one condition. You agree to have dinner with me."

What was one night of my life if this led to Daddy's freedom? "I'll do it. After the results come back."

"Woo doggies! Put a rush on the analysis, Sis." The sheriff thrust the wilted flowers at Alice Ann and walked me outside. "Does Friday suit you?"

Friday sounded soon. But soon was good if it cleared Daddy's name. "Friday works for me."

"I'll be ticking off the minutes until then." The sheriff gave me a bone-melting smile.

His eyes twinkled dangerously. "Whatever you say."

Was Ike insatiable? *Yikes.* This wasn't helping. I drove my fresh rosebuds to the office.

Ellen startled with recognition. "I know where you've been. The judge's rose garden."

Her blush scattered my thoughts in another direction. "Did he give you roses?"

"He surprised me with a half a dozen some time ago. The vase is still here. Let me get it for you."

Ellen walked by in a citrus-scented rush. Citrus . . . oranges. I stared after her. Ellen and the judge? Nah. He was old enough to be her father. But the orange fragrance might be relevant. "You smell good, Ellen. What is that?"

She glanced shyly over her shoulder. "It's the one thing I do for myself. I use a scented shampoo from Misty's Beauty Shop. I just got a new bottle."

Hmm. If Ellen bought the shampoo locally, so could other women.

An hour later, I had a list of Misty's recent shampoo purchasers and a hair appointment next week.

While I recognized the names, I didn't know much about these women's relationship status. I walked to the Post Office. Luck was with me. Aunt Fay's friends, the Barrington sisters, were keeping her company. With their pastel blouses, tan pants, and sneakers, all three ladies looked like they shopped at the same places.

After we said our hellos, I asked for their help. "This list of shampoo purchasers might be relevant to our murder investigation. Which woman might be a likely affair prospect for Judge Sterling?"

Peggy Barrington took first crack at the names. "Forget Betty Furbee. She's settling her mother's estate in Florida. And Ginger Taylor moved in with her Colorado daughter five months ago to provide daycare for her new grandson."

Her sister Bernice snatched the list. "Myrtle Lowell. She's ninety and on oxygen. No way the judge was doing her."

Aunt Fay looked over Bernice's shoulder. "Thelma Riley is meaner than a wet snake. Forget her."

"Sally Ditterman moved in with Ramona Blossom," Peggy volunteered. "Wrong persuasion."

Bernice snatched the list. "Wynelle Johnson. Not likely. She smokes cigars and keeps to herself."

"The next person on the list is your friend Ellen," Aunt Fay added. "She's too young for him."

Peggy peered over Bernice's shoulder. "Connie Whitehead moved in with Chester Smith around Easter. Can't picture her satisfying two men."

Aunt Fay frowned. "All you got left are Willingham twins. June's battling stage four breast cancer, and Dena's her caretaker."

"I was hoping to identify the mystery woman. Rats." Desperate for a lead, I tried another avenue. "Cousin Janey says most of the town's affairs are conducted at The Oaks Motel."

"True," Bernice added, "and Number Ten was Alan's private love nest."

"I didn't know." I didn't need a love nest image in my head either. "Thanks for your help." I ducked outside into the heat. The shampoo lead was a bust, but with any luck the rose analysis might yield useful information. If it did, dinner with Ike would be a fair trade for Daddy's freedom.

Chapter 12

The next day Trish Sterling was in the office renewing her newspaper subscription when Aunt Fay phoned. "They found the deed. Meet me at the Courthouse," Aunt Fay said. "Bring Trish. I see her car over there."

I hung up and relayed the news to Trish.

"Who owns the motel?" Trish asked in a breathy voice.

I shrugged. "Aunt Fay didn't say. Why don't we ride over there in my car?" No matter who owned the motel now, the news would be emotional for Trish.

"Sure, but mine is roomier. You drive." She handed me her keys.

In the car, Trish buckled her seatbelt with a stoic air. "I have a bad feeling about this. If Alan owned the motel when he died, the deed wouldn't have been missing."

Silently, I agree with her logic.

"I blamed Angie for Alan's indiscretion, but it wasn't her fault he was a tom cat," Trish continued.

"Angie knew he was a married man."

She made a face as I parked. "Maybe she didn't have a choice. Alan probably made servicing him a part of her job description."

Sobering thought.

A small crowd awaited us inside the courthouse. Aunt Fay, the clerk, the sheriff, and tax assessor Chester Fitzwater stopped talking when we entered. Chester took Trish's hand. "Sorry, Miz Sterling. I didn't realize the deed was in my car. I misplaced it while moving my mother the other day."

Trish wrestled her hand free. "Is The Oaks mine?"

Chester shook his head. "The judge deeded his property over to Angela Johnson last month. This wasn't a joint holding."

"I see." Trish sagged like she'd been gut punched. Aunt Fay wrapped an arm around Trish's shoulders.

"I'll release the escrow, and send your lawyer a copy of the deed, in case you want to challenge this," the sheriff said.

"What's the point?" Trish sighed. "She earned the motel the hard way."

"Come on, Trish. Let's go," I said.

Trish needed a friend, and I only knew one of her friends. "She's had a bit of a shock," I told Daddy at the door when I dropped her off.

He nodded. "I'll take care of her."

I headed back to the paper on foot. Perspiration dripped from my chin before I walked three blocks.

A Jeep slowed. "Want a lift?" Ike asked.

"I would kill for a ride." *Oops.* Unfortunate choice of words. "Figuratively speaking, of course."

"Of course." His sunglasses hid his eyes, but his lips curved into a smile as he drove. "You did a good thing with Trish."

I lifted the sodden mass of hair off my neck. "Trish deserved better than Alan. She had plenty of motive to kill him, but she didn't."

"I see." The sheriff parked his Jeep next to my car at the newspaper.

From his tone, he didn't see at all. "My family has weathered tragedy and loss. Daddy blames himself for Colin's disappearance at sea. Mama couldn't save Colin or Daddy so she left to save the world."

The sheriff drummed his fingers on the steering wheel. "What about you?"

I turned to watch cars barreling across the bridge. "I ran away."

"But you're back."

"Because there's a new mess." I sighed. "Now Trish is adding her mess to our pot."

"You worried about your parent's marriage?"

"Daddy claims it's been over for a while, even though they haven't divorced, but it still shocked me to hear that."

"They'll figure it out. All you can do is love them both."

"Sounds like you've been to counseling, too."

He frowned and I wished he'd take off his sunglasses so I could see his eyes. "Two years' worth. If your parents are no longer compatible, it's best they cut ties."

I didn't want more heartbreak. "You want a Coke or something?"

"Nah. I've got to get back."

"Thanks for the lift and the advice."

"Anytime."

~*~

My coworker sat at my desk, her face buried in my roses. "Ellen?" I asked.

She jumped to her feet and clutched her heart. "I didn't expect you so soon."

"You like the roses?"

"Yes. They remind me of . . ."

Maybe it was the heat, but facts lined up in a new array, one I'd refused to consider before. Ellen used orange-scented shampoo. Ellen received roses from the judge. "Did you have an affair with the judge?"

Color drained from her face. "None of your business."

"I wouldn't pry if Daddy wasn't charged with murder."

She wrung her hands. "I don't want anything to happen to George."

"Please. I need your help."

"All right. Yes. I had a brief fling with the judge, months ago. Mama took the kids to her sister's, and I had two weeks alone." Ellen laughed. "It was wild. It was wicked. But it was over as soon as it began. I have responsibilities. I couldn't conduct a long-term affair."

So Ellen was the mystery woman. "I see."

"The judge knew how to treat a woman. He brushed his roses all over me. I wasted eight years on Thomas and never experienced passion like that. Do you think that's fair?"

"No."

"Alan said Trish understood. I wanted a walk on the wild side. I got that and more. Best of all, once I knew what good sex was like, I realized Thomas is a crappy lover."

"Did anyone know of your affair?"

"We were careful. Alan picked me up for lunch in the park every day and drove us to The Oaks. On the weekends, we stayed at Mom's. I ended it when the kids came home from Florida with my mother."

"Was he bitter?"

"No. He wanted to continue, but I couldn't juggle him and the kids."

"What about your mother or the neighbors?"

"It was a secret, but maybe someone saw us."

Ellen's ex had been following her around recently. What if he'd watched her for months? Could jealousy incite him to murder a rival?

The phone shrilled. "Lindsey, my accountant called," Trish said. "Alan withdrew ten thousand from an investment account two weeks before he died."

My heart raced at the good news. "Call Sheriff Harper. This is important."

I hung up and glanced out my window. The rusty pickup was parked at the dock, and Thomas was inside it, busily talking on his cell phone. I was in luck, because Thomas practically lived on the *Pamela Sue*, and the dock was near the crime scene. If evidence connected him to the judge, it might be on his boat.

I needed to take a quick look. "I'm taking Bailey on a walk," I told Ellen. "If we don't return by quitting time, lock up. I have my keys."

Bailey romped along the water's edge. Since it was Thursday, the boats wouldn't unload today. If Thomas was in his truck waiting for Ellen to leave, I could search his boat. Only problem was I'd avoided boats for ten years.

I could do this. For Daddy. And, if I fell in the water and was too scared to swim, I could yell for help, I rationalized. The Inverness River wasn't the Atlantic Ocean. I wouldn't drown.

Glancing over my shoulder, I saw that Thomas was still sitting in his truck. Bailey and I ducked behind the oleanders lining the riverbank and made our way to the *Pamela Sue*.

It was dead low tide. I set my purse next to a wooden piling and stepped way down onto the raised cap-rail of the boat. Bailey stutter-stepped like she wanted to jump, but the distance to the deck of the boat was too far.

"Shh," I whispered. "Stay, Bailey."

I threaded through the nets and machinery in the stern and traversed the narrow outside passageway to the pilot house door. Locked. Peering through the window, I saw the oaken captain's wheel and the vinyl covered captain's seat. I needed to get in there.

Skirting the anchor in the bow, I tried the opposite door. It swung open.

I ignored the bank of monitors and electric wires lining the low ceiling and focused on the clutter. Two stained coffee cups, an almost empty roll of toilet paper, duct tape, and random parts filled the countertop. I pawed through the stuff, but nothing stood out.

A faded flannel shirt with button down flaps hung over the captain's chair. One of the pockets bulged. With trembling fingers, I unbuttoned the flap and reached inside.

Bailey yelped outside, but I ignored her. My fingers closed around a circular metal item, and I pulled it out. The distinctive stainless steel band gleamed brightly. I recognized the crown symbol on the watch face from my Atlanta power lunches. A Rolex.

The judge's missing watch. I shoved it back in the pocket. I needed the sheriff to find it.

Suddenly, the doorway filled with a large, angry male. Thomas was blocking my exit. The fevered look in his eyes took my breath away. Why hadn't I studied martial arts?

I turned to run, but a beefy paw grabbed my shoulder. I opened my mouth to scream but his other fist smacked my temple. The world went black.

~*~

I awoke to a headache, darkness, vibration, an engine roar, and the rhythmic sway of waves. My hands and feet were hogtied behind me with duct tape. I lay on a thin foam mattress.

Memory flooded back. Thomas had found me on his boat. He knocked me out, and now he was taking me somewhere in the ocean. I was in deep trouble.

Tears filled my eyes as I struggled against my bonds. If only I hadn't acted on impulse.

Even though it was August, I shivered with icy fear. As my vision sharpened, I made out the pilot house's walls in the dim light coming through the narrow window. Full moon tonight, which meant that it wasn't pitch black outside.

Realization clunked in my empty stomach. No one knew where I was. I had to rescue myself. Stealthily, I inched my bound hands and feet to the edge of the foam, until I felt the crack between the mattress and the wall.

I found crumbs, cellophane wrappers, something that felt like an old sock, and a beer bottle cap. The edges of the bottle cap were sharp.

I grabbed it and began working on the tape. I was making progress when I heard footsteps. I palmed the bottle cap.

Light flooded the room. An involuntary sob of terror spilled from my throat.

Thomas swung his fist back to hit me again. I scooched back on the bunk, retreat my only defense. "Don't hit me," I pleaded.

He reached in and shook me so hard my teeth rattled. "I saw you sneak out of your office. Why are you on my boat?"

"You followed Ellen. I wanted to know why."

"I always follow Ellen. She's my wife."

"Ex-wife. She doesn't belong to you."

"Ellen is mine."

This guy was certifiable. "Why don't we forget about this misunderstanding?"

"You McKays are so stinking proud." His gaze narrowed. "You're being punished for working at that lousy newspaper."

This made no sense. "You're punishing me because of the *Gazette?*"

His face neared mine. "I'm killing you because you're a McKay."

My mouth went dry. "Killing me? Why not write a letter to the editor like everyone else?"

"You're gonna die."

I held my breath and watched his hands. How would he kill me? A knife, like the judge? Terror took over, and I struggled against my bonds, but the duct tape held.

He laughed, and the rasping sound made me tremble. "You're afraid. Good. At least you know I'm the master. Sterling never acknowledged I was his master, and he's dead now."

Would he confess? "You killed Alan?"

"I know you already figured that out. You McKays don't care about Ellen. You stole her from me, and you're gonna pay for that. When I get finished, there won't be a McKay left in this county."

He'd targeted my entire family? I had to do damage control. "We didn't tell Ellen to divorce you. She did that on her own."

"You people ruined my life, so you're going to pay with yours."

"Killing me won't bring Ellen back. She left for personal reasons."

"She left to fornicate with other men. That's not allowed."

"You'll never get away with this."

"Who'll stop me? Not you. You're shark bait."

My heart stalled. I would drown, same as my brother, unless I planted a worm of doubt. "Trish found ten grand missing from her investments. These new nets and your story of extra hauls won't hold water. Besides, forensics will convict you. This mattress is full of my skin cells. They'll catch you even if you kill me."

He swore and punched the wall. "Shut your lying trap."

"You can't erase my DNA."

"I gotta think." He glared at me. "What else did you touch?"

"Nothing. I came inside, saw you weren't here, and then you hit me. And I heard my dog yelp. You hit my dog, didn't you? Your DNA will be on my dog." I didn't know that for sure, but it sounded good. I was desperate.

"I kicked your mutt, and it ran off." His face darkened, and he grabbed me.

"What are you doing?" I hollered as he started walking with me in his arms, all the while I clutched that palmed bottle cap.

"End of the line for you. I'm going to find and shoot your dog."

"But the mattress! Even if you kill me and go back for my dog, you'll get caught."

"Right." His laugh was cruel.

Salt air hit my face as he exited the pilot house with me in tow. "Don't do this," I begged.

He twisted at the waist as if preparing to swing a golf club. He was going to throw me overboard! I cringed and flailed, but it didn't matter.

I sailed through the night air, gulped in a big breath, sank in the ocean, and sawed feverishly at the tape that bound me hand and foot.

Chapter 13

Dark water surrounded me as I sank, hands and feet hogtied behind me. Using the bottle cap's sharp edges, I sawed the duct tape bindings. I would drown as soon as I ran out of air if I couldn't free myself. My body trembled. Was I already too deep? *Please, please, let this work. I don't want to die.*

Another slice with the bottle cap, and my feet ripped free. I let out a little air and followed the direction of the air bubbles on my face. I kicked for all I was worth, losing my shoes in the process. With every microsecond, doubt and horror raged inside me. What if I'd misjudged the direction in the dark? But I couldn't quit. I wouldn't quit.

Finally, lungs burning, I broke the water's surface and gasped in a huge breath. I bobbed in the swells. The salt water stung my face, but I was alive.

I sliced through the remaining duct tape, and my wrists came apart. Treading water, I checked the moon's position low in the western sky. It was late at night, and land wasn't visible. I'd been missing for hours. Was anyone looking? With my known avoidance of boats, would they search the ocean?

Fear smacked me like a fist, and I gulped a mouthful of seawater. *Stop that, Lindsey McKay. Don't give in to fear. Use your head.*

Waves buffeted me. Thomas Mattingly had killed the judge. He tried to drown me. But here I was. Alive. He hadn't beaten me. Not yet. But I was so scared. What if a shark found me? What if I swallowed too much water? What if I got too tired to keep afloat?

71

Get a grip, woman. Think. Shrimp boats didn't travel very fast. If I was offshore, it likely took hours to get here. I didn't think I could swim to shore. Not this far out. My best chance for survival was to find a flotation device. If Thomas had thrown that old foam mattress overboard, I could use it. I prayed he had tossed it, and that I'd convinced him it wasn't safe for him to keep it.

The mattress would be somewhere between me and the departing boat. I swam until I tired. My heart pounded a mile a minute. I couldn't stay afloat if I exhausted myself with swimming. Some people survived a few days adrift in the ocean, but I had to keep my head above water. If I kept calm, I could float for hours, maybe longer. But would that be long enough for me to survive?

Out of the corner of my eye, something pale glowed in the moonlight. The mattress! I sent up a prayer of thanks and swam for all I was worth.

I was exhausted by the time I reached the mattress, but it didn't matter. I hooked my arms around it. The mattress would keep me afloat until help came. Or so I hoped.

Did my brother float like this in the sea? Did he have anything to support him? Was he even sober when he went overboard? There was so much we didn't know about Colin's death at sea. But I wasn't my brother. I wouldn't quit. No matter how hungry, thirsty, and tired I was. I would not give up.

Dawn came and went in a rosy glow. My hope of rescue faded as the sun inched higher. I was so thirsty. Water surrounded me, yet I couldn't drink a drop of it. The sun scorched my ears, neck, and arms.

Exhaustion fuzzed my thoughts. It would be easy to let go and slip under the waves. I could drift into the hereafter and wouldn't feel a thing. It was tempting.

But Thomas would get away with murder, and Daddy would go to prison. Thomas would shoot my dog. I had to make sure Thomas paid for his crimes, and Daddy went free. I clung to the mattress with renewed determination. My life mattered.

I drowsed until a sound awakened me. The *chop-chop-chop* of a helicopter. I hollered. I kicked in the water, but the chopper flew away.

They hadn't seen me on this pass, but someone was searching. Tears welled in my eyes. I had to believe they would come back.

The sun was heading toward afternoon when the chopper returned. My cramping feet barely churned through the water. Even so, the helicopter banked toward me and hovered directly overhead. The words "U.S. Coast Guard" on the cherry red helicopter were the sweetest I'd ever read.

A man splashed down beside me. "My name's Michael. You must be Lindsey."

Relieved, I could only nod. He secured a life jacket and a harness around me.

"If you release the foam pad," he said, "you'll fit in the basket."

"Can't," I croaked. "It's evidence."

He made a hand signal to the chopper and then pried my fingers open. "I won't leave it behind."

Dizzying moments later, I sat in the chopper wrapped in a blanket. A small bottle of water appeared in my hand. As I drank greedily, Michael returned with the soggy mattress.

He closed the chopper door, and the pilot headed for shore. Michael took my vitals and started an IV drip to hydrate me. Though we flew on a level heading, I felt as if I were still bobbing in the ocean. "Thank you for rescuing me. You're my guardian angel."

"It's what we do, ma'am." Michael massaged cool ointment onto my neck. "The Morrison County Sheriff is waiting your arrival at Coast Guard Station Savannah in relation to a murder case."

I smiled but my sunburned face had no stretch. "Thanks. Did you catch Thomas Mattingly?"

"We seized him and the *Pamela Sue* this morning."

It was over. I had survived, and Thomas was in jail. I'd done it. Daddy would be cleared. Relieved, I let my eyes drift shut and dozed fitfully until we landed.

Coast Guard personnel wheeled my gurney into the station. Once inside I saw a familiar face. Ike Harper galloped toward me. "I'm all wet," I protested, "and sunburned." He still managed a loose hug.

"But you're the best thing I've ever seen," Ike said. "Thank God you're safe."

As I took his outstretched hand, his warmth flooded through me like a heat lamp. I felt grateful for his solidness. Despite my time in the sun, I was shivering. Perhaps the shock of all that had happened was catching up to me. Ike's fingers gripped mine lightly, but they felt like they would never let me go.

"Thomas Mattingly isn't going anywhere. I got him." There was satisfaction in Ike's voice.

"How'd you find me?"

He squeezed my hand. "I'll start at the beginning. Your flower samples tested positive for the judge's DNA. Seminal fluid."

"Seminal fluid?" I shook my head. "That must have been his special tonic. Gross. Trish told me she'd seen him paint the flower bushes with fluid from a Mason jar. Why would he do that?"

"Because he was a pervert. Everyone knows he rubbed those flowers on women's faces. He was laughing inside as he marked his territory all over town. Once I knew about Trish's missing money, it was a matter of finding out who spent the ten grand. Mattingly was the only person who fit the bill, so I went to have a talk with him, but his boat was out. Then I saw your purse, abandoned on the dock. Your car was still at the *Gazette*. With Bailey hiding under it. She was shaking and upset. The only thing that made sense was that Thomas had taken you, so I notified the Coast Guard."

"Enough about the judge. How's my dog? Is she okay?"

"Bailey is fine. The vet checked her out. She's at my house with Trent."

Thank goodness. "And Daddy?"

"I offered him a ride here, but he wouldn't come. Said his heart couldn't take the strain. He's pretty shaken up."

"Poor Daddy."

"You should be saying Poor Ike. I've been living a nightmare ever since I found your abandoned purse. You're lucky Mattingly didn't stab you before he threw you overboard."

I shivered. "Don't I know it."

"Why were you on his boat? Why didn't you come to me first?"

"After I learned that the judge had an affair with Ellen, I figured Thomas had a strong motive. But I needed to bring you proof. So I snooped around on his boat and found the judge's missing Rolex."

"I warned you about investigating. I was worried you'd get into trouble," Ike said, but there was no anger in his voice. Only concern.

"I was coming to get you when Thomas clobbered me." I paused. "You seem to have all the loose ends wrapped up."

"We monitored the ship-to-shore radio and heard Thomas talking on one of the channels. The Coast Guard got a fix on his location, sent a cutter to intercept him, and took him into custody. Thomas denied you were ever onboard, but he couldn't explain the missing mattress, the Rolex, or the explicit pictures of Alan and Ellen hidden in his boat

74

registration papers. Thanks for bringing the mattress back with you by the way. During interrogation, Thomas confessed that he threw you overboard. He used the photos to try to blackmail the judge."

"But why would the judge care? Ellen is a divorced woman."

"Because Alan Sterling was in the process of deeding the motel to Angie. He'd made a promise years ago, and he knew if Trish found out, there'd be trouble."

That made sense. Trish Sterling had put up with a lot over the years. Losing a valuable piece of property might have been the last straw. If she'd taken her philandering husband to divorce court, she might have won more than her freedom.

Ike continued, "After Alan Sterling handed Thomas the ten grand, the judge's ego got the best of him. He made the mistake of bragging to Thomas about shagging Ellen. Thomas went nuts and stabbed him. He'd stolen your father's knife and taken it with him just in case. He claims he didn't expect to use it, but…he did. The Coast Guard Search and Rescue Team found you, and the rest is history."

He gave me a long searching look. "Next time, leave the investigating to me."

Next time. I liked the sound of that. Because of Ike I had a future. If he hadn't kept following leads, no one would've looked for me until too late. "Thanks for saving my life. All I want now is to go home. No hospitals. I'm refusing treatment. Can you make that happen?"

"I can, after you're medically cleared."

Chapter 14

The morning sunlight filtered into my room. I opened my eyes, relieved the horizon had stopped moving as it had when I was in the ocean. My dresser, crowded closet, and cluttered bedside table had never looked so wonderful. I was glad to be home, although I'd had to fast-talk the ER doc out of hospitalizing me for exposure yesterday.

Every muscle in my body ached, my skin felt like it had been shrink-wrapped, but I was blissfully alive.

A rumble of voices filtered into my bedroom. I needed a shower before I faced anyone. Fresh water pounded the salt from my pores and washed the baked-in seawater from my hair. Afterwards, I rubbed aloe everywhere, slipped on a tee and yoga pants, and headed for the noisy kitchen. "What's going on?"

Aunt Fay gave me a gentle hug and handed me a painkiller with a glass of water. "Saints be praised. You're safe and sound."

"I'm okay." I gladly took the pills and drank the water. It would take a while to get over this horrible sunburn.

"I'm not," she said, dabbing her eyes.

"My turn." Cousin Janey wedged between us. "You scared us."

"I was pretty scared myself."

"Of course you were," said Aunt Fay. "Sit down, and I'll pour your coffee."

"Where's Daddy?" I asked.

"Oh, he'll be out directly." Janey cleared her throat. "We want details. How did you solve the case?"

"I wasn't certain it was Thomas until it was too late." I recounted how his new shrimp nets had started me wondering about where he was getting his money. "He owed Ellen back money for child support, so it didn't make sense that he had plenty to spend."

Janey cracked eggs in a bowl. "How did Thomas get the money?"

"Blackmail. Thomas knew the judge's secret." My mouth watered as bacon sizzled. "Sterling paid Thomas ten thousand dollars, but Thomas killed the judge anyway."

"Back to the blackmail part," Janey said. "What did Thomas have on the judge? Alan Sterling didn't care who he slept with or who knew it."

"Except that when the judge started sleeping with Ellen, Thomas snapped photos. For all we know he might also have taken photos of the judge and his other conquests."

Aunt Fay frowned. "I wonder why Thomas left a photo of a rose by the judge's body, instead of a picture of the judge and one of his lovers."

"Because the judge was a pervert," I said. "What did he care about most?"

Janey stared at me over the island stovetop. "His Inverness Pinks?"

I nodded and munched a piece of bacon. *Heavenly.* "You remember he rubbed roses across women's faces?"

Aunt Fay sat beside me. "Oh! This is going to be juicy. Tell us."

I blotted my greasy fingers on a napkin. "Seems the judge brushed a special elixir on his roses. Bailey seemed more interested in some rose bushes than others, so I asked Ike to test three roses from those bushes."

They hung on my every word. "And?" Janey spooned the scrambled eggs on a platter and joined us at the table.

I heaped my plate with food. "And the roses bore the judge's DNA."

Janey's face scrunched in confusion. "He spit on the flowers?"

I swallowed some eggs. "He made other biological deposits on the roses."

My cousin danced out of her seat, her ponytail bobbing wildly. "Yuck. Ick. Omigod. That's horrible."

Aunt Fay howled with laughter. "He marked every woman in town with those roses. What a field day the bridge club will have with this."

"Good thing he's already dead," Janey said.

"This is the best meal I've ever eaten," I said, as I dug into my eggs with abandon.

Janey grabbed my arm. "How did Thomas learn about the judge's secret juice?"

"A few months ago, Ellen had an affair with Alan. Thomas was livid. He followed the judge and photographed the whole process. Ike said they found intimate pictures on the boat."

"What a story," Aunt Fay said. "But you're safe, and the charges against George were dropped. Congratulations, Lindsey."

My father wandered into the dining area. Deep creases lined his pale face, and his silvered hair stood on end. "Welcome home."

"Daddy!"

He looked me up and down. Taking care not to touch my burned skin, he put his arms around me.

I could feel him trembling as he whispered in my hair, "I thought I lost you. It's a miracle you survived."

"The whole time I was out there, I kept thinking this couldn't be the end," I said. "Surely fate wouldn't do this twice to our family."

"Fate had nothing to do with it. Sheriff Harper put it together. I'm ashamed to say I'd had too much to drink and didn't know you were missing." Daddy's arms fell to his sides. "I'm making changes in my life, Lindsey girl. Will you keep the paper on course while I get help?"

"Are you returning to the *Gazette*?" I asked. I loved my dad, but I wouldn't work for him.

"No." He held my gaze. "I'd rather enjoy my golden years."

"Then I want the editor-in-chief job."

"It's yours, sweetheart. I'm officially retired."

"I thought about everything," I said. "I had a lot of time out there, bobbing around in the ocean."

"And?" Aunt Fay asked.

"Dorothy in *The Wizard of Oz* was right. There's no place like home. Danville is where I want to be."

"Another answered prayer." Aunt Fay clasped her hands together theatrically.

"Amen," said my father as he caught Aunt Fay's eye. "Let me know when you want to leave, Fay."

"You're leaving already? Why?" I blinked in surprise.

Daddy gripped a kitchen chair. "Fay has had a recovery place on speed dial. She's offered to drive me there tomorrow. I'll be gone for a while."

"I'm stunned. But…that's great, Daddy. Really it is."

"Say you'll take care of everything."

"You know I will." It was a solemn promise, and he could tell I meant it.

There was a knock on the door, and Trish Sterling entered carrying her terrier under one arm. She gave me a happy smile. "I'm so glad to see you, Lindsey. Thank you for catching my husband's murderer. When I heard what Thomas did, I could've spit nails."

"I wasn't too happy with him either," I said.

Trish turned and smiled at Daddy. "Which reminds me, my sink is dripping. George, would you look at it?"

"This isn't a good time." Daddy sent me a panicked look. It only lasted a second, but I read his mind. He needed to settle things with Trish, and he couldn't do that in front of us.

"Don't worry about me," I said. "I've got plenty of company."

He managed a wry smile. "All right then. Now's a great time."

After they left, I beamed at Janey and Aunt Fay. "Between Daddy being cleared, my almost murder, and Thomas being caught, we'll have to work hard to get everything on the newspaper pages."

Ellen and her three little girls arrived. "I'm so happy you're safe," my co-worker said, while her oldest handed me a basket of my favorite junk foods.

I couldn't say much with the little girls there, so I thanked them politely. My cousin took the hint and invited the kids outside to play on the swings with her.

As soon as we were alone, Ellen's face quivered. "How could I live with Thomas for years and not know he was capable of murder?"

"No one blames you," I said, and I meant it. "Thomas will be held accountable for his actions."

"I put you in danger." Ellen blinked back tears. "I shouldn't have asked you to find out about those nets. You'll have my resignation letter today."

"Don't be ridiculous." I wiped away the moisture on her cheeks. "We're a darned good team, and I'm going to need your help."

Ellen tried to smile. "You're staying?"

I nodded. The sunburned skin on the back of my neck pulled, and I swallowed a grimace. "I'm the new editor-in-chief. Speaking of the paper, who's there now?"

"My mother is holding down the fort until I return."

Another car arrived, and I heard a distinctive bark. The front door opened, and my dog bowled into me. Despite her delirious wiggles of joy, I checked Bailey for injuries and found none.

Rising, I smiled at Ike and his son. "Thank you both. Bailey means the world to me."

"Me too," said Trent. "Dad says I can get a dog like Bailey."

I ruffled the boy's hair. "That's great. Meanwhile, you can visit Bailey any time you like."

"You're staying?" Trent asked. At my nod, he pumped his fist in the air. "Awesome."

"Would you step into the front yard with me?" Ike murmured in my ear.

"Sure." I owed him my life. I bent over to Trent's level. "Would you and Bailey like to join the other kids out back?"

"Yeah," he said, tapping the side of his leg. "Come on, Bailey."

Ike opened the door and led me under the canopy of a large live oak. I'd played childhood games under this tree, but what Ike wanted from me was no game. He'd been very direct about his interest over the last few weeks.

"You owe me a date." He held my gaze. "I've got big plans for us. Be forewarned. Crazy and naked are on the menu."

Liquid fire singed my insides. No longer would I deny my attraction for him. I slid my arms around his neck. "Crazy and naked suits me fine."

His arms wound around my waist, and I lost myself in his kiss.

--The End--

Turtle Tribbles

A Lindsey & Ike Mystery, Book 2 of 3

Maggie Toussaint

Chapter 1

"I've got turtle tribbles," an athletic young woman said.

"Come again?" I glanced up from the ad log I'd been wrestling with to see a visitor in my office doorway. I waved her in as I remembered her name. Selma Crowley, our Turtle Girl, a summer posting coveted by college interns. Each of the Georgia barrier islands had students who monitored the yearly loggerhead turtle migration to our shores and subsequent egg hatching.

She perched on the edge of a chair. Her bright blue eyes matched the skin tight tank she wore over running shorts. From her boyish haircut to the rings on both second toes, this gal set her own style.

Selma made a funny face. "Oh. Sorry, Miss McKay. I forget everyone wasn't raised with geeky parents in suburbia. Mom and Dad are whacko about Star Trek everything. I grew up on a steady diet of the TV shows, movies, and Trekkie conventions. The episode about tribbles is my favorite."

I closed my laptop and reached for a pad of paper. "Please, call me Lindsey, Selma. We're not big on formalities here at the newspaper. What are tribbles, and what do they have to do with our endangered loggerheads?"

"Tribbles are adorable space creatures, but they multiply faster than rabbits. Just like the TV show, my tribbles are out of control. I desperately need your help."

I sat in stunned silence. No way was she talking about space creatures on the island, was she? There would've been sightings of spacecraft. Unless they were sneaky and were just here for our turtles. Crazy possibilities spun through my head. Selma and her boss could've called the TV networks in Savannah or Jacksonville to break this story. Instead, they'd chosen our small weekly? The skeptic in me raised its ugly head.

I settled on what I hoped was a professional expression of interest. "You've got alien creatures in the turtle nests? Do you have photos?"

"Sorry. Didn't mean to alarm you. Substituting tribble for trouble is a bad habit I picked up ages ago. So far, I haven't seen aliens, but we can't rule them out either." Selma shook her head, her expression glum. "I don't exactly know who or what is causing the tribble, I mean trouble, but eggs are disappearing from the turtle nests. It happens every year, but this year's been the worst ever."

Disappointed, I absently rolled my pen in my fingers. "So we may or may not have aliens on the island, but we positively have fewer turtle eggs?"

"You got it."

It wasn't much of a story, except for an earnest young woman's word that eggs were disappearing. "You sure it's not natural processes?"

"Real sure. When raccoons, feral hogs, or fire ants invade a nest, they don't cover everything back up. But, the nests with the missing eggs look undisturbed."

"How do you know anything's missing? Do you have a device like ground penetrating radar to detect the eggs?"

"All you have is a geeky kid's word. I know when the turtles lay their eggs because of the crawl marks on the beach. I dig up each new nest to make sure it isn't a false crawl, then cover up the eggs and mark the location. We're still early in the nesting season, but more nests should've hatched already. I dug up two of the first nests I marked before I decided to come over here." She passed me her hot pink cell phone and showed me the images of sandy holes. "Look at the photos. No eggs."

All I saw was a sandy pit in each image. Was there a story here? If the egg theft didn't pan out, I could slant this into a nature piece about turtle nesting. "I'd like copies of relevant images, including those of an egg hatch for the story, and your permission to use them." She nodded eagerly. I hated to bust her bubble, but this question had to be asked. "Don't take this the wrong way, but could you have missed the hatch?"

"Nope. I hit the beach first thing every morning and monitor the nests after dark each night. If turtle eggs hatched, I would see the signs. Eggshells would be cracked and left behind. The sand from the nest to the sea would be full of turtle tracks. The nests would look disturbed. I didn't see any of that at those locations. It's like the eggs got beamed into outer space."

I leaned back in my chair and briefly contemplated the domed ceiling light. No way was I writing a headline about turtle-egg stealing aliens. I needed an angle for this story, or else I should encourage Selma Crowley to leave. Time was always in short supply now that I ran the *Gazette*.

Though it was technically my family's newspaper, I was editor in chief. Daddy had retired last fall, and Mama lit out for seminary after their divorce. So the newspaper became mine, and I loved the work, loved telling people's stories. Selma's tribbles appealed to me, but I needed more from her. Sometimes it was a matter of asking the right questions.

"You mentioned this happened before," I said, returning to the missing egg puzzle at hand. "Are there historical records of empty nests I can report?"

"The last two turtle girls made notes about nests that didn't hatch, but only last year's gal documented that eight of the no-hatch nests were positively empty. The previous year, several nest markers went missing, which dropped them out of the count, so the stats don't reflect those occurrences."

"Eight out of how many?"

"The number of nests on my island are usually a hundred or so. As you may know, turtles return to the same beach every time they lay eggs. I'll scrounge up the data and email it to you."

I sensed she was holding back. Time for me to tighten the screws. "I need concrete facts for the paper, Selma. I can't report on feelings or impressions." And I certainly couldn't report on aliens with transporter machines. "Why would anyone steal turtle eggs?"

"Because there's a black market for the eggs. Some claim they're an aphrodisiac, while others say they're a delicacy. With about a hundred and twenty eggs in each nest, a poacher can pocket several hundred dollars off the theft of one nest."

Black market. Egg heist. I was starting to get an idea of where this story could go if it got legs. "Can you use a hidden camera to catch the thief in the act?"

"Too many nests to monitor. They're along the entire length of the beach. That's a couple of miles."

Disappointed, I blurted out the first thought in my head, unfiltered. "Too bad we don't have drones to keep watch or something."

"Too bad we can't afford armed drones to shoot poachers," Selma said. "They have no right to do this."

The cute little blonde had a bloodthirsty bent. Interesting. "What can be done about this issue? Who have you notified?"

"Only my co-workers, my boss, and a wildlife agency contact know about the thefts. We didn't want the news getting out at first, but my boss gave me the go-ahead to contact you for an article. Dr. Jernigan said it would be cheaper to scare the thief away than it would be to prosecute him or her."

Hmm. I didn't like being used, but I was in the business of selling papers. A photo of this pretty girl on the beach would be eye-catching. Unless we had a deluge of homicides or other major news, there was no reason her picture couldn't be above the fold on page one.

"Do you have a plan going forward?" I asked.

"Sure do. I'm in the process of removing the traditional markers from the nests. First, I have to record all of the nests' GPS coordinates in my phone and in my spreadsheet. If that thief doesn't already know where the nests are, he or she will have a lot of digging to do to find eggs."

"What do the nest markers look like?"

She showed me an image on her phone of a small wooden stake. Not much of a thing, really, but if you knew what to look for, the stakes reveal the location of the nests.

"That should stop your thief all right. Anything else?"

"The wildlife folks have been monitoring ferry passengers for a few days. They're especially interested in people who might suddenly carry a duffle bag or cooler on or off the island. According to apprehension reports elsewhere, stolen turtle eggs are usually transported in plastic bags inside a container. They've made a list of folks who carry these containers infrequently on our ferry. They have a way to detect the eggs, but I can't talk about that yet."

"Why not?"

"Until they catch the thief, I'm sworn to secrecy. They don't want to tip anyone off. The goal is to get this poacher, not send him or her underground for a few weeks."

A secret. All my journalistic instincts were firing as I scribbled down her words. This could be big. If I was this excited about the story, everyone else would be too. I flashed a bright smile her way. "I'd love to see the nests firsthand. Let's set a time for me to catch the ferry over to the island this week. What's a good day for you?"

Selma waved off my question, her lilac nails catching the light. "My schedule is flexible. You tell me when you want to come."

Sooner was always better in my book. "Let's plan for tomorrow. I'll take the early ferry. Meanwhile, send me the stats from past years on turtle nests and counts. Oh, and I'd love a quote from your boss. Will you share her phone number with me?"

A few minutes later, I had Dr. Jen Jernigan's number at the university, and Selma had my business card tucked in her hand.

Once she left, my office manager, Ellen Mattingly, joined me. "I heard most of that. You believe her?"

I shrugged. "What's not to believe? She thinks aliens are stealing her turtle eggs to light up their nights."

"I'd love it if someone lit up my nights," Ellen said, "but mostly nighttime is about getting my three kids out of my bed. At least you have a boyfriend, though I haven't heard an Ike report recently."

Sheriff Ike Harper had swept me off my feet when I moved home last fall. I enjoyed his company and our extracurricular activities, but I valued my independence too. "He's still pressuring me to move in with him and his son."

"I don't see why you're resisting the idea. You're at his place all the time, or else Alice Ann is staying with his son. Why not go all in on the Ike train?"

Indeed. Why couldn't I move in with him? I'd pulled out a suitcase several times, but I'd never packed a thing. Something about our relationship wasn't to my liking. Darn if I knew what it was.

Chapter 2

The next morning, Selma met me at the island ferry landing in a utility vehicle and drove us to the research quad. We were loading gear into the Gator when a young man approached. "Y'all headed out?" he asked.

Selma introduced me to her friend Buzz, a mechanic in grey coveralls with the sleeves ripped out. His closely shorn hairstyle matched his name. He took the tote of tools and the cooler from Selma and easily hefted them into the vehicle.

"Thanks. I'm taking Miss McKay out to see the nests," Selma said.

"She writing a story on you?" Buzz asked Selma.

"I'm doing a feature on the turtles," I said, handing him my business card. "The *Gazette* periodically highlights the research here on the island."

"Good to know. Make sure y'all have plenty of water in that cooler. Gets mighty hot on that beach." He flipped my card a few times in his hand, pocketed it, and waved goodbye. "Catch you ladies later."

"He's sweet on you," I said as we motored toward the beach.

"Not interested. Buzz is a hunk, but he's not my type. I want a guy who gets me. Someone who doesn't expect me to change who I am to be with him."

"Sounds like you're speaking from experience. Bad breakup?" An involuntary shudder ran down my spine as I said breakup. Thinking about turtle eggs and turtle babies was doing weird things to my biological clock. Ike was the first serious boyfriend I'd ever had. Last night, he asked me again to move in with him, but I told him not yet.

Would he give up on me because of my commitment issues?

"Yep. A guy at college. Ozzie will probably be the next president or something, but he's a jerk. All over campus, girls flag him down and write their phone numbers on his hand."

"Does he call them?"

"No, but it annoyed me." She hesitated. "Ozzie visited a few days ago, hoping I'd changed my mind about our breakup. But if anything, this summer internship has given me clarity. I need to focus on things and people I enjoy being around. With him, it's always about doing what he wants. I don't miss being his girlfriend."

God knows I had no crystal ball. Ike and I were still finding our way, but that was the point. Love wasn't a one-size-fits-all process with the same answers for everyone.

I shot her a reassuring glance. "It sounds like you reached a decision about Ozzie. Good for you on knowing who you are and what you want."

"I'm glad you agree. I hope one day I'm as well respected and settled in my career as you are."

She made me sound older than dirt. We were barely eight years apart, but that must seem like a generation to her. Even so, it took an effort to pry my back teeth apart. "I'm sure you'll do fine."

On the beach, Selma pointed out the wooden markers on nesting sites. About every third nest, we stopped for her to catalog the spot with her phone's GPS and to remove the physical marker. I took pictures of her recording the data. She explained how she coded the sites and logged the data. I took copious notes on the process, knowing this wouldn't all fit in the story, but not wanting to misunderstand anything in case it had relevance to something she said later.

After we skipped a few more nests, I asked her the reasoning behind the hit-or-miss approach. From my previous career in writing for a scientific journal, I knew science demanded similar data sets among control and test populations, so leaving certain nests flagged struck me as unscientific.

"My boss suggested this strategy," Selma said. "Partly to keep from tipping our hand too soon. I left the markers in place near the beach access point. Unless our thief comes out here daily, he or she shouldn't notice what I'm doing."

"Will you put the markers back once you catch the thief?"

"If it were up to me, no. But Jen says that having the nests marked keeps good people from inadvertently pitching a tent or having a bonfire there. I get where she's coming from, so I'll replace the markers. I want to protect my turtles from all threats."

Her boss, Dr. Jen Jernigan, was in Athens this week. I'd gotten a nice quote from her yesterday over the phone. She commended the thorough job Selma was doing and remarked on how discouraged she was about anyone disturbing the turtle nests.

I took photos of the nests and of Selma driving the Gator, making sure to get the lighting right to display her passion for this work. I was glad for the sunscreen I'd applied on the ferry because the June sun was already brutal at mid-morning. Even so, I knocked back two bottles of water before we reached the south end of the beach.

A nice cross breeze cooled the sand flats around us. Water sparkled everywhere, as small waves built and crested on the sand. Gulls winged happily overhead, and little plovers chased after each retreating wave. The Turtle Girl may have a lowly job on the scientific totem pole, but dang if the benefits weren't spectacular.

I wished I'd been more adventurous during my college years, but my brother's death at sea and my subsequent fear of water kept me from seeking intern opportunities like this. That's how I'd ended up writing for a science journal in Atlanta. The job had been safe, not scary. I'd gotten over my fear of water recently, but I would always have a huge respect for the sea. Fishing, boating, or swimming in the ocean would never be my first choice for recreation.

"I may have news for you on Friday," Selma said.

Two days from now. "Oh?"

"The wildlife agency is going to try something."

"Their top secret test?"

"Yep."

"Can you give me a hint?"

"You'll have to be patient. This is for the good of my turtles."

~*~

Friday came, and each minute ticked slowly off my life clock as my phone didn't ring. By noon, I couldn't take the suspense any longer. I phoned Selma, and my call went straight to voice mail. I tried her again at three. Same result. Since I had her boss's number, I tried that, only to be told that Dr. Jernigan hadn't heard from her. I phoned the research center's onsite answer gal. "Do you know where Miss Crowley is?" I asked.

"She's probably on the beach with her turtles," the receptionist said, her voice cheery.

Her good mood darkened mine. "I tried her phone already. Left messages. She isn't returning my calls. I'm concerned about her."

"I'll take a message and put it in the lab, hon. That's all I can do."

I hung up, miffed. Selma was so passionate about her turtles. I couldn't understand why she wasn't returning my calls. Needing to talk to someone about this in person, I whistled up my dog, Bailey, a rescued black lab mix, and walked over to the Morrison County Sheriff's Office.

Ike was delighted to see me. He told his Deputy Alice Ann Harper, his sister, to hold his calls and watch Bailey. The office door locked behind us, he drew me into his arms for a senses-drugging kiss.

"I've been thinking of you all day," he murmured in my hair as his hands went to work on my clothes.

The need to be with him thrummed in my head, in my heart, and I gave myself up to the heat of the moment.

~*~

Afterward, we cuddled together in his chair. "We should do this more often," Ike said. "Instead of lunch."

"Did Alice Ann hear us?" I asked as my thinking cleared.

"Not if she knows what's good for her."

"Oh."

"So, did you come over here to seduce me, or is something else on your mind?"

"The Turtle Girl is on my mind. Selma Crowley isn't returning my calls."

"She might be busy."

"All day? I doubt it. She has a flexible schedule. There was supposed to be a break in the turtle egg case by now. She said something was happening today."

"Is she on the island?"

"I don't know. The receptionist was vague."

Ike snorted. "She's always vague. Not much between those ears."

I playfully punched his bare chest. "Get serious. I'm concerned about Selma. Something's wrong."

"You got spidey senses now?"

"No. But it's like when I knew who killed the judge last fall. My gut says Selma's in trouble. She really wants to catch this egg thief."

91

Ike gazed out the window for a few moments. "We could watch the ferry unload this evening."

That was a good idea. Selma hadn't confirmed what time she'd have news today. Maybe she'd hop the last ferry and call me from the safety of the mainland.

"I should go out there by myself. Since you're a cop, you might spook her or whatever's going down."

Ike's arms tightened around me. "I insist on going with you."

The atmosphere in his office shifted from fun to stifling in a heartbeat. I tried to get clear of him, but his arms caged me like jail bars. "What gives you the right to insist? This a free country."

"You nearly died investigating the judge's murder. I can't take that chance again. I know you have this Nancy Drew, girl detective, streak in you. I can handle that. As long as I get to come with you. I can't risk losing you, Linds."

The way his voice cracked melted my heart. He wasn't locking me behind bars. He was helping me do my job. "Okay. You can come."

Chapter 3

In the end, Ike's eight year old son Trent and my dog accompanied us to the ferry landing. It was exciting seeing the large vessel power up the creek, the setting sun glazing the boat a golden hue. A dark-haired woman with a German shepherd also waited at the landing. She made it clear from her tight grip on her dog's leash that she didn't want the two dogs to socialize.

Bailey whimpered and tugged at her leash, so she quickly became Ike's responsibility. When she couldn't get free, she sat and wagged her tail at every passerby.

About twenty people disembarked. For the most part, the folks were dressed in business casual attire, and I assumed they worked at the research center. None of them stood around chitchatting. Everyone hurried to their cars and quickly departed.

I recognized the cheerful secretary for the center, an ecologist I'd interviewed about rising sea levels, a couple from high school who'd gone native, and the maintenance guy who worked with Selma. But there was no Turtle Girl.

"She's not here," I said to Ike when the last person trudged off the boat.

"I'll talk to the captain, find out when he last saw her," Ike said, eyes narrowing as the other woman with the dog walked onboard the ferry. "Hmm."

He wrapped Bailey's leash twice around my wrist. "Stay here. I need to check something out."

I meant to stay out of the way, but before I knew it, Trent, Bailey, and I were standing on the dock beside the ferry. Inside the cabin, Ike, the woman, and the captain searched around one particular bench seat.

"What are they doing?" Trent said. "Is it a scavenger hunt? I'm good at finding things."

"I'm not sure, but your dad was clear we should wait outside."

Trent gave me an odd look. "You always do what he says?"

Uh-oh. How would I get out of this jam? Then the answer popped in my head. "When it comes to you, I do. You're his treasure."

Trent kicked the dock piling and jammed his hands in his pockets. "Are you going to be my new mom?"

Now I was truly speechless. Ike had asked me to move in, but marriage hadn't been offered. After a bad divorce, Ike was justifiably gun-shy. I was—I didn't know what I was. Confused, mostly.

I cleared my throat. "Your father and I haven't talked about that, but I'm sure if it's something Ike wants to consider, he'll talk to you about it first."

"Well. It wouldn't be terrible. I wanted you to know."

"Thanks." With an endorsement like that, would I ever be mother material? Another disappointment in a strange day.

My gaze returned to the boat. The woman gave her dog a treat and unclipped the leash. Her dog dashed onto the dock to see Bailey. Both dogs wagged tails. With the pedestrian and vehicle traffic cleared out, I removed Bailey's leash so that they could play.

Ike waved us aboard and introduced me to Rosa Rapido. She worked for the wildlife agency, and she was checking the boat and its passengers at Selma's request. Both of us tried calling her phone again. No response, and her voice mail box was full.

"According to the captain, the last time Selma rode the ferry was Tuesday when she came to the mainland to talk with you," Ike said. "She returned to the island on the late ferry that day. He saw her meet you at the island's ferry landing on Wednesday, but he didn't see her yesterday or today. Unless she hopped a ride in someone's boat, she's still on the island."

"What's special about this bench?" I asked.

"My dog alerted on this location," Rosa said. "Whoever sat here handled turtle eggs recently."

How long did scents hang around, I wondered. "It might be someone from the center who works with turtle eggs."

"Or it could be the egg poacher," Rosa said.

94

An egg-sniffing dog. That was the secret weapon. And it worked. Someone on the ferry had handled turtle eggs. "I thought the thieves used large containers to haul the eggs. I didn't notice any big coolers or duffel bags. Most everyone had a briefcase, a small tote, or a backpack."

"I had Jamie sniff near the larger bags as people came by," Rosa said. "We didn't get a hit."

"This is so odd. Where is Selma? She put all of us in motion to be here. Why doesn't she answer her phone? I'm concerned about her." I turned to Ike. "Is it too soon to report her as a Missing Person?"

"There's no indication of foul play, violence, or danger. I have to follow protocol. I'll check with her work and call her family to get a timeline of her activities," Ike said.

I wanted to go to the island right now. Why was I the only one feeling any urgency? "Something's wrong. Selma wouldn't have missed Rosa and the egg-sniffing dog for anything."

Ike studied the horizon before turning to me. "If you're determined to search for her, I can requisition the law enforcement boat tonight, and the two of us can search the island for her, but it would be best to search in the daylight tomorrow. Less chance of missing something. We could take the first ferry over, and leave the speedboat at the ready on the mainland in case other responders need to join us."

A couple of hours of daylight remained. Probably not enough light by the time we got Trent situated with his aunt, made arrangements for dinner, and rode in the boat over to the island. And we wouldn't have ground transportation over there on short notice. Those things had to be prearranged.

I understood the time constraints. Sometimes I didn't care much for being a grown-up. A sigh slipped out. "Tomorrow it is."

Chapter 4

Overnight the wind shifted direction until we had a strong northeaster blowing. Spitting rain fell from the leaden sky in fits and bursts. On the beach the sand shifted and swirled until it felt like needles were pelting my skin.

As soon as we hit the island this morning, we'd checked the dorm, talked to Selma's friends, and looked around the research center. No leads. Periodically, I called her number as we searched, in case the phone was nearby. No luck.

The Gator she used for transport was parked amongst the fleet, and it was pristine clean. As a precaution, Ike asked that no one touch that vehicle until we found her. After an exhaustive search of the center, we had no answers and a missing Turtle Girl.

No one could place Selma after dinner on Wednesday. Her parents in west Georgia hadn't heard from her, and they were told how to file a Missing Person's Report. Ike called the mainland to put his deputies on alert.

Ike checked out a Gator and drove us to the beach. We traversed the entire shore's length near the tidal zone. There was no one walking on the beach this morning, no one was in sight. No large objects bobbed or rolled in the surf either. Every now and then, Ike stopped and scanned the sea and the sky.

"What are you looking for?" I asked.

"Birds."

I gestured down the beach. "Plenty of shorebirds out here."

"Not those kind of birds. Vultures."

96

Oh. The kind of birds that fed on road kill. "You think she's . . . dead?"

"Looking that way."

"I know turtle eggs are valuable and all that, but killing someone over turtle eggs seems farfetched."

"Unless she caught the thief in the act. He might have had priors or a reason to avoid arrest."

"In my book, a human life is worth way more than some turtle eggs."

"Which is why you're not a criminal, hon. Not everyone thinks the way you do."

His distracted tone was at odds with his comforting words. A glance at Ike confirmed he was in full hunter mode. Everything about him was on high alert. No doubt about it, he had the skills for this job. But at what cost?

I found my voice. "Does this job keep you awake at night?"

"Not usually, but some cases are personal."

From the intense way he glanced at me, I surmised I was personal to him. Without his stubborn determination to find me a few months ago, I'd be sleeping with the fishes. His tenacity served me well. How would Selma fare?

Ike stopped the Gator. "This isn't productive. She showed you the nest locations, right?"

I nodded, and he continued. "You drive, and as best you can remember, show me every nest."

We swapped seats. "The ones with the low stakes are easy to spot, but some nests aren't marked now." I explained Selma's system of removing the markers and using GPS coordinates to catalog the nests.

"What about new nests? Do you remember where those are?"

"There were several she pointed out as less than a week old. I'll try to find them for you." I angled away from water's edge, taking us to the high beach. The sand was really blowing up here, but the misting rain had stopped. I was glad for the vehicle's windshield protecting my eyes.

We zigged and zagged from nest to nest, hovering in the high beach area as we searched. Nothing looked undisturbed. Nothing looked like a Turtle Girl. I stopped at the tail end of the beach, out of ideas and out of luck.

"This is pointless," I said. "She's not here."

Ike shook his head. "She's here all right. I smell something."

We were in the most downwind position on the beach. I sniffed and got nothing. I sniffed again, deeper. There it was. A faint tinge of something spoiled. My gut knotted at the implications. "You sure?"

"Positive. I can take you to the research center. You don't need to help me search the dunes for Selma's body."

Her body. I cringed inside. I'd feared the worst, but I had trouble accepting the finality of it. We were too late. The compassionate young woman who spent all hours of the day and night protecting our endangered turtle nesting sites was no more. She'd been the picture of health. If she was dead, it wasn't likely from natural causes. Such a tragedy.

Selma had been right all along. She had tribbles in large measure, and now they'd killed her. Furry space creatures weren't to blame. A person did this to her.

It was hard to breathe, hard to swallow. I'd compounded her problems with my story demands, not knowing the consequences would be so costly. I had responsibility here. Selma had come to me for help, and I'd let her down. I wouldn't fail her in death.

My gaze lifted to the heavens momentarily as I said a prayer for her. "I want to help. Selma tried to get evidence for me because I couldn't run her story with conjecture. She knew I need proof of the theft. If I hadn't demanded proof, she might be alive."

"Blaming yourself won't change anything. Ms. Crowley made her choices. She could've let the wildlife dog sniff out the egg thief before she checked the nests again. She could've been more aware of her safety. You're not responsible for whatever happened to her."

Easy enough for him to say as we rolled toward the dunes. Something about the dune line bothered me. That short one. It wasn't here before. "I see something odd."

"Got a bead on it myself," Ike said. "Sure you don't want to wait elsewhere?"

I gritted my teeth. "I'm certain." I parked a little ways from the new berm and steeled my nerve.

Ike bolted out of the Gator and headed to the north end of the berm. I followed in his footsteps, but truthfully, the sand around the berm looked pristine. No tire tracks, no footprints. If this was a crime scene, the wind had scoured the scene.

With an oyster shell he found on the beach, Ike carefully moved sand from the upwind side of the berm. The smell of death was strong here. No doubt in my mind that this was Selma's untimely grave.

Another swipe of his oyster shell scoop and human toes showed. As Ike carefully brushed sand away, more of the toes became visible. The second one bore a toe ring, and the nails were painted a familiar lilac. Ike's head sagged, and his shoulders stooped. "Found her."

Chapter 5

Deputy Alice Ann Harper and her boyfriend Jimmy had been fishing in the nearby sound, so they arrived on the beach in fifteen minutes, anchoring their boat in the creek behind the island and trekking over the dunes to meet us. They set about defining the crime scene and photographing the uncovered corpse.

As he assisted the deputies, Ike handled calls to the coroner and other authorities regarding the discovery and notification process. I phoned Selma's boss at the university. Dr. Jernigan was appalled and said she would drive down to the coast the next day.

A small crowd gathered on the beach as the news spread. Most were islanders but some worked for the research center. The young adults wept openly. I envied them that freedom of expression. I was heartsick about Selma, but I would grieve for her in private. It was the McKay way.

Noontime came and went, as did the ferry. Ike made arrangements for the island women to provide sandwiches and sodas for his team. I wasn't allowed near the crime scene, though I knew in one glance that Selma hadn't been shot or drowned. Someone had smashed the back of her head with an object. Blunt force trauma.

Had she known someone was behind her? Had she died at once or was it a slow death? Should I have insisted on coming over here last night? No, Ike had been right on that. I wouldn't have seen the Selma-shaped berm in the dark.

My newspaper camera was in my tote bag, but Ike had cautioned me against using it. I knew the drill, and there was no way I'd blow this case for him. I snuck a few "safe" shots of the crime scene tape and the people standing on the beach. The dark sky overhead added to the grim scene.

I wanted to help, but what could I do? The cops focused on the immediate area around Selma. Seemed to me that her killer had either lain in wait for her, arranged to meet her, or been surprised by her presence.

Unless it was the laying-in-wait option, the crime had been spontaneous, meaning the killer had used an object at hand to strike her. There were no obvious blunt force objects in sight. No rocks. No baseball bats. No hammers. I shuddered thinking about the horrible pain Selma must have endured.

I'd have nightmares after this, for sure, but so far, I'd managed not to throw up after seeing another dead body. We were far from the main beach access that most people used. I started walking in the high beach area and stopping at any nest marker I found. All were labeled in the last four to six weeks.

The island was narrow here, the forest and the homes were north of us. Behind the dunes were beach meadow plants, if I was remembering right from my college ecology class. I tried Selma's phone a couple of times as I walked. It hadn't been on her body. There was a slim chance it had been lost during a confrontation.

After my tenth dialing attempt, I heard a faint reply. I turned in the direction of the sound. A few more calls, and I had it. The bright pink case glimmered in the sand. I phoned Ike and told him. Minutes later, Alice Ann and Jimmy arrived in Ike's Gator. They went through the routine of photographing and bagging the evidence.

"Way to go, Lindsey," Alice Ann said. "The battery in this phone is nearly dead. A few more hours, and we wouldn't have found it at all."

"I hope it's helpful," I said, sighing out my frustrations. "I feel so bad for Selma. Her summer job got her killed. In what world is that right?"

"We can learn a lot from people's smart phones. We'll get this charged. Jimmy's kid brother is really good with tech stuff. With a few keystrokes, he can tell us where she went and who she talked to."

"Great. We need to catch this thief-turned-killer."

~*~

The rest of the weekend flew by. From Ike, I learned Selma's parents drove down from north Georgia on Sunday and identified her body.

The coroner officially ruled her death a homicide, and Ike became too busy to talk to me. Was the distancing because I was The Media?

Whatever the reason, I still had a paper to run. I wrote a press release on Selma's death for our *Gazette* website and also started the longer article I would run in Wednesday's paper. We would find this killer, and he would pay for his crime.

I hoped.

Selma's smiling photo while driving the Gator would go on page one. No, I couldn't do that. That would be tacky to sensationalize her death. Did I want to be *that* kind of paper? I could use one of my pics of the crowd viewing the crime scene, the one with the darkest sky in the background. Then I could offer the lovely picture of Selma to her parents for the full obit.

Fortunately, I was saved from a morality introspection by a phone call. My assistant Ellen announced that Dr. Jen Jernigan was on the line.

We talked for a few minutes before Selma's boss got around to why she called.

"We recovered Selma's log book from her locker," Jen said. "I had Buzz cut the lock off this morning with the cops watching. I'm not sure why the log book was locked away if she'd been working at the time of her death. Be that as it may, I don't understand her shorthand. The cops took the logbook, but they allowed me to copy the pages so that I could give them to our replacement Turtle Girl."

"The replacement doesn't understand the abbreviations either?"

"No. Selma invented her own nomenclature. Worse, she didn't keep the online log current. The bulk of her research to date is on these pages, but we're not sure what it says."

Odd. When I spoke with Selma last week, she sounded like an organized person. "I'll help any way I can. I took notes on her process while I interviewed her, but I may not have all the information you seek."

"Anything would be better than the nothing we've got now. When can you return to the island?"

"I'm birthing a paper. I should be clear in the morning though. Can I catch the noon ferry over for an afternoon visit?"

"That works. Meanwhile, I'll have Minnie Lee start with taking an inventory of the marked nests."

"Selma removed ten markers the other day when I was there. Those nests are tracked solely with GPS positions."

"I'm hoping that's what most of this gibberish is."

"We can match the data in her log with my Wednesday interview. I know what those numbers mean."

"Sounds good."

"Listen, I've been wondering about this. What kind of tools did Selma routinely carry in her Gator for work?"

"Nothing fancy. A flashlight. A shovel. Resealable plastic bags. A first aid kit. I don't know what all else."

"When I saw her Gator on Saturday morning, it held no gear. Where did it go?"

"I'll have Minnie Lee look for it. She should know where Selma kept things."

"Why's that?"

"She worked on the island on another project until last week when her grant money ran out. Last year her best friend was the previous Turtle Girl, so she knows the job. I contacted her straight away to fill Selma's position, and she accepted. Even moved into Selma's dorm room."

"I see." And I did see. Minnie Lee profited from Selma's death. She was familiar with the island and the intern job. She'd been out of work, and now she had a job. That sounded like motive to me.

Chapter 6

"Keep your news-hound nose out of my case," Ike said over burgers and sweet potato fries with his son that evening.

The heat of the day had eased and where we dined on his screened back porch was lovely. You'd never know this was a guy's home. Everything had a place, a neatness quality I admired. Even the yard was tidy and trimmed to perfection. Ike had built a home here in the woods for him and his son after his divorce. Off and on all evening, I'd been looking around, wondering if this could ever feel like my place.

I wanted clarity about our future, but being with him was like getting caught in a riptide. We were both strong, independent people, and his tendency to boss me around chaffed more than my pride. I understood that this was his case, but he hadn't given me a chance to explain.

Communication was essential in relationships, and this was as good a time as any to state my point. "I'm not sticking my nose into anything. I was invited to the island. Dr. Jernigan asked me to help her and Selma's replacement, Minnie Lee, to decipher Selma's shorthand on the nesting records. I'm taking the ferry over there tomorrow."

"I wish you would wait a few days."

At least he wasn't forbidding me. That was a step in the right direction. "Are you close to making an arrest?"

He pushed his empty plate away and gave me his full attention. "Are you asking as my girlfriend or as the newspaper editor?"

"Depends." I grinned. "Is the answer different?"

"This is an ongoing investigation. The Crowleys have political pull, as it turns out. The wife is the governor's cousin. They're threatening to bring in one of those TV docudrama shows to solve the homicide. The mayor's calling several times a day. He wants the case to be solved before the upcoming festival."

"You can handle the pressure, Ike Harper. You were always cool under fire on the football field."

"That was then and this is now. In the innocence of youth, I thought I couldn't be hurt. But now I know that I bleed just like the next guy. Worse, if I make the wrong move or arrest the wrong person, I'm doing everyone a disservice. I need to do this right."

He wouldn't guilt me into caving. I sat back and barred my arms across my chest. "So do it right. I'm not pressuring you to solve the case yesterday. But, this Minnie Lee girl benefitted from Selma's death. Seems like motive to me."

"Motive." He snorted. "Far as I know, she wasn't on the island when Selma was murdered. I reviewed the ferry's passenger logs for the two weeks before to the homicide. Minnie Lee left the island the week before Selma went missing and if she returned to the island before we found Selma, she didn't use the ferry."

I absorbed those thoughts, wishing I had my notepad. Ike must have seen a certain gleam in my eye. "You can't print any of that, you hear? I'm thinking out loud," he said.

"You should do more of it." I gave him my most encouraging smile. "What else did the ferry logs tell you?"

"We've identified everyone who rode the ferry recently. All except for one guy, Ozzie Shaniman. No one knows who he is."

Ozzie. Not a common name. Could that be Selma's Ozzie from college? "How old was he?"

"That wasn't on the log, but I talked to the skipper. Said he was a college kid. Went over on one ferry and returned on the next one. I don't think he's relevant."

"He sounds like Selma's ex-boyfriend. He came down to rekindle their relationship, but she wanted nothing to do with him."

Ike startled. "How do you know this?"

I relaxed, sipped my tea, and perversely enjoyed his discomfort. "She confided in me that he'd visited her."

"People tell you things. How do you get them to talk?"

"It just happens. At the time, I was peeved, if you want to know the truth. Selma wanted to be responsible and respected like me one day. I'm barely eight years older than she was, and her comment chaffed. It made me feel twenty years older than I am. I was jealous of her youth and naiveté, and now she'll never be my age."

"You look pretty hot if you ask me, despite your advanced years."

I playfully punched his arm and nodded to where his son played with my dog. "Trent might hear."

He leaned in and lowered his voice. "You know what I'd rather be doing."

Hard to miss that particular heat in his eyes. We both enjoyed the constancy of our physical attraction. He was ready for the next step. I'd gotten cold feet. I stacked the dishes to settle my thoughts. "I do, but we're on good behavior right now. What about the turtle egg thief? I haven't heard a peep about it."

"I asked Rosa to keep her investigation under wraps. The turtle egg thief might be our killer, or it might be someone from the island."

"Or the new Turtle Girl. Or the ex-boyfriend," I added helpfully.

"Neither of whom is on record as using the ferry for transport."

Reading between the lines, his wry tone came just shy of calling my ideas worthless. Why was he being so short-sighted? "You could find out if either of them has a boat or knows someone with a boat."

"If my other leads run dry, I might."

Talk about a brick wall. I tried another approach. "What about Selma's phone?"

"Nothing unusual in her calls or messages."

Hmm. "What about the missing gear from Selma's Gator? Did it turn up?"

He shook his head. "I didn't know anything was missing."

"Well, it is. Dr. Jernigan confirmed that this afternoon. All of Selma's Turtle Girl supplies are gone."

"That is odd," Ike began slowly, "but those items could have been stored elsewhere by someone trying to be helpful. It doesn't necessarily mean the turtle egg thief is behind her death."

"I disagree. Why would gear be missing if it wasn't relevant? I need to look around over there. Besides, the turtle egg thief does his dirty work when no one's looking. It's unlikely he would kill me in broad daylight. I see no good reason why I can't go over to the island tomorrow."

Ike rubbed his chin and studied me with cop eyes. After a long moment he nodded. Another woman might've backed down from his steely glare, but this was a turning point in our relationship. I knew it, and if he had the sense I credited him with, he knew it too.

"Let me clear a few hours from my day to accompany you," Ike said. "We can take the law enforcement boat and not be constrained by the ferry schedule."

A boat ride with Ike. A compromise, but precious time alone with my guy. I smiled. "Works for me."

Chapter 7

The wind still blew out of the northeast, giving a solid chop to the sound. As Ike kept the throttle maxed out, I found it easiest to absorb the bounce of the boat if I stood.

I'd packed a picnic lunch hoping we could take a break and enjoy the peaceful solace of the island before we returned. Ike looked so at ease captaining the boat, I felt guilty for having any residual nervousness about being on the water. To his credit, Ike hadn't batted an eyelash when I insisted on wearing a life jacket. He'd also slipped one on, though his wasn't belted.

I had a super healthy respect for what a tiny speck a small craft was on the surface of a vast, rippling body of water. If I ever found myself adrift in the sea again, I needed the security of a life vest. I wasn't scared anymore. I was prepared.

When the island's landing came into view, Ike moored at a floating dock behind the main pier. The Dockmaster helped with the lines. Behind him stood Buzz, the mechanic from the research center.

I removed my life vest, changed from a ball cap to a wider brimmed hat for sun protection, and gathered my reporter gear. Ike hefted our mini-cooler onto the dock, and I shouldered my tote. Ever the business professional, I'd worn a jaunty blue capris slacks set with a breezy cotton tank and matching sneakers.

"Dr. Jernigan asked me to be your escort today," Buzz said, reaching for my tote after I stood on the dock.

The feminist in me wanted to hang onto the tote, but even as my knuckles tightened on the straps, I caught the glare Ike sent me. We were supposed to observe and not make waves.

Ike had made a slight concession to being low profile. He hadn't worn tactical gear or a belt full of people-stoppers. His badge and gun were clearly visible, however.

I summoned a smile and followed Buzz to a new-looking, four-seater Gator. "Thanks. We're headed to the center to meet with Dr. Jernigan and Minnie Lee."

When Ike climbed in the back, I had a choice of seats. It was a no-brainer for me. I climbed in the backseat with Ike, which elicited a smile. He reached for my hand, and I slipped my fingers in his. He was here because he cared about my safety and well-being. That meant something.

That meant everything.

As the utility vehicle traveled down the road, my thoughts about Ike cleared. I loved him. He loved me. Even though he'd never said the words, he'd shown it in many ways. When I first said the L-word to him, his eyes had glistened.

I loved his man of action style, but words were my life's stock. I didn't need a ring on my finger. This was the twenty-first century after all. I should be satisfied with the status quo, but I couldn't quite gloss over my neediness. It kept bubbling back to the surface.

Turning from my personal thoughts, I surveyed our surroundings. The enclave of buildings around a central courtyard had a dated feel, but in a good way. The old-fashioned architecture signaled a slower pace over here. It reminded me that everything wasn't geared for speed. This research center was a place of creativity and intellectual dreaminess. A place that spoke to my muse.

Inside the office, the bubbly receptionist greeted us like we were long-lost family. Dr. Jernigan came out of her office, shook hands, and invited us into her office. She was a pant-suited, thirty-something woman with a prowling stride. Her chin length hair was stacked and sprayed just so. If she wore makeup, it was applied to look invisible. From her lean and muscled physique I guessed she ran marathons.

"So nice to finally meet you," Dr. Jernigan said after we were seated around a small work table. "Thank you for helping us with the data interpretation. Minnie Lee, who will be here in a few minutes, has no idea what Selma's notations mean."

No idea? That seemed beyond odd. I set my tote down by my chair. "Have you reviewed the entries, Dr. Jernigan?"

"Please call me Jen. I glanced at the pages, but I didn't spend much time with them. Minnie Lee needs to understand the process or she isn't a good fit here."

Reading between the lines, Minnie Lee's job was on the line if she didn't interpret her predecessor's data in a useful way. From this, I inferred Jen Jernigan ruled her domain of interns in a Darwinian manner. Survival of the fittest.

I kept my expression bland. "I'll do what I can."

Minnie Lee blew in like a gusty storm. Laughing, smelling of sun lotion and sea breeze, long, honey brown curls mussed, feet sandy and bare, logbook in hand. "Sorry. It took me a little longer than I thought to complete the nest inventory this morning. I started at two a.m. today, and two turtles came ashore and nest. That was awesome. There's nothing like the magic of a turtle crawling out to sea at dawn. I have pictures!"

"I'd love to see them later," I said, catching Jen's immediate scowl. Jen Jernigan was not a happy camper. Was her irritation at me or her employee?

On the other hand, Minnie Lee seemed puppy friendly. The dynamic between these two women was strained. Jen was clearly the boss, but she seemed dismissive toward her recent hire.

"Oh. Sure thing," Minnie Lee said. She raised a marbled composition book in the air. "I have the logbook. Anything you can tell me will be appreciated."

I pulled my reporter pad from the tote. "It won't take long to go through this. I took three pages of notes on how Selma recorded data."

Minnie Lee nodded and asked Jen for a pen.

After she handed the intern a pen, Jen turned to Ike. "Would you like a walking tour of the research facility while they talk shop?"

"Sure," Ike said, surprising me.

Soon as they left, Minnie Lee shook her wrists as if to get feeling in her fingers. She leaned forward. "I don't know if I can do this job. Selma was a saint to work directly for the dragon."

"The dragon?" I repeated, feeling as if I'd fallen into a fiddler crab hole.

"Dr. J is a fire-breather. You don't toe the line exactly, and you're out. I was trying to get my stipend extended, which I should have done ahead of time, but she made me pack and leave the island. Said I was taking up needed space. My project supervisor is out of the country so

I had no one to run interference for me. Dr. J stuck a post doc in my dorm room the next day. Rumor is she's about to pull the plug on the entire intern program. Even though she gets us cheap, as in free, we don't meet her professional standards. In her eyes, post docs are the wave of the center's future."

Wow. Such drama in this group of scientists. And here I thought the center looked so tranquil and reflective. Instead, everyone avoided the dragon so they didn't get canned. "I had no idea. What else can you tell me about her?"

"Besides being hard on her staff, she, uh, has a thing for men."

"What do you mean?"

"The sheriff's probably getting hit on right now."

I stiffened instinctively. Minnie Lee's remark sounded unprofessional. My impression of her dropped several notches. But Ike – how would he handle her making a pass at him? He must be used to that by now. Surely he wouldn't be tempted.

Loving someone made you vulnerable. I'd never expected to revisit teenaged insecurities again when it came to guys, but that's exactly how I felt right this second.

But my insecurities were private. "I don't think she's his type."

"You never know. I saw what happened when Selma's ex-boyfriend visited. Dr. J gave Ozzie her phone number."

My brain went nuts trying to fit these tidbits into a decision matrix. Sounded like Jen, Selma, and Ozzie were in a twisted love triangle. Did Jen fixate on Selma's ex-boyfriend, and he turned her down because he wanted Selma?

I wasn't sure Minnie Lee was a credible source for island shenanigans. Sure, she was friendly, but she could have an ax to grind against her new boss for booting her off the island. On the other hand, Minnie Lee could've gotten rid of Selma for another chance at an island job. I needed another source for corroboration. Otherwise, this was merely juicy gossip.

Either way, I needed to get us back on track. "I'm sorry to hear of the discord, but I'd rather we focus on the data set. Here's what I know about Selma's notetaking system."

I showed her my notes on what Selma had recorded in the logbook that Wednesday. It didn't take Minnie Lee long to catch on to the coding system, which gave me second thoughts about her helplessness. Was she posing as a dummy? It seemed Selma's death could be related to other island troubles.

"I heard Selma's gear is missing," I began slowly once we'd deciphered Selma's shorthand. "Will you show me where it was stored?"

Minnie Lee nodded and gestured for me to accompany her to the maintenance barn. "Selma loved lilac. She put purple hearts on everything. Sometimes she used stickers, but most times she used nail polish. And she got to where she rarely used her shovel anymore. She was crazy about a little hand rake from a gardening set she brought over. Said it was better for checking the nests. We knew what items were hers because she made a big deal out of claiming them."

"Nail polish can easily be removed. So can stickers," I said as we entered a big barn. Several mowers and tractors were slotted at the far end. Nearer to us were several utility vehicles in various stages of repair. A soldier-straight array of tools lined the back wall.

"But that's the thing. I know these people because I've been here for two summers," Minnie Lee said. "They're decent folks. No one would take Selma's gear. There's no need. See for yourself. We have plenty of rakes, shovels, and other hardware."

I stepped forward to inspect the long row of tools. Which one of these implements had blunt force trauma written all over it? Any of them could be lethal. Did Ike's deputies swab every tool for Selma's DNA? If so, what would that tell us? We had no way of knowing if Selma touched these items recently.

Worse, if Minnie Lee was to be believed, Jen Jernigan was a tyrant of a boss and a man stealer. Minnie Lee, who landed Selma's job, was back on the island where she wanted to be. As for Selma's ex-boyfriend Ozzie, it wasn't clear if he'd returned to the island after Selma said no. On top of that, a host of other people worked here, people who regularly came and went on the island. And the turtle egg thief was still at large.

Selma had been dead for five days, and we weren't close to solving her murder. We had to do better.

Chapter 8

Ike and I were sitting at a seaside pavilion on the island eating a picnic lunch of my homemade chicken wraps and the fresh blueberries I'd picked at the berry farm. With the tide ebbing and the breeze dying down, the overhead covering provided little respite from the June heat. My clothes clung to me like plastic wrap, but my thoughts spun with the information Minnie Lee planted in my head.

"Could Jen have been in a love triangle with Selma and Ozzie?" I asked Ike.

"This is the first I've heard of it. Why do you ask?"

"As soon as you and Jen left the office, Minnie Lee ratted out her boss. She said Jen showed an interest in Selma's ex-boyfriend."

"Jen seems like a woman with a more discriminating palette."

"She gave you her number, didn't she?" Oops. I didn't mean to say that out loud. Didn't want him to know I was channeling my teenaged self. Or that I had doubts about him.

Ike stilled. He raised his eyes slowly to mine. "What if she did?"

"I wouldn't like that."

"Good. I wouldn't like it if a guy gave you his number either."

He'd avoided answering the question. I chewed my lip to keep more insecurities from tumbling out. I knew he liked me. I knew he wanted us to move in together. I knew I loved him.

"I wish you could say it," I whispered to my plate.

After a silence that went on forever and a few seconds, Ike answered. "You know what I wish? I wish you'd leave crime detection to me."

That he'd dismissed my wish so easily rankled. My retort came out hot. "Selma was getting proof for me to run a story. I owe her."

"These people aren't what they seem. I can't put my finger on it yet, but I will. Meanwhile, I don't want you anywhere near them."

I popped out of my seat to pace the pavilion. "I don't appreciate you telling me what to do. Crime investigation is like journalism. It involves asking a lot of questions to different people who are connected to the subject matter. Then it's a matter of stringing the facts together into a plausible story."

"Except journalists don't carry weapons for self-defense. Someone killed this young woman, Linds. I don't want you in harm's way."

"I'm careful. Besides, people like me. They open up to me."

"One of them is a killer."

"You don't understand." My voice cracked with emotion. "I need to do this."

"Where's this coming from?" he asked, still sitting and eating. "Why are you upset?"

I shrieked in frustration and hurried away from him. It was embarrassing to lose control like this. I'd just learned how to live again, after surviving a lonely existence in Atlanta. I wanted him to admit I could make a contribution. To admit I mattered. I didn't want my wings clipped.

He vaulted from his seat and crossed to me. "What's really wrong?"

The faster I blinked, the faster the tears flowed. I tried to answer, but words failed me. Miserable, I turned from him and let it out. Moments later, his arms encircled me, and he stroked my back. "Easy, gal. I've got ya."

Despite the heat, I nestled into the comfort he offered, needing him. Needing us to finally be honest with each other. He kept stroking my back, rubbing my shoulders, and making quieting sounds. Finally, the outburst quieted, and I felt like even more of a fool.

Between sniffles, I thanked him. He lifted my chin and looked me square in the eye. "What's this about?"

I thought we were about enjoying each other's company and committing to a future, but I wasn't certain of his understanding of our relationship. "I need clarification. About us."

"I threw her number away." He made a dismissive gesture with his hand. "I'm dating you."

That was good, but it wasn't enough. "Ike, why should I move in

114

with you?"

Despite the heat, his silence chilled me. I wished I could stuff the genie back in the bottle, but I'd asked the question. Now I had to live with his answer.

"Don't box me in a corner," Ike said. "Annette did that, and I'll never be another woman's property again."

"Forget your ex-wife. I'm a different person, one whose life is based on words. I love you. Is the feeling mutual?"

Ike raked his fingers through his hair. "I care for you. But the L-word. Annette flung it at me every time she wanted something."

A motor rumbled in the distance. Buzz was returning in the four-seater Gator. I didn't have much time to say my piece.

"You're a good guy, Ike Harper, a guy I want to spend time with," I said, laying my heart bare. "I think we have a future together, but I can't move in with you without you saying those words. Our commitment level feels unbalanced."

His jaw clenched then his mouth flapped soundlessly, as if he was working the rust off his heart. I waited and waited some more.

Footsteps on the deck planking brought me back to reality. We were on the island and no longer alone. Buzz was our ride to the ferry dock.

"Y'all finished here?" Buzz asked cheerfully.

I turned to Buzz. "I believe we are." Quickly I stowed our lunch in the cooler, despite Ike scowling at me.

Once again, Ike climbed in the backseat, and I had my choice of locations. I clambered in beside him, which I hoped he took as a show of support. But he didn't reach for my hand, and I didn't reach for his.

My thoughts churned all the way to the boat. We'd reached an impasse. Would our relationship survive? From the stern set of Ike's jaw, he wouldn't change his stance. Past events had seared his heart. He had my empathy up to a point. I had to protect my heart too.

I couldn't bear to think of breaking up with Ike. To see him every day for the rest of my life and know we weren't a couple. No killer had come after me on this trip, thanks to Ike's presence. I risked a glance at him again. Tension radiated in unrelenting waves from his body, his spine rigid beside me in the vehicle.

We'd come this far together. Was it the end of the line for us?

Chapter 9

"I need some time," Ike said when he dropped me off at home. "Stay out of trouble."

Not trusting myself to speak, I nodded and let myself out of his Jeep. He'd been so quiet all the way back that I didn't know what to think. "Stay out of trouble" didn't mean he was dumping me. But still, I'd managed to stun him, and from his immediate withdrawal, I'd hit a nerve.

One day passed without a word from him and then another.

I kept busy so I didn't obsess about Ike. I filled the newspaper with fresh copy, kept the house clean. The shower grout sparkled, the silver service gleamed. At some point, I should move out of my parents' house on River Road, but they were divorced and headed in different directions. Mama to seminary, and Daddy on cruises with his lady friend Trish.

Right now, it suited everyone for me to house sit until they decided what to do with this place. But I kept thinking about the property Daddy set aside for me at mid-county. I'd recently paid to have that lot bush hogged and had several pines removed. If I built there, Ike couldn't easily cruise by my house to see if I was home.

I didn't like this separation at all. I picked up the phone almost hourly that first day to call him. But he needed time. I loved him enough to give him the time he needed.

~*~

"He's acting like a jerk," Cousin Janey said the following Thursday evening. "You should hand Ike his walking papers."

At Janey's arrival, I'd stopped trimming, weeding, and edging everything in the yard and offered her a Chardonnay. We sat on the front porch steps. "I don't own him. His ex-wife tore his heart out and stomped on it."

"Patsy from the salon has been over at the jail every day since y'all broke up."

Irritation flashed. "We didn't breakup. We had a discussion, and he said he needed time."

"Still. His truck isn't here in the mornings. His sister spends her evenings with Jimmy at the bar. People know there's a rift between you."

"Ike and I will be fine," I insisted. "I have to believe he misses me as much as I miss him."

Janie let those words die in the breeze. "Are you going to the bonfire kickoff of the festival tomorrow?"

"No."

"He'll be there."

"So what?" I frowned at my sharp tone. "I'm not chasing after Ike. If that's what he expects, forget it. Enough about me. What's this I hear about you and the bail bondsman?"

"Junior Curtis is an interesting man." Janey smiled and sipped her wine. "I've shown him property all over the county, but he hasn't decided on a location."

"By my count, y'all have had four lunch dates."

"Now who's listening to the county grapevine?"

"I'm delighted for you, but what about his alleged mob ties?"

Her lips quirked. "Not true."

"But the limos from Florida?"

"That's a secret, but he isn't dirty. He's actually a nice guy."

"He kissed you yet?"

"Maybe."

"You like it?"

"Maybe."

My cousin glowed like the fireflies on the lawn. Whatever Junior Curtis was, he was good for her. "Be careful."

"I will. And I asked him to snoop around in your Turtle Girl case because he has friends in low places. He didn't want to at first, for fear of crossing Ike, but he says there's a network of captains who routinely take charters to the island and keep the passage off the books."

I hefted my wine glass, noticed it was empty, and set it down. "Why would they do that?"

"Income declaration on their end and privacy of the charter clients."

Secrets. That was progress. "What did he find out?"

"First is that head honcho woman. Dr. Jen Jernigan. She uses a certain retired fisherman exclusively to run her back and forth to the island. You may have seen his shrimp peddling truck all over the county. Junior says she pays for his services in a nontraditional way."

Janie's crude hand gesture clued me in. The guy was twice our age and more than twice Jen's weight. I did not need that image in my head. "Too much information."

"Also, the victim's ex-boyfriend uses the same skipper for secret trips to the island. Junior says Ozzie has made regular visits since mid-May. He usually rides over late Friday and returns early Saturday morning."

Interesting, but was it relevant? "What about the turtle egg thief?"

"Junior couldn't get any traction on that. Folks are close-mouthed about this person, though it seems a certain segment of the population knows what's going on."

Dusk thickened, but my thoughts centered on the new data. "How so?"

"I believe he's selling them turtle eggs."

It was a guy! Junior was amazing. I only hoped Janey wasn't trading sex with Junior for information. "We should follow him around."

Janey shook her head. "Probably not a good idea. Junior already went to Ike with his suspicions on the turtle egg guy."

"We don't know if the turtle egg thief and the killer are the same person. Those clandestine trips to the island intrigue me. We could stake out the charter captain. That would be easy. He docks at mid-county, and my lot there has a good vantage point of the docks."

"Bad idea. Didn't Ike tell you to butt out of his investigations?"

"You know what?" I vaulted to my feet. "I'm flippin' tired of waiting for Ike Harper to make up his mind. I need to take action. And I have Bailey. She'll protect me. The weekend's coming, and I'll bet the secret travel network will be hopping."

Janey downed the rest of her wine. "No way are you taking this spy adventure alone. I'm coming too."

"What about your daughter?"

"She's on vacation in Florida with her other grandparents. I'm free as a bird."

My eyebrows arched. "And you want to spend your time with me instead of the hunky bail bondsman?"

"He shouldn't think I'm on speed dial to answer his every call."

"Thatta girl. Now who has a tent we can borrow for tomorrow night?"

"I'll ask Junior."

Chapter 10

With Junior's help, the tent went up quickly. The campsite was soon ready for our stakeout, but I had no idea how the tiny portable stovetop worked. Junior provided it, saying it was a bad idea for us to have an open fire if we were spying on the dock.

I tried not to ogle Cousin Janey and Junior as he said goodbye. Pretending to inspect the stove, I had a clear shot of them in my peripheral vision. From the way Junior crowded her close to his SUV, the way she let him smooth her hair back from her shoulder, I was pretty certain the attraction between them worked both ways. Funny though, last fall when we were dealing with Junior for Daddy's bail, Janey wanted nothing to do with this man. She wouldn't even step foot in his bail bonds office.

The tide had turned, that was for danged sure.

My cousin returned before I figured out how the little camp stove worked. Her light and ready smile spoke volumes. "Don't say a word," she cautioned.

"Can't help it. You and Junior are an item."

"We are. Which is why I arranged for my daughter to be away. Then I got cold feet and glommed onto your stakeout. Junior knows I chickened out. I like him. But I don't know nearly enough about him. At my age, it can't just be about attraction. I need to know if he has a criminal record, or if he's still sleeping with Angie out at The Oaks Motel."

"Have you asked him about Angie?"

"No."

"Why not? You're usually direct."

"With you. But not with men. I've had guys show an interest in me since the divorce. There's something about our crazy relative lineage that positively excites men. It's like they believe we're tornados in the sack or something. Nothing could be farther from the truth. I'm a plain jane with an average amount of passion."

The tremble in her voice got to me. I drew her into my arms, and she clung fast. "You're not plain. You're beautiful. Even though starting a new relationship is terrifying, you have plenty of zippity-doodah for the bedroom. You haven't met the right guy yet."

She pulled away with a sniffle. "Junior is a complex guy and reticent about his past. Will you ask Ike to run a background check on him?"

"You ask him. Ike and I are on a timeout, remember?"

"He's probably at the bonfire in town right now. Every single woman will make it her business to see him and be seen. Doesn't that drive you nuts?"

"Ike makes me nuts. He's locked in a defensive mindset based on how his ex-wife acted. That barrier is what's come between us. On an instinctual level, he believes my motivations are the same as hers."

"Y'all are nothing alike."

"Exactly." I mulled his stubbornness around in my head. "But, I know firsthand how easy it is to run from your fears. It takes real guts to face them. I let my brother's death keep me from coming home for years. I created another life for myself, albeit an empty one."

"I'm glad you came home. Ike is too. He's different now that you're back. Less man on the prowl, more man in charge."

Bailey lifted her head, cocked her ear, and whined. "Shh," I whispered to Janey. "Someone's coming."

We'd set up our campsite at the back end of my lot, the farthest from the dock. We darted forward from tree to tree to see who was approaching the dock. A red pickup idled up to the shrimp factory house and parked. It was the guy we expected, Cap'n Nick. I fumbled for the camera around my neck and waited. A young man in jeans and a white tee climbed out of the passenger door.

I zoomed in on the guy's face as he shouldered a bookbag and then grabbed a large cooler. I snapped a few shots before he hurried after Cap'n Nick. Less than five minutes later, a speedboat roared out the creek. With Cap'n Nick and his passenger on the move, Janey and I were alone again.

"Who was that guy?" I asked.

Janey squinted in the thin light. "Never seen him before."

I reviewed the image in my camera and turned it off. "Me either."

"Could this be Selma's ex-boyfriend?"

"I've never seen a photo of Ozzie Shaniman, but this guy fits his description. What's his business on the island? And why the cooler? Turtle egg thieves use coolers, but he doesn't fit the profile of a turtle egg thief. People say a disgruntled former islander is behind this."

Janey's head rocked back. "You mean Ozzie doesn't fit the racial profile?"

The edge in her voice concerned me. "I mean he can afford college, so why bother stealing turtle eggs? You know I have no racial bias." Janey's lip poked out a little more. Were those tears in her eyes?

I guided her to our camp chairs. "Tell me what's going on. Now."

"I can't. I promised."

"Unpromise. Whatever it is, it's tearing you up. I mean it. Tell me right now or I'm calling Aunt Fay to grill you."

"No! Don't do that." Janey let out a shaky breath. "I'll tell you, but you can't tell a soul. Not anyone. Junior is . . . Junior has a . . . Junior used to . . ."

Horrible fill-in-the-blank words danced in my head. Sadist. Polygamist. Serial killer. Psychopath. "Janey, spit it out. I can't take the suspense."

"Junior has two children with a black woman."

I was so relieved I nearly slid out of my chair. "So?"

"So, Aunt Fay and my stepdad always assume we'll marry anyone we date." She held her silence for a long while. "We've never had a person of color in our family before."

"Then it's time we did." I reached over and took Janey's hand. "If it works out for you guys, fine, or if you move on and fall in love with a black man, a Hispanic dude, or a Chinese guy, it's okay with me. I promise you it will be okay with them too."

She placed her other hand atop mine, gripping me tightly. "You're sure? Because I really like Junior."

I spoke from my heart. "Life is short. Go for it, Cous."

Chapter 11

The sand gnats and mosquitoes found us at dusk, so Janey and I zipped ourselves inside the tent with my dog Bailey. We talked like school girls, joking and giggling and binging on snacks. I hadn't done a sleepover with my cousin in nearly twenty years. She was the closest thing I had to a sister, and I wouldn't let so much time go by before we did something fun like this again.

In hindsight, it was clear that distancing myself from the family these last ten years had hurt others. I had selfishly avoided home so that I wouldn't have to deal with my brother's loss. Not once had I thought about the far-reaching impact of my decision.

More to the point, I hadn't considered how Janey felt about me staying away. We used to tell each other everything, or we did before my brother's fatal boating accident. Afterward, I focused on getting away from painful memories and not thinking about my family at all. Now that I'd moved back home, Janey and I had fallen back into our best friends' mode.

I felt bad for abandoning her for nearly ten years, but the time away had seasoned me. In some ways, I felt like I was waking up after a long nap. As for Janey, I'd cradle her dreams and encourage her every chance I could.

After dark descended, I wished we'd ignored Junior's advice and started a campfire because at least then we could move around freely outside the tent. Janey checked her cell phone a bunch of times, and I checked mine because that seemed to be the thing to do. No calls. No Ike. Did he even know I wasn't home? It hurt that I couldn't answer that question.

"When is Cap'n Nick coming back?" I asked at midnight.

"How should I know? Maybe the guys hooked up with someone. They could've had beer or wine in that cooler."

"I don't believe Cap'n Nick and that young man are friends. Even if the trip is about island romance, it doesn't take this long to ride over there, have some dinner and fun, and return to the mainland. The longer they're gone, the more I feel like something else is happening."

"We should call Ike," Janey said.

"Based on what? A feeling? No way will he investigate that, especially in the middle of the night. Nope, the sheriff requires cold hard proof. He waited a day to go look for Selma Crowley because all I had was a feeling."

"Say the guys come back on the boat. What's our plan?"

"We document their coming and going from the dock."

"But nothing else, right? You're okay with letting them go?"

"I might've confronted them in the daylight. But not at night. It feels creepy."

"No kidding. I'm glad we're not camped beside the dock, and I'm double glad we've got Bailey for protection. Are you thinking to build out here?"

I ignored the personal question. "I want something to happen. That's what I want."

"Is it always about the story?" Janey asked, her voice softening.

"It has to be."

"And what's your story?"

Janey would dog this topic to death. Might as well get it over with. "My story is a mess right now. I'm a to-be-continued. I thought Ike and I had something, but now I'm not sure he feels the same way."

"Hmm."

Bailey stirred, went to the front of the tent, and whined softly. "What is it, girl?" I asked, crawling after her. "Do you hear something?"

"I hear a faint buzz," Janey said. "A boat motor. They're coming back."

"About time." I fumbled for my shoes, my camera, and my binoculars.

"You're going out there?" Janey asked.

"I am."

"Shouldn't we wait here until Cap'n Nick's truck leaves?"

"I can't see anything from back here. If you want to hide in the tent, fine. I'm taking Bailey and observing from that big oak."

"You're not spying on them alone, but we'll be careful, right?"

"Absolutely."

We pulled it together and hustled outside, little flashlights showing us where to step. "If I wasn't scared," Janey said, "this would be fun."

Would our snooping amount to anything? My heart said yes. My head said be careful. Janey and I were vulnerable. We had to be smart about this. I clung tightly to Bailey's leash.

"Shh." I clicked off my flashlight at the big oak. "They can't know we're watching."

Janey grinned, her teeth gleaming in the dark.

I groaned inwardly at her delight. She'd been born to sneak around at night. I'd rather be home in my own bed, except for needing justice for Selma and her turtles.

A lump formed in my throat as I peered around the tree at the moonlit creek and the approaching boat. I tried to clear the lump without making any noise. Not working. I swallowed hard and managed to work it free.

We were fine, I reasoned. They wouldn't know we were here. This was scary, but we were safe enough. Besides, I wasn't doing anything wrong. This was my property.

The boat slowed to approach the dock. After mooring his boat, Cap'n Nick caught his passenger by the shoulder. "Not so fast, hot stuff. You owe me another $200 for this trip."

The sound carried across the short expanse of water crystal clear.

"I'm good for it, bro," the younger guy said.

"You're not good for it, and you're not my bro. You're paying now, or I'm calling the sheriff about this duct-taped cooler with your fingerprints all over it."

"You can't do that to me. You're part of this too!"

The young man's voice rose with each word he spoke. Was Cap'n Nick shaking him down or was it the other way around? I caught Janey's eye and made a motion like I wanted to take a picture. Janey held Bailey's leash while I tried to get a shot. It wouldn't take. Not enough light. Inspiration struck. I could use the camera to record the conversation. I switched the camera to video mode.

"Think again," Cap'n Nick drawled. "I may talk slow, but my brain is as good as any of you college kids' brains. You want custom transportation to the island like a high roller, fine by me, but you gotta pay."

"I'll catch up next time," the young man said.

"How do I know there'll be a next time?' Cap'n Nick asked. "Your gal got dead."

"Let me go."

"Only if you give me your car keys. You get them back when I have the two hundred."

No one spoke for a few long seconds. "Is there an ATM at the dock?"

Cap'n Nick laughed. "Good one, city slicker."

"Where's the nearest ATM?"

"The bank in town, which is a pretty far piece to walk. Go ahead. I'll wait."

"But my car's in the other direction, at your place. You made me leave it there so you could shake me down tonight. I should've known you'd double-cross me."

"You have two choices. I keep your car as collateral for the two hundred you owe me. Or I keep the cooler."

"The cooler stays with me. Thanks to you, the broker knows my name and where I live. I can't have him coming after me or my family," the guy said. "Don't call the cops."

"And?"

"You'll get your money."

I glanced over at Janey, and she was fooling with her phone again. Bailey lunged on the leash and broke free of Janey's grasp. The dog made a beeline for the dock, barking as she ran.

Fear struck hot as a fire poker, jolting me into action. Swearing under my breath, I tossed the camera to Janey. "Keep this on. I'm taping the conversation. I'll get Bailey. If something happens, call Ike."

"Wait!" Janey said.

"I can't take the chance they'll hurt Bailey. She's already been kicked by one bad guy in her life." I stayed her second protest with a finger to my lips. Honestly, she'd had one job to do, hold onto my Labrador retriever, and she blew it.

I handed my binoculars to Janey. "I'll be right back." Clicking my flashlight on, I jogged to the dock, calling the dog as I went. Both men huddled in the speedboat, quiet as field mice.

Bailey paced alongside the boat on the floating dock, barking. I hurried down the ramp to the lower dock, apologizing profusely for the dog bothering them as I caught her leash and brought her under control.

"Evening, Ms. McKay," Cap'n Nick said. "What are you doing out this way?"

"Camping on my property with friends. Bailey must've heard y'all talking and that's why she wanted to go out in the middle of the night. I'm sorry she bothered you."

"Y'all having a party up there?" Cap'n Nick said.

The hopeful note in his voice irritated me. Was he angling for an invitation? Not going to happen. "A few friends getting together. That's all. Good night."

For a large man sitting in a boat in the dark of night, Cap'n Nick proved to be amazingly agile. Before I walked four steps, he charged up behind me. Bailey went nuts, lunging back at him, snarling and growling and biting the air. My emotions warred. Save the dog, or save myself? I wanted to do both, but in that instant, Bailey yanked the leash from my hand. Self-preservation took over. No one was taking me captive again.

My heart threatened to burst from my chest. I screamed at the guy and ran the last few steps to the main dock. Thanks to Ike, I knew self-defense moves. We'd practiced them over and over. I could confront a larger, enraged man, or I could run and hide in the midnight shadows of the shrimp house.

I ran.

"Come back here," Cap'n Nick yelled.

Over Bailey's barking, I heard the younger man yell, "What's going on?"

"Get off your butt, and hand me an oar," the captain snapped. "This gal's the sheriff's girlfriend. She calls him, and we're both up the creek."

Call Ike. That's what I needed to do. But I didn't have my phone. I didn't have anything except the flashlight, which I'd switched off as soon as I hit the shrimp house. From memory, I summoned the layout. The conveyor machine that washed the shrimp and dumped them into a weighing pan was on my right. The ice crusher was on my left. Beyond on the right were large tables used in the past for heading shrimp. Further ahead on the left was a tiny office with a phone.

A phone. I tiptoed to the office as quietly as I could. Outside, Bailey yelped, followed by a splash. I grimaced and hoped she was okay. If I went back for her, I'd seal both our fates. Calling for help was the best plan, but the office door wouldn't budge. Locked.

My hopes plunged. I stood near the front door, and even though there was faint moonlight, making a run for it was my only option. Heart thumping madly, I dashed out, heading straight for the nearby thicket, away from my cleared lot. I had to keep Janey safe.

I darted from tree to tree, fighting briars and palmetto fronds. Behind me, I heard a vehicle door snick open, then the unmistakable retort of gunshot.

Chapter 12

I froze, paralyzed by that sharp blast. I couldn't move if I wanted to, except for my heart, which beat so loud I couldn't hear myself think. Despite sweating in the humid heat, an arctic chill turned my blood to slush. Did they shoot my dog? Did they shoot my cousin?

"That was a warning shot," Cap'n Nick shouted. "Come out of those woods, Ms. McKay, or the next bullet goes in your dog."

My brain rebooted, and I crouched behind an oak for protection. This stakeout had taken a wrong turn, and I had no idea what these guys were up to.

"What kind of monster are you?" the other guy asked. "I'm not shooting a dog."

I heard the unmistakable sound of flesh smacking flesh. "You will shoot the dog if the woman doesn't show herself in the next ten seconds."

Bailey. I couldn't fail my dog again. I resigned myself to being captured, but doubts surfaced. They didn't have Bailey. How could they? My dog went overboard. I would've heard her yelp if they'd caught her. All I heard was eerie silence. Bailey was brave, to a point. Then she hid. Like me. We were survivors.

Was Janey a survivor? I sure hoped so.

Cap'n Nick swore up a blue storm when I didn't step forward. "There's a ten-foot diamondback rattler lives in there, girlio. We leave her alone because she eats rats. You make one misstep near her hole, and you're dead. I won't even have to shoot you."

A rattlesnake? My knees turned to putty. Wait. Was he trying to flush me out of hiding? I wasn't that far in the tree line. They'd hear me if I moved.

Snakes. Since my property had been cleared recently, if there were snakes out here, chances were they'd moved over here for cover. How fast did snake venom work? I was forty minutes from the nearest hospital.

Think. How could I survive this? Where was Janey? Did she summon help? We were fifteen minutes from town, but the sheriff's deputies should be patrolling county roads. I had to believe Janey phoned for help.

"She called your bluff," the young guy said. "Now what?"

"I'm getting the hell outta here. Get your stuff off my boat, Ozzie, and vanish if you know what's good for you. This place's gonna be crawling with cops in ten minutes."

"You can't abandon me in the middle of nowhere. I've done everything you asked. I won't let you ruin my life."

The gun rang out again. The young man screamed. "You nearly shot me."

"Get in my way again, and I won't miss," Cap'n Nick said. "Forget you ever saw me, that you ever did any business with me."

"What are you doing?"

Metal creaked. "I'm taking the cooler, and I'm making a run for it. No one will believe I was here. My wife will alibi me."

"That woman in the woods knows you were here."

"Not worried about her, she made a beeline for the snake den. If she survives, it'll be her word against mine. I pay my taxes and keep my nose clean. Plus, the sheriff owes me a favor."

"What about her camping friends?"

"No one followed her to the dock. No one came when I fired the gun. She's here alone, and rumor says her and the sheriff are on the outs. I like my chances. Keep your trap shut, and you'll have that future in politics you want."

"Take me with you," Ozzie begged.

"You're on your own, college boy." A vehicle door opened and slammed. An engine roared to life, and the truck left. I heard a sob, then the sound of someone running after the truck, away from the dock.

That must mean Cap'n Nick left and the kid fled on foot. Or were they tricking me? It sounded like they were partners. One of them had a gun. I wanted to believe I was safe, but I wasn't sure of anything. Dare I turn on my flashlight? No. It might give away my position.

My knees ached from crouching for so long. My heart raced out of control, and my hands trembled. Sweat made an interstate highway down the channel of my spine. My skin felt as if a thousand bugs crawled on it, and mosquitoes buzzed my ears.

I had to get out of these woods. I didn't feel safe here.

"Lindsey?" Janey said in a near normal voice. "You can come out now, they're gone."

"You sure?" I asked.

"Cap'n Nick left in his truck. The other guy chased him."

So great was my relief, I sagged into the oak, and my wobbly legs gave out. I sank to the ground. We were alive. "Bailey? Is she okay?"

"I watched her from the tree I climbed. Bailey swam to the bank and ran to the campsite. Everyone and everything's safe. Come out of there."

"I'm shaking all over."

A flashlight beam shone my way. "Shock. Move now before you can't."

I moved one foot and planted a hand on the ground, but a rustling sound beside my left hand stopped my heart.

Chapter 13

"S-s-s-nake," I managed to get out.

"Don't move. Don't even breathe," Janey said. "You hear me? You are not dying on my watch."

I heard her stomping her feet and yelling as she came my way. The rattling continued, but the intensity lessened. I'd lived twenty-eight years. Was this the end of me? With as many buttons as this snake probably had, she could be full of venom.

A mosquito landed on my neck and dug in. I tried twitching my skin, but the critter stuck fast. What was a mosquito bite compared to a snake bite? I'd survive a mosquito bite.

I started to see stars. I had to take a breath, but I made it as slight as possible. Between the mosquito bite and Janey raising cane, I'd forgotten to listen for the snake. The rattling ceased. *It's working*, I said to myself. It's working.

Janey stopped yelling, but she kept stomping hard on the ground. "Lindsey?"

"Still here," I whispered.

The flashlight moved in an arc. When it passed near me, I whispered louder, "Right here."

Janey went nuts yelling again, stomping the ground, and flashing the light in my general area. Moving my other hand ever so slowly, I squashed the mosquito feasting on my neck. I listened intently for rattling again, heard nothing. Emboldened, I switched on my flashlight and checked the ground. I saw movement on the ground, but it was headed away from me.

I scrambled to my feet, ran around the pine, and smacked into Janey. "Thank God for you," I said, clinging to her. "Otherwise, I'd be a goner."

"I'm glad you're all right. Let's get out of these woods." With that, she dragged me to the dirt road.

I tried to get my head right to be conversant and grateful, but I couldn't. I kept my flashlight beam on the ground because I feared stepping on another snake. "I want to go home."

"Good, because I was gonna take you back to town no matter what. I've had enough excitement for one night."

We were okay, I repeated silently. No one was shot. No one was dead. Some of the fog in my brain lifted.

"It sounded like Captain Nick and Ozzie were up to no good," I said.

"I wonder what was in that cooler," Janey said.

"We'll never know. Those guys are long gone."

She flashed me a sidelong glance. "Maybe."

"You know something?"

"I called for backup."

"Some backup. Nobody came."

"Once the men left, I rerouted our help. I thought it was a simple matter of getting you out of the woods and into your car. I didn't know we'd encounter a big rattler."

We veered off the road onto my lot. My skin itched and prickled. Not from the bugs and ticks that were probably crawling on me, but from knowing snakes climbed trees. One could drop out of a tree on us. I wanted a roof over my head right now.

Janey had saved the day. I wouldn't be walking around right now if not for her. Of that I was quite certain. "You were amazing. I owe you my life. Without you raising a ruckus, that snake would've nailed me. I am never living out here. Daddy can sell this property because I don't want it. I don't like being so far away from town. Nobody but us heard the gunshot. That's no good."

"You don't owe me anything. I'm glad you're all right."

"I am, thanks to you." Bailey came running, soaking wet and wagging her tail. I bent down and greeted her. We'd barely escaped another ordeal. I should feel relieved. Instead, I felt empty. Spent.

Meanwhile, Janey rummaged in the tent, gathering our possessions. She tossed our purses and clothes in the car, then she ran back to the tree for the camera and binoculars. When she returned, waving the camera, I was surprised. "Did you tape the guys? Cap'n Nick threatening me and everything?"

"Yeppers."

"I can file charges against Cap'n Nick. He threatened me with a gun."

"You can and should file charges. We're taking this to Ike." She took my arm, led me to my car, and positioned me in front of the headlights. "Tick check."

She had me slowly turn around so that she could check my clothing, and then I did the same for her. We checked out okay, so I sat in the passenger seat. With my nerves shot, I was in no condition to drive.

Her words slowly percolated in my head as she spread a blanket over the backseat and invited Baxley to climb inside. "Ike? Why?"

"'Cause he's at the head of the road, reading Cap'n Nick and Ozzie Shaniman their rights for assaulting you."

I tugged on my ear, not sure if I'd heard correctly. "Ike's here?"

"Yep. Him and Junior Curtis. Junior told Ike about our campout, and Ike asked to be kept abreast of developments. I've been texting Junior all night. Soon as things went sideways, I sent him a SOS, then I scrambled up that oak tree. I got it all on tape. Though the video is too grainy, the audio is fine. I already checked. We've got 'em cold."

Ike. I wanted to see him, but I was a wreck. My emotions were swinging like Spanish moss in a gale. I didn't know if I'd clobber him for being out of touch this week, or if I'd run to him and hug him because he was supposed to be my boyfriend. Or not.

Between the scratches, bug bites, and wet dog smell, I was no prize. But I was alive. That mattered. Janey cranked the car, and we pulled away from the campsite. Can't say I was sorry to go.

We edged along the dirt road until we hit the pavement. Then Janey accelerated. A few bends of the road later, I could see the commotion. The head of the road blazed with cop lights. The red truck was there, but Cap'n Nick and Ozzie were nowhere in sight. Good. I'd had enough of them.

Janey eased through the maze of emergency vehicles, stopping when Ike stepped in front of my car. She rolled the driver's window down. "Got something for you," she called.

Ike trotted over and leaned down. I couldn't look at him. I couldn't bear to see the rejection in his eyes. Janey shoved the camera at him and explained she'd recorded the details of my encounter with the men.

"I need your statement, Lindsey," Ike said.

"Tomorrow," Janey answered for me. "Between almost getting shot by Cap'n Nick and then fighting off a rattler, she's exhausted. Ta-ta." She hit the gas, and Ike jumped out of her way.

"I could've given him a statement," I said.

"Nah. Let him sweat. He screwed up, and he knows it. You solved one of his cases for him."

"I did?"

"Yeah. Junior texted me while I was gathering our stuff in the tent. That cooler was full of stolen turtle eggs. Cap'n Nick and Ozzie Shaniman are the turtle egg thieves."

Chapter 14

My sleep was fitful, to say the least. Snake heads big as oaks reared and struck at me. Handguns with barrels the size of semi tires pointed at me. I awakened with silent screams and frozen limbs. As I came to my senses, I realized I was safe and that Cousin Janey was sleeping in the next room. The first time I drifted back to sleep. The second time, I tossed and turned until dawn's rays brightened my bedroom walls.

Janey and I did a second tick check on our skin last night before we showered and went to bed. I had three, while she had none, but I needed to look again. After I reassured myself I was tick-free, I took another long shower. My briar scratches and the monster mosquito bite got treated with anti-bacterial ointment. This was Saturday, so I didn't have to dress for work. I donned fresh pjs and let my hair air dry naturally.

Padding down the stairs, I heard muted voices. One of them sounded male. My steps quickened. Janey and Junior Curtis looked quite comfy on the sunporch sofa. No Ike. Rats.

"Morning," I said from the doorway.

"Morning." Janey glowed with happiness. "Hope we didn't wake you."

"Couldn't sleep," I said. "Nightmares."

"Me, too. Coffee's made, if you want some."

I nodded and retreated. Coffee. Yes. Coffee would help me feel normal. Cup in hand, I padded out to join them. Neither of them made a move to sit up straighter. You couldn't have wedged a sheet of tissue paper between them.

I settled into a cozy rocker. "I didn't know you slept over, Junior."

"I got here two hours ago to relieve the sheriff." Junior's face seemed softer, friendlier. His smile reached his eyes. "Ike spent the night in your yard, watching the house."

My heart stutter stepped, my hopes spiraled. "He did? Why?"

"He did. Because all the pieces of this story don't fit together yet. Anyway, I sent him home to rest. He's got suspects to question today and your statements to take. That was brilliant, by the way, using the movie function of your camera. Stealing turtle eggs is a federal offense. Those guys are going down."

The fact that Ike spent the night in my yard meant something. Okay, it meant a lot. He wouldn't do that for everybody. Despite our week-long separation, he cared for me.

Last night crystallized my thoughts. No living in the country for me. No camping ever again. No more fussing with Ike. I could compromise. If he could forgive me enough to resume where we left off, fine with me. We may not have forever, but we had right now. I wanted to make every day count.

I rewound Junior's last words for an appropriate response. "Cap'n Nick threatened me with a gun. I won't forget that."

"All the charges should stick." Junior stroked Janey's arm repeatedly. "Ike said a night in jail would loosen their tongues. He's hoping they'll roll on each other. The kid was spinning wild tales last night about a sex club on the island. Ike took a preliminary statement from both men last night, and he'll go at them again today after he talks to you."

"A sex club? In Morrison County?" I snorted in disbelief. "Y'all believed him?"

Junior shrugged. "Anything's possible."

I sipped my coffee in silence. Anything *was* possible. Junior Curtis was sitting in my house at seven in the morning all cozied up to my cousin. Ike spent the night in the yard watching my house. It was almost too much to take in. Almost, but not quite. Coffee made it seem possible. Pancakes would make the lingering doubts go away.

Decision made, I rose. "I'm cooking pancakes. Who's hungry?"

"Me." Janey raised her hand. "Lindsey makes the best pancakes ever."

"Me," Junior said, his voice deep and resonant. "I haven't had homemade pancakes since I was twelve."

"Coming right up."

~*~

I doubled the recipe and reserved two stacks in case Ike showed. Junior ate everything I put on the table. Janey and I watched with fascination as he downed nearly a pound of sausage and three stacks of fluffy pancakes.

"You could put the pancake place out of business with cooking like that," Junior said, pushing back from his empty plate.

"Sure. So long as my customers only wanted pancakes, fudge, or baked wings. Everything else I make is average."

"I adore her fudge," Janey said. "It took her years to perfect the recipe. I'll tell you about that sometime."

Junior's phone buzzed. He glanced at the text message. "I'll look forward to the story, but right now I need to carry you ladies to the sheriff's office. They're ready for you, and we gotta arrive before they close the street for the festival parade."

I policed the kitchen super-fast, stashing Ike's breakfast in the fridge. Then I stood in front of my closet deliberating what to wear. Dressy? Sexy? Casual? I settled on a pair of flattering capris and the top Ike always complimented when I wore it. No reason not to stack the odds in my favor.

The wardrobe choice paid off. Ike's eyes heated when he saw me. It took every bit of self-restraint I possessed not to jump him as he held the door for me. Every eye in the lobby watched us. My skin prickled, and I clutched my purse like a lifeline. My breath trembled.

Ike looked terrible. Dark circles ringed his eyes. He caught my hand as I passed and leaned in close so no one could hear. "Are we good?"

Not trusting myself to speak, I nodded. He pulled me close, and I lost it. Absolutely lost it. He drew me into his office to give me privacy. I cried for nearly losing him, for being so scared last night, and for nearly dying.

The whole time, he made soft sounds and rubbed my back. Finally, my outburst ran dry. "I'm sorry," I mumbled into his chest. "I have a habit of crying on you."

"You can cry on me anytime you like, but we're never doing this again."

I didn't know how to take that. The silence stretched out wafer-thin. Our entire future hinged on what came next. I'd survived close encounters with armed men and a snake, but could I survive if he rejected me? I held my breath.

He cleared his throat gently. "I don't know if I can be the man you want me to be, Linds, but I want to be with you. I've been miserable all week, not knowing how to make things right. I can't eat. I can't sleep. You're under my skin. Please tell me it's like that for you."

"It is." Relieved, I cupped his face. "Whether you admit it or not, Ike Harper, you love me, same as I love you. One of these days you'll say the words."

He stiffened. "Don't corner me."

"I'm not. I'm telling you I want you just as you are."

"Thank God."

He kissed me, and it felt like I'd come home. When he broke off the kiss, regret filled his eyes. "I know," I said, feeling the same longing. "We'll make up properly later."

"Damn straight. Meanwhile, let's nail these bad guys."

Chapter 15

Janey and I wrote our statements in Ike's office, then Junior Curtis joined us to watch the interviews through the observation window. Ike started with the young man.

Ozzie Shaniman claimed Cap'n Nick was a criminal who forced him to do his bidding. Ozzie admitted he knew turtle eggs were in the cooler, but reiterated he had no choice. His "Nick made me do it" defense was all Ike got out of him because the next word out of Ozzie's mouth was "lawyer."

After Ozzie was escorted to a cell, Cap'n Nick sat in the interview room. At first he denied any knowledge of the turtle eggs, but Ike played him a few audio clips from last night, and the fisherman realized he was snared.

"It's not my fault," he said. "I've got a disease."

"You committed a federal crime. What kind of disease makes a person steal turtle eggs?" Ike asked.

"She made me do it."

"Who made you?"

"The witch."

"I need a name."

"Lady Jay."

"Real name."

"I never knew her real name. Didn't want to know. It wasn't about names anyhow. Once she got her hooks in me, I couldn't stop. She turned me into an addict."

"Go on."

Cap'n Nick hesitated. "It's embarrassing."

"As embarrassing as spending time in federal prison for stealing turtle eggs?"

"My family can't know."

"Shoulda thought of that before you cut loose and broke the law. What's the deal?"

He shook his head. "I can't."

"Yes, you can. I got you cold on the federal crime, and you're my top suspect now for killing Selma Crowley. She catch you stealing the eggs?"

"I didn't kill nobody."

"Try again."

"I did wrong, but I never intended to hurt that gal. She wouldn't let anyone touch her. That was the problem. She wouldn't play along."

"With what?"

Cap'n Nick clamped his lips together.

"Is this about the sex club?" Ike asked. "Is that why you're embarrassed? You don't want to be caught with your pants down?"

"I like sex. Sue me."

"And there was plenty of sex on the island."

I inched closer to the speaker because I needed to hear every word.

"For a price," Cap'n Nick said. "I used my shrimping profits to buy time with the girls, but the madam was something else. She cost four times as much, but she was worth every dollar. I can't get enough of her."

"She lives on the island?"

"She's there most weekends. But she's booked way in advance. I begged her for more time, but she laughed. Said I'd have to grovel and do her dirty work and then she'd think about it."

"Where'd you meet her?"

"I ferry her and her after-hours customers back and forth across the sound. That's how I discovered she had a sex club over there."

"How's it work? You drop the johns off at the ferry landing?"

"No way. I hauled her guys to the back of the island. A golf cart would be parked near the drop site, and the GPS was programmed to her location. Customers knew the drill, but business fell off when the new Turtle Girl wouldn't play along."

"She was on the beach at all hours of the night. She see you?"

"Once, and I thought nothing of it. But the last time she saw me,

I'd carried lover boy over there, and it wasn't to see her. She recognized him."

"Are you referring to Mr. Shaniman?"

Cap'n Nick scoffed, made a dismissive gesture with his hand. "Ozzie. I wish I'd never laid eyes on that kid."

"Why?"

"Because he's addicted to sex, same as me."

"Y'all are together?"

"No. We're monotonous. I mean monogamous. Hell, I don't know what I mean. We like women."

"You're heterosexual?"

"Yes."

"Why did Miss Crowley get upset about Mr. Shaniman's presence on the island?"

"Because she thought he was stalking her. But he'd been shagging a bouncy blonde chick all night, same as I'd been with the madam. Let me tell you, those little blue pills are magic. Then, when Selma saw us, I had the bright idea of doing her on the beach. Ozzie didn't like that.

"We fought. He grabbed a shovel from her Gator and came after me. I wrestled it away from him and swung at him, but the little gal…" his voice drifted off.

"What about her?"

"She leapt to his defense. When the shovel came down, I struck her head. Hard. I didn't mean to hit her. I was raised better than that. She stepped in the way. It was an accident."

"Why didn't you report it?"

"I couldn't. I was supposed to be at my buddy's house playing poker. My wife's gonna kill me."

His words aggravated the heck out of me. I glanced over my shoulder at Janey. "What an idiot. He's more scared of his wife than prison?"

"His wife's a Lowe. He should be scared," Janey said.

Good point. The Lowes were a violent bunch. I turned back to the drama in the interview room.

"Where's the shovel?" Ike asked.

"I don't know. Me and the kid buried her and scratched off."

"You left the shovel on the island?"

"I dropped it off at a thrift shop in town. Why waste a good tool? But I told the kid I had it and his fingerprints were on it from helping

142

me bury her. That's why he helped me steal the turtle eggs this time." He hung his head. "I needed more money for another visit with Lady Jay."

~*~

Afterward, I joined Ike in his office. "The bouncy blonde must be Minnie Lee. She's the only person over there who fits that description. Will you go after the sex club?"

"Prostitution is illegal," Ike said. "But this Lady Jay sounds savvy about due process. She won't confess to anything."

"Cap'n Nick can visually identify Lady Jay. Bet if you got the prosecuting attorney in here and waved some kind of deal at him, you'd have leverage with her."

"You know who she is?"

"Don't know for certain. My best guess is Dr. Jennifer Jernigan. There is a lot of hostility between her and Minnie Lee. Perhaps they are rivals in this sex club business."

"The last prostitution rings in this county were shut down nearly seventy years ago."

"Out at the truck stop?"

"Yeah. And run by my great great grandfather. We don't need this kind of news getting out about Morrison County."

The hackles on my neck rose. "You're letting this slide?"

"Never. This is my town."

~*~

Lady Jay aka Dr. Jen Jernigan came in that afternoon all cool and collected. Her façade fell once the facts were revealed. Ike had sworn statements by two men who had used her services, and Cap'n Nick supplied a list of customers he'd ferried to the island for her.

Jen was led away in handcuffs, making ugly noises about suing everyone in this backwater town. With her academic polish stripped away, I didn't think she was pretty at all. Not unless you counted pretty desperate.

Minnie Lee admitted she'd worked tricks for money, said she needed the funds to pay for college, and she was working on a plea bargain when I walked home. Good for her. Clearly, that young lady was a survivor, though I didn't agree with her personal choices.

I'd done what I set out to do. Selma's killer was in jail, and the turtle egg thieves were caught. So many troubles, or tribbles, as Selma would say, stemmed from bad choices. Cap'n Nick would spend the rest of his sorry life behind bars for killing Selma. With a federal charge against him, Ozzie could never run for dogcatcher much less President of the United States. Too bad for both of them.

Jen Jernigan could breathe fire all she liked in the big house. The Island Madam, as I'd dubbed her in my mind, threw away her academic career and her authority, all to gain a steady supply of customers in her sex club. She'd lost more than those things. She'd lost her freedom and the right to make personal choices. Too bad for her.

Three ruined lives, four when you added Selma's senseless death. She'd died defending her ex-boyfriend. I hoped there was a special place in heaven for her.

I knew enough juicy details about these people to fill an entire newspaper, but if I included the good stuff, I would burn my bridges with Ike. That wasn't going to happen. Things were finally getting back to where I wanted them with Ike.

About time.

~*~

A few hours later Ike let himself into my place with his key. My man of action showed me how much he missed me. Afterward, I fed Ike pancakes and asked about his son, who was spending the weekend with his mother. While I finished the dishes, walked the dog, and locked the place up tight, Ike drowsed on the sunporch sofa.

He roused from sleep when I joined him. "Let's talk to your folks about buying this place," he murmured in my ear.

I wiggled out of his arms. "What?"

"It's the best solution. You won't move in with me. I want to be with you, but I can't live in someone else's house. We move in here together. You and I put our names on the deed."

His idea shocked me. "Won't it be messy if things don't work out?"

"Life is messy. I'm used to it."

"It's a good idea," I began slowly, interlacing our fingers. "I found out this weekend I don't want to live in the county. I like living in town."

"There's plenty of room here for Trent." He gazed around the living room with interest. "And Bailey is accustomed to living here."

"My dog will be fine anywhere. She's the least of my worries."

"What do you say, Lindsey? My heart can't take you getting lost in the ocean or getting threatened by an armed killer at the docks. You have an uncanny knack of finding criminals."

A smile split my face. "Must be my investigative journalism skills kicking into action. You and I are a good match personally and professionally."

His fingers tightened around mine. "Say yes to my idea. I need to have this settled."

There were so many things we hadn't talked about: shared bank accounts, down payments, mortgages, babies, dreams, just to name a few. And Ike wouldn't say he loved me. But he wanted to be with me, and he wanted to buy a house with me. Those were commitments. More importantly, I wanted to awaken in his arms every morning.

I cinched my arms around his neck. "Yes. Yes to you. Yes to the house. Yes to us."

"This means the world to me, Linds."

"Me too."

--The End-

Dead Men Tell No Tales

A Lindsey & Ike Mystery, Book 3 of 3

Maggie Toussaint

Chapter 1

Despite the distant rumble of thunder, the first dinner in our new home on River Road was amazing. I couldn't stop smiling at Ike and his eight year old son Trent. Sure, we'd grilled burgers and hot dogs here before, but tonight everything tasted extra special.

I'm Lindsey McKay, editor of the *Gazette*, Danville, Georgia's, weekly newspaper. Sheriff Ike Harper is my partner in housing and love. He'd been burned in matrimony once so we were trying a less traditional route with our nearly nine-month romance. We'd joined our names on a property deed and called it good.

In principle, I agreed with Ike. A piece of paper saying we were married wasn't a guarantee of happiness, but I also valued tradition. Living in the moment was challenging.

Forks clanked on plates, drawing me from my musings. I passed the platter of grilled meat since the baked beans and watermelon bowls were empty. "Seconds?"

Trent dug in like he hadn't eaten in a week. Ike settled back in his seat, a goofy smile on his face. "We should've done this months ago."

We'd struggled with our commitment level this summer, or so I'd thought. Turned out we had communication and processing issues. Since summer had turned to fall, I'd been learning to speak guy, and he'd been doing his best to make me happy. How was it possible to be deliriously happy and yet worried that I might mess it up?

"What?" Ike said. "You scowled."

"I did? Sorry. Thinking of something else."

"You must not like that something else."

"It's no big deal," I said, hoping he'd let it drop.

Lucky for me, Trent distracted his dad with a question about football tryouts, and less than five minutes later, an emergency call came in for Ike. Hunting accident.

After Ike left, I thought how my role had shifted. Before, I'd chased cops to a scene to get the story for the paper. Now I lived with a cop and had more information than I could print. Best of all, I chose to stay home with Trent when these afterhours calls occurred.

From the incident details I overheard, one man accidentally shot the other in the swamp when he heard a noise. I didn't know the name of the shooter yet, but Dispatch mentioned he seemed broken up about the tragedy.

The victim, John Starling, tended bar at Fiddler's at the north end of the county. I'd met him once when he came into the office to buy a newspaper, not long after he moved here this spring.

Time flew as Trent and I played cards, bathed, and got ready for bed. Ike returned in time to tuck his son in for the night. "Was it bad?" I asked when we were cozied up on the sunporch sofa.

He drew me into his arms. "Seemed straightforward. Both men were hog hunting in the swamp. Neither was aware of the other. Sonny Mowrey shot the bartender, thinking he was a hog. Mowrey was so upset he could barely hold it together to give his statement."

"I've shot a gun before, at targets mind you, but I've never shot a person, and I hope it never came to that. I'd be a wreck too."

"Seemed cut and dried to me. Accident all the way."

An accident. Many people today thought "accident" meant no one was responsible. Surely that wasn't the case for a human life. "Will Mowrey face charges for killing someone?"

"I'm running his fingerprints right now, something he isn't happy about."

"Why? He said he shot the guy."

"Learned this lesson a long time ago. Tie up loose ends or they'll bite you in the butt. Whatever happened out there, I'll get to the bottom of it. It's always best to follow procedure."

"I want to see the police report tomorrow."

He nuzzled my neck. "I expected no less, Madame of the News."

I swatted him playfully, enjoying his attention. "You make me sound like something dirty."

"You make me think wild thoughts." His hands drifted lower. "How about we take ourselves up to our bedroom and let the world take care of itself?"

"Sounds good, but I have one more question."

Ike groaned. "What is it?"

"Where was the bullet hole?"

"Straight through the heart. Two kill shots."

Swamp hogs came in all sizes and were ferocious. You did not want to be charged by one, so you made sure you aimed at the right spot. "A person is taller than a hog."

"So?"

"Shouldn't Mr. Mowrey have aimed lower if he was hog hunting?"

"Good observation, but these people barely knew each other. Let's not look for murders. The simplest explanation is usually the best."

"I'm not looking for anything. My mind went there on its own."

He studied me for a long moment. "You have good instincts, Linds, and I've learned to trust them. We'll find out the angle of the shots at autopsy. Now, can we let the dead sleep long enough for us to have some privacy?"

I pulled free of his embrace and rose. "Race ya."

Chapter 2

Cousin Janey, my best friend and sleuthing buddy, stopped by my office first thing in the morning. Her face glowed from all the time she was spending with Junior Curtis, so things between her and the bail bondsman must be going strong. "I heard."

Though I was pretty sure I knew where she was headed, I couldn't resist teasing her. "About what? The first night Ike and I spent in our home?"

She slouched in a guest chair and propped her sandal-clad feet on my desk. "Well, that too. Nothing like buying property to cement a relationship. Or destroy it."

Janey was a Realtor. She'd seen it all with the clients she'd chauffeured around in hopes of a sale. "We're going for cementing our relationship. Don't jinx us."

"Got it, but you guys are golden. With home ownership, you and Ike are legally bound. You're as good as married now."

"Keep that on the down low. Ike's scared to death of the M-word."

"At least you got a commitment out of him. My guy goes home every night. No hint of a ring or a future."

"Junior makes you happy, and he lights up when you enter the room," I said. "I'm glad he turned out to be a nice guy."

"Me too. If he'd been with the mob as rumored, I'd be in deep trouble by now because I can't stay away from him. He's got this magnetic pull."

I chuckled. "They're called pheromones, Cous, and you are hooked on his."

Janey took her time answering, as if she were considering the matter at great length. "Junior's all-consuming. We talk, we make out, we, you know, and then he goes home. Both of us want that so we don't have to explain that he slept over to my daughter or to my ex."

"Y'all are finding your way. It'll work out."

"I suppose, but I didn't come over to talk about either of our relationships. I heard about Sonny Mowrey. I know him."

My curiosity spiked, and I leaned forward. "You do?"

She nodded. "I sold Sonny and Deena that foreclosure house out on the point a few years ago."

I grabbed a notepad and a pen, eager to take notes. "What can you tell me about them? Where'd they come from?"

"They were vague about their hometown, but they moved here from Florida. Just wanted a place on the water that was off the grid."

"Lot of people come here for that reason. Who'd they get their loan through?"

"No loan. They paid cash."

Even though my folks gave us a good price on the house, Ike and I had to get a mortgage to buy this place. "Cash? For a house?"

"It was an easy sale and a quick closing. They offered on the house and owned it less than a week later. They told the people they could leave any furniture they didn't want in the house. First I ever heard of anyone doing that."

The furniture part wasn't too weird. Mom and Dad left a lot I still needed to go through. But we were family. "Weren't you suspicious?"

"I needed the money," Janey said. "But now, I'm wondering if I should mention it to Ike."

"Ike already believes I read murder into every 9-1-1 call. Are you thinking Sonny Mowrey didn't have an accident? That he meant to kill John Starling?"

"Something is strange about the Mowreys. Both of them had short bleached blonde hair when they moved here. Now Sonny's totally dark-haired with a full beard and a ponytail. Deena's sporting a pink doo at the moment. I don't know how she walks with so many rings on her toes. Have you ever worn a toe ring?"

"Nope."

"Me neither. What's wrong with us?"

I shrugged. "I dunno. Seems like with our racy ancestress, we'd be on the forefront of every trend. Guess the Episcopalian upbringing

153

trumps the Beulah McKay exhibitionist genetics."

"Speak for yourself. I've been letting my inner exhibitionist have free rein lately. It's more fun, and Junior likes it."

I did not want to know what they were up to at her place in the deep dark of night. "Enough about us. Can you think of any reason Sonny Mowrey might've shot John Starling?"

"Well. The obvious thing is two men and one woman."

"Deena came between them?"

"Not saying she did. You asked if there was *any* reason. Deena seemed very flirty and . . . accessible when she was my client."

"She flirted with you?"

"She turned on the charm everywhere we went. I always had the sense she was working a room when we hit a restaurant or the Bar and Grill for lunch."

"Extroverted wife. Introverted husband." I weighed the ideas in each hand. Given Janey's observations, I had no trouble picturing a love triangle. "What was Sonny's response?"

"He didn't react to her flirting, but he always sat beside her in the back of my car."

"Doesn't sound like he'd go into a killing rage if she strayed. Do you ever see them out and about in town?"

Janey studied the ceiling for a moment. "I waved to them at last year's Fall Festival, but I was in the kid area with CeeCee. They didn't wade through the screaming children to speak to me, and I couldn't leave my daughter there alone to go speak to them."

"So they keep to themselves. They haven't been in trouble with the law since I moved back home last fall. I ran their name through our archive and there's never been anything in the paper about them. Then it occurred to me that I was looking in the wrong place. I searched for their names online. You know what I found?"

Janey grabbed my orange stress relief ball, squeezed it several times, and returned it to my desk. "What?"

"Nothing. I even checked the Census listing. I was stunned. They should have some digital footprint other than property ownership. Is Sonny a nickname or his legal name?"

"It was the name he signed on the contract and the name on his Florida driver's license."

"I wonder if Ike knows about this," I mused, thinking out loud.

"He doesn't like you nosing around in his cases."

"I'm fact finding for my feature story. He can chase all the bad guys he wants. I want nothing to do with that end of things."

"I'm sure he'll discover this much on his own," Janey said. "How come there's no other information on the Mowreys?"

"Perhaps they're not newsworthy people. If not for Aunt Fay's membership in the DAR and her property deed, I couldn't find her online. I checked."

"Get real. The Mowreys are our age. Look up any late twenty-something online and you get a ton of hits from the search engine. Something's fishy about this duo."

"I'm getting that sense myself. What about the bartender? You know John Starling?"

"He asked me out once. I was attending a high school classmate's birthday party at his bar not two months ago."

"Did you do it?" I reached for the stress relief ball and massaged it absently.

"Nah. No chemistry. After my divorce, I thought I wouldn't date again. I was devoting myself to being the best Mama ever."

"And look at you now. How do you explain Junior to your daughter?"

"I just say we're seeing each other. CeeCee doesn't have a problem with it one way or another."

"And your ex?"

"He's steamed about Junior, but he's keeping his mouth shut. Junior's badass reputation is serving me well."

"My, how the tide has turned."

We were grinning at each other like silly fools when the front door burst open. I heard my assistant's voice go from placating to loud in the lobby. Ellen is a good gatekeeper, and she keeps the public at bay when I'm busy. She only allows people back if they're blood relatives, Ike, or someone we're interviewing for our next paper.

A buxom woman appeared in my doorway. She was pretty in an overdone, big pink hair and fake eyelashes kind of way. The short dress, bare legs, and high heels made a feminine statement. A closer look revealed shiny rings on her toes.

Deena Mowrey had come to me. Oh, joy.

Chapter 3

"Ms. McKay, I'm lodging a complaint about the sheriff." Deena breezed in, pushed Janey's stacked feet off my desk, and took center stage. "My name's Deena Mowrey and there's been a huge miscarriage of justice."

It was hard to take all of her in at once. Her various assets bounced as she walked, and her red-tipped fingernails fluttered and stabbed through the air punctuating her words. On top of that, her mouth was working ninety miles an hour on a wad of gum.

There were so many questions I could ask. It wasn't often that folks connected to Ike's cases wandered through my doors. I'm sure Deena Mowrey would have some one-sided fairy tale about Ike. Not that I'd print something like that, but I walked a fine line of disclosure between what I could put in the paper and what I would put in the paper.

I stood. "I'm Lindsey McKay, Ms. Mowrey. You're here to pitch a story idea to me?"

"Yes. I want you to rip that sheriff a new one. He locked Sonny in jail. Says things about the accident don't add up. I'll tell you what doesn't compute. It was an accident. Sonny can't be held on charges because he didn't mean to do anything wrong."

I worked my back teeth apart and hoped I could manage a civil tone. "I don't know the specifics of the law, ma'am, but the sheriff knows the score. Your husband will be treated fairly."

"Nothing fair about him being held against his will. Write a scathing story about that, about how he's put an innocent man behind bars."

"I can't write specifics about an active investigation. There will be

156

a factual story about the shooting, and if the investigation is resolved by press time, I'll add the sheriff's findings. Until then, I can only gather information. If you know something about the case, I urge you to go over to the sheriff's office and speak to him."

Deena stomped her foot. "I'm not going over there. I'm trying to spring my husband, not fall into the sheriff's clutches. Who's to say he wouldn't lock me up just for darkening his doorway?"

Not wanting to lose an opportunity, I shifted to a related topic. "If you have background about Sonny you'd like to add to my story, I'm happy to interview you."

"No. I want you to expose the sheriff. He's a bad cop."

I didn't like her attitude or her one-track mind. "I don't print unsubstantiated accusations in my feature stories. If you write your complaint as a letter to the editor, I'll consider it for publication. However, submission isn't a guarantee of acceptance, just so we're clear. I have final approval of everything that runs in the paper."

"We're clear all right. You filter news about the sheriff because he's your boyfriend. Never mind. I'll find a real newspaper that isn't afraid to print the truth."

With that, Hurricane Deena sailed out of my office.

"Well, la-dee-dah," Janey said. "Someone's got her thong in a twist."

I sank into my seat, feeling relieved that Deena left but worried about her claim. "Do I withhold news because of my relationship with Ike?"

"No way. Deena was trying to get your goat. She wants Sonny out of jail."

"If Ike's still got Sonny, he has a reason for holding him. I wonder what it is."

"You'd be better served to discover what Deena's hiding."

"Why's that?"

"When you asked her for background on Sonny, her skin blanched. She doesn't want you to know a single thing about him."

"She may get her wish because that's exactly what I have about the man right now."

Janey let those words sink in for a moment. "She wouldn't have gotten in here if you still brought Bailey to work with you."

"Bailey is morphing from a news hound to becoming Trent's dog. Ike and Trent are even talking about using her when they go marsh hen hunting later this month."

"You okay with that?"

"Bailey will always have a special place in my heart, but I love my dog enough to share her with Trent and Ike."

"How are you handling having a child underfoot?"

"Okay, I guess."

"What's he call you?" Janey asked.

"Ike told him to call me Ms. Lindsey."

"You want him to call you mom?"

I rocked back in my chair, nearly tipping over. "Heavens, no. That's Annette's honor. I'd be happy with Lindsey. Mostly Trent tries to catch my eye before he speaks so that he doesn't have to call me anything."

"Mark my words, he'll call you mom before long."

Warmth flooded my entire body. "Oh my. That'll cause problems."

"You want my advice?" Janey asked on her way out.

"You're going to give it to me regardless." I braced my shoulders. "Go ahead."

"Trent's a kid. If he calls you mom, roll with it. Don't make it a big deal."

Alone, I scrubbed my face with my hands. Mom. Was I mature enough to be anyone's mom? And what about that subtle ticking I heard from my own biological clock? Was conception in my future?

Chapter 4

"I was sitting in my office minding my own business," I told Ike on the phone a few minutes later, "and Deena Mowrey blew in here, madder than wet fire ants. She swears Sonny's innocent. Plus, she wants me to write a story about the gross miscarriage of justice because you're keeping Sonny in jail."

"And?"

"When I said I wouldn't do it, she said she'd find a real newspaper."

"You are a real newspaper. Where's she get off attacking you like that?"

"It's okay, Ike. I can fight my own battles. Get this. I offered her a chance to fill me in on Sonny's background, and she clammed up immediately."

"That is interesting."

"You found it too?"

"Found what?"

I ignored his suspicious tone. "Sonny Mowrey has no digital footprint. Cousin Janey says Sonny is his legal name."

"You brought Janey into this?"

I had information that might help him, and he jolly well would hear it. "She dropped by. Sonny and Deena were her real estate clients, so she knows them. They paid cash for their place out on the point."

"Interesting. And, off the record, a lot about Sonny Mowrey doesn't add up."

He paused, and I so wanted to know what facts he knew. "You can trust me."

"I trust you. But I don't reveal details of an active case with the press."

Another silence. I was learning that was how Ike processed information, so I didn't rush to fill the void. Patience prickled my skin like a mohair sweater.

"You were right about the angle of the shots," he said in a bit. "Once the coroner took a close look, I sent Alice Ann and Jimmy back to the scene. We now believe John Starling's death wasn't accidental."

Which meant the shot had been intentional. Someone took aim at the bartender with intent to kill, and they pulled the trigger. Twice.

"But the gun Sonny gave me doesn't match the bullet in Starling," Ike said.

"He gave you a different shotgun to confuse the issue?"

"Rifle. He gave us a different rifle. I asked him what he did with the other rifle, and he said nothing. The bullets and the distance of the shots suggests a sniper."

I stared at my office wall. "Sonny Mowrey is a sniper?"

"Didn't say that. He could be, but there's no evidence of it."

"Was there evidence the rifle he gave you had been recently fired?"

"Affirmative."

"And he had gunpowder on his hands?"

"He tested positive for GSR, yes, but so did Starling."

My mind went to a strange place with two armed men discharging weapons in the swamp. The shootout at O.K. Corral, redneck style. "Was it a gunfight?"

"No evidence of that either. I have to charge Sonny with something today or let him go. If he's a pro, he'll run."

My thoughts spun like a boat propeller. "If the rifle doesn't match, what about his identity disconnect? Can you get faster results investigating that?"

"I've got deputies searching for another rifle, but it's slow going in the swamp. Meanwhile, I'm running Sonny's prints through the system, but nothing yet." Ike's voice trailed off. "John Starling had a record."

"What'd he do?"

"Larceny and burglary, over in Alabama. I'm not sure if he turned over a new leaf or if he's robbed locals who haven't reported it."

"Interesting. Since it appears Sonny doesn't have a past, maybe John discovered his secret. People talk to bartenders. Sonny or Deena might have let something slip. Sound feasible?"

"Maybe. Even so, we'd have to figure out what John had on Sonny. I've got a team at his place now, but nothing there seems worth killing over."

"He might not have noted anything on his calendar. Someone who's opportunistic isn't a planner. What about money in his bank account?"

"Looking into that too. I've got a call in to Henry at the bank."

"You thought of everything. You don't need my help."

"You have a way of helping me focus, and I appreciate your insights," Ike said. "But what I wish I had was Deena's fingerprints."

I basked under his compliment before I tried to help again. "Deena didn't touch anything while she was here. I could invite her to lunch and save her drinking glass."

"I don't want you near her. I'll get her prints."

"Are you going all Tarzan on me?" I asked.

"I . . . I did it again, didn't I? You're a thinking, intelligent, beautiful woman. You do amazing things. And you're street smart too. But the thought of anything happening to you freezes my insides. I can't think. I can't sleep. I can't function. Your safety has a direct impact on my well-being. Promise me you'll be careful."

I reveled in his heartfelt emotion. "I feel the same way about your safety, and your likelihood of coming in contact with a dangerous person is much higher than mine."

"We'll each be careful. Hang on. I've got another call."

He clicked back on a minute later. "That was Henry. He won't tell me about the Mowreys' banking history without a warrant. Reading between the lines of what he didn't say, the Mowreys aren't big depositors at The Danville Bank. They might bank online."

"Where does that leave you?" I asked.

"Heading home for an early *lunch* with you. Can you take off now?"

My pulse jumped. "Meet you there in five minutes."

Chapter 5

We ate cold pizza directly out of the refrigerator. I'd acquired the habit from Ike. He was right. Pizza tasted good cold.

I chased a mouthful of pizza with iced tea. Ike reached over and drank from my glass. "What are you working on today?" he asked.

His heated gaze swept my length. My thoughts turned to how we'd passed the first part of our *lunch* upstairs. Even though we had dressed again, Ike had a way of looking at me that made me feel like I was the sexiest woman on the planet.

"Background on the homicide, of course," I said. "Thanks for the police report, by the way. The rest is routine. Two obits came in this morning, so I formatted them and uploaded to the Web. I'm headed out this afternoon for more church door photos."

I encouraged my readers to post pics of the door of the week on our social media page. Keeping readers engaged on multiple fronts was the name of the newspaper game these days.

"I might be late tonight," Ike said. "If something breaks on the case, I'll see it through."

My turn to nod. "I understand."

~*~

I noticed the flashy red car after I stopped at the post office to return an online purchase. The coupe stayed behind me when I veered onto the spur, and again when I turned down New Faith Road.

Not wanting to alarm Ike, I called Janey. She answered on the first ring. "Ike's busy with the case, so I didn't want to bother him. Cherry red sports car. Ring any bells?" I asked.

"That's Deena's car."

"She's following me, and I'm on my way to the North End Baptist Church."

"Odd."

"Very odd, considering how her visit to my office ended this morning. Anyway, I wanted someone to know she was following me in case anything happens."

"Should I drive out there?"

"I don't anticipate a problem. Deena could be headed this way for personal reasons."

"What're you doing out there, anyway?"

"Getting a church door pic for my series. It won't take long."

"Call me back in ten minutes, or I'm calling Ike."

"I will."

After I ended the call, I parked in the church's empty parking lot. The red car slotted in beside me on the passenger side. Great, I groaned to myself. *The one person on the planet Ike told you to avoid followed you to a remote location.*

Nothing to be gained by hiding in my car. I grabbed my camera and stepped out of my vehicle for the door photo, making sure I had my phone with me. Oak-filtered sunlight bathed the church's paneled double doors. This picture would come out nice.

I took a few door shots from the parking lot, before moving forward to snap more. Deena's car door snicked open behind me. My shoulders tensed in anticipation of another vicious verbal assault.

"No one took me seriously," Deena said, her voice petulant. "I called two other newspapers and the TV news in Savannah. Did you blackball me?"

I turned and surreptitiously snapped a picture of her leaning against her little car. Her cotton candy pink hair didn't quite go with the fast car look. "There is no story. Despite what some people think, print and digital media strive to report facts. You have no facts to support your claim."

She gestured broadly with both arms. "Sonny's behind bars. That's a fact."

"Talk to Ike."

"Can't you put in a good word for me?"

"I'm not a police officer, and I don't know the facts of the case."

"It was an accident. Case closed."

"Someone died. Even if it was an accident, there are consequences. John Starling had a family. They will demand justice."

"He said he wasn't married."

Bingo. She knew the bartender. I moved on, so she wouldn't realize she'd let something slip. "He had parents, possibly siblings or children. I haven't received his obituary yet, or I'd tell you exactly how many people survive him. His loved ones expect accountability for his death. That's basic human nature."

"It isn't fair. I need Sonny. I don't want him locked up."

She wasn't listening, which begged another question. "Why did you follow me?"

"I didn't."

"Try again. You were behind me in town. Your red car shines like a beacon."

"Maybe I did follow you." Her chin lifted. "I need someone to help me."

"I can't help you. Talk to Ike. He's running the investigation."

Her eyes rounded. "What investigation?"

"Of the accident," I said. "If you won't talk to him about your husband, tell him what you know about the bartender."

"John was fun, but I don't know much about him. He was a Scorpio to my Leo. He liked singing along with the radio. He hit on me at the bar, even though he knew I was married."

"Did you encourage him?"

"I like male attention. I like all kinds of attention. Why else would I drive a red car?"

I assumed her question was rhetorical and nipped past her. "I have to get back to the office."

As I buckled my seatbelt and prepared to drive, I felt the weight of her gaze. I refused to glance at Deena. I disliked her direct manner, though I'd known others with the same flaw and liked them. But the edgy aspect of her personality worried me.

I got the sense that if I crossed her, I'd be sorry. It wouldn't take much to provoke her into an over-the-top reaction.

Her palm splayed over my closed window. She called my name, startling me from my thoughts. I cracked my window. "Yes?"

She leaned close, her brown eyes burning into me. "Is there anything I could do to change your mind about Sonny?"

A knot formed in my stomach. "What are you asking?"

"I know five hundred reasons why Sonny's innocent."

This again? "His fate is out of my hands."

"What about a thousand reasons? Does that sound more likely?"

I had a light bulb moment. "Are you bribing me?"

Her tight expression remained. "Will you convince Ike to let Sonny go?"

"Ike Harper makes up his own mind."

"Very well, I can go two thousand, but no higher."

"I don't want your money." Disgust stiffened my spine. "I believe in our justice system. Now if you'll excuse me, I must return to the office."

Without waiting for her reply, I reversed the car and spun out of there. I sped all the way to town, all the way to Ike's office. I burst in, nearly beside myself with emotion. "Deena tried to bribe me, and I've got her fingerprints!"

Chapter 6

"We agreed you'd steer clear of Deena." Ike closed his office door.

I walked over to his window, instinctively retreating from the stormy emotions flashing across his face. "You told me to stay away from her. I did that, but Deena didn't get the same memo. She followed me out to the north end and waylaid me. She offered me three amounts of money. She called them *reasons*, but she meant money. I didn't take the bribe, of course."

Ike drifted closer, his gaze intent. "What did she want? To quash a story about her husband?"

"I wish I had enough details on Sonny's life to suppress them. At least then her behavior might make sense. Deena wanted me to exert my feminine wiles on you."

An eyebrow arched. "Yeah?"

"Yeah. I was supposed to convince you to let Sonny go."

"Curious."

"She thinks I wield all kinds of influence around here."

"She was right about one thing." Ike's tone turned grim. "If anyone could persuade me, it would be you."

A chuckle slipped out, followed by a grin. "Ike Harper, that's the nicest thing you've ever said to me."

"Don't let it go to your head. I respect your opinion, and you discover information that helps me piece together crimes. You are influential because of your integrity, not because we're sleeping together."

I tried to put a positive spin on his words. "Thanks. I think."

He drew me close for a kiss. "You are also sexy, beautiful, and smart."

"I like the sound of that," I said when we surfaced for air.

"I like the feel of you, and you know what I want to do right now." His voice softened. "Only the certainty that I get to hold you tonight will tide me over. Meanwhile, you said you had Deena's prints?"

"I do." Oops. The matrimonial phrase. I hurried to add something else. "Deena placed her entire left hand on my driver's side window. Dust it and you'll have her prints."

"Wait here." Ike went to the door and instructed a deputy to dust my car window immediately and run the prints through the system.

He returned, a thinking look on his face. "As a matter of intellectual curiosity, how much did she offer for us to look the other way?"

"She started at five hundred and went up to two grand."

"Huh."

"She thinks you're being mean because it was an accident. So, no harm, no foul."

"Doesn't work that way. And it wasn't an accident."

"You making progress on the homicide investigation?"

"I've got my sister and Jimmy combing the scene for the murder weapon. Talked with the District Attorney. He said Sonny's statement admitting he shot Starling and the autopsy results are enough to charge Sonny Mowrey with murder."

"But?"

"But I'd prefer to have more evidence. Finding the murder weapon would be huge. Finding Sonny's fingerprints on that gun would be even better."

"What did Sonny say about the gun's whereabouts?"

"Said he gave me the gun. Since that's obviously a lie, I need to find out why. That gun has to be around, somewhere."

A crisp knock sounded on the door, and a fresh-faced deputy looked in. "A man out here says he's Sonny Mowrey's lawyer. Said you know him. Crash Considine."

Ike's face brightened. "Send old Crash in here."

"Are y'all talking about Bobby Considine?" I asked.

Before I finished speaking, Bobby "Crash" Considine, the senior voted "Most Likely to Succeed" in our class, swaggered in and bumped fists with Ike. Bobby matched the sheriff in height but won the prize for being the heaviest and having less hair. Ike and Bobby had been friends in school, and it looked like that hadn't changed.

"Lindsey McKay!" Bobby grabbed me in a bear hug, whirling us both in a dizzying circle. "I'm glad you're making my man Ike here so happy these days."

"Uh, sure." I held onto the back of a chair until the room stopped spinning. "What have you been doing since high school?"

"I tried to be a cop, but they canned me after I crashed two squad cars, hence the new nickname," Bobby said, as charming and roguish as ever. "Then I went off to school and became a lawyer. Now that I'm all educated, I've come home. Sonny Mowrey is my first client."

"How'd Deena find you?" Ike asked.

"I've been moonlighting as a musician out at the north end for a few months while I studied to take the bar in July and then while I waited for the results. Deena and I frequent the same watering hole."

"Would that be Fiddler's?"

"It would. And yes, I knew John Starling. Deena and I closed down his bar a coupla times in the last few months."

"Deena. Not Sonny?"

"Only Deena. Sonny didn't hang out at the bar."

Ike didn't say anything, so I offered my opinion. "Seems odd for a married couple. Were Sonny and Deena having marital problems?"

Bobby cleared his throat. "I can't speak to that, seeing as how I represent Sonny Mowrey. Speaking of which, I understand no charges have been filed. I need to see my client. And I need to spring him from jail, like now."

Ike went all squinty-eyed on Bobby. "They teach you to talk like that in law school?"

"Nah. I figured it out myself. Charge my client or release him."

Ike glanced at the clock on the wall. He must be weighing how much to tell his friend. As I well knew, being on opposite sides in a case was hard on a friendship. I hoped the investigation wouldn't wreck their lifelong ease with each other.

"I'm arresting your client today," Ike said.

"On what charge?" Bobby countered in the next breath.

"Murder."

"You mean involuntary manslaughter."

"Nope. Felony murder."

"Get real. This was an accidental shooting. Sonny Mowrey didn't plan to end the bartender's life."

"We believe otherwise."

Bobby swore fluently. The air seemed bluer when he wound down. Riveted by the conversation, I hoped neither man remembered I was still here.

"You done?" Ike asked his friend.

"In more ways than one. No way will Deena keep me on as Sonny's lawyer. She needs a topnotch criminal defense lawyer, not a fledgling goober like me."

"Don't sell yourself short, Bobby," Ike said. "You're smart and you know people."

"Yeah, but Deena and I thought I'd waltz out of here with Sonny."

"You saying she hired you for more than one reason?"

Crimson stained Bobby's neck and face. "I might have mentioned I knew you."

"Be careful," Ike said. "Deena tried to bribe Lindsey earlier today. Deena's working every angle to get her man released. That makes me think these people have a lot to hide."

"I can't tell you anything." Bobby hung his head. "Attorney client privilege."

"She thought of everything," Ike said. "But I'm good at my job. I'll bring Sonny to the interview room. Go ahead over there."

"I've got a newspaper to write," I said, sensing my time to leave. "I'll see myself out."

Ike grabbed my hand and reeled me in for a kiss. "See you tonight."

As I exited Ike's office, Bobby ribbed Ike about being bitten by the love bug. I certainly thought so, but Mr. Ike Harper still wouldn't say those all-important-to-me words. *I love you.* How hard was that?

Monumental if you were Ike Harper.

Loud voices in the lobby caught my attention. My stride quickened automatically.

"If you don't release that S.O.B. so I can kill him, I'm gonna get myself arrested and kill him in your jail," a man hollered. "I'm coming for you, Mowrey. Nobody kills a Starling and gets away with it."

Chapter 7

John Starling's little brother Ray looked like he'd been engineered with pro basketball in mind. His head was higher than most doorways, and I couldn't imagine where he found pants long enough to fit those three miles of legs.

Two deputies restrained the angry man. Ike hurried past me into the lobby. I tried to make myself as small as possible by the admin desk so the raging man didn't notice me.

"I'll sue everybody in this backwater town, if you don't let me see him," Ray Starling shouted. "Let me at that yellowbelly. I'll show him a thing or two. Save you the cost of a trial too."

"Mr. Starling, your brother's death is an active investigation," Ike began in a soothing tone. "Why don't we discuss it privately in my office?"

"I don't want nothing done in private. That's how things get covered up. I want the whole world to know Sonny Mowrey is a stone cold killer."

Oh, boy. Ike would kill me if I took notes, but he wouldn't know if I recorded this conversation on my phone. I clicked my phone's apps until I found the right one. This would be one heck of a scoop. The story might get traction with the big city dailies.

"Lucky for you, I have the newsletter editor in the building. If I ask her to join us, will you consent to talking privately?"

"The newspaper will be there?" Ray asked.

Ike shot me an entreating look. With a sigh, I reached into my bag for a business card before cautiously moving toward the red-faced man. "I'm Lindsey McKay, editor of the *Gazette*."

Ray ducked his head in acknowledgement as he palmed my card. "You gonna write down every word I say?"

"If that's what you want," I said.

"What I want is my brother back home in Alabama alive and well. That ain't happening. He's going home in a body bag tomorrow while the coward who shot him is still breathing air. Johnny said he'd found a way to turn his luck around. That's why I know someone murdered him. For the money."

"In my office. Now," Ike said.

The two deputies accompanied Ray, one on each arm. Though Ray looked like he could easily lift both men and not break stride, he allowed himself to be guided along the brightly lit corridor. He ducked his head to enter Ike's office.

Since Ike was allowing Ray the courtesy of being interviewed in his office, Ray wasn't in imminent danger of arrest. However, it'd be front page news if this guy lost it and wound up in jail.

Ike directed me behind his desk and into his chair. He sat on the front edge of the desk and said, "Ray, you're mad at the wrong people. I'm working hard to discover what happened to John, but your behavior is a problem. Three cops are babysitting you instead of following leads."

I put my phone on the desk and flipped open a notepad, knowing full well Ike would ask me for the notes. But he wouldn't think to ask for my phone.

"John's all the family I have left," Ray said, tugging free of the two deputies at his side and slumping into one of Ike's guest chairs. "I can't believe my brother's gone. We had plans to go fishing offshore next weekend. He'd even lined up dates for the both of us."

"Tell me about the fishing plans," Ike said. "Where were y'all headed?"

"To Gray's Reef."

"And he invited two women to go fishing with you?"

"Yes, but that's not important now."

"On the contrary," Ike said. "It's very important. Who were they?"

"He was seeing some woman named Louise. He kept raving about how she really got him. And she likes the things guys like. She's even done well in fishing tournaments. Me and John like fishing, but we never caught much. Louise was our ace in the hole."

"What's Louise's last name?"

Ray shrugged. "Louise didn't kill him. They were doing it like bunnies all the time. John was crazy about her, and it sounded like she felt the same way about him."

I scribbled "Louise?" on my notepad. I couldn't call any Louises to mind, but my father, Uncle Henry, or Aunt Fay would know if Louise was a local. They might even know her if she was an import.

"I need to talk to Louise," Ike said, handing Ray a business card. "If you remember her last name, call me."

Deputy Sam Hicks knocked on the door, then breezed in with a tray of canned sodas. Everyone took a beverage, including Ray, who gulped his down like it was his last meal.

"The hell with Louise." Ray's eyes glittered with malice. "I want to talk to Sonny Mowrey. I heard he confessed to shooting my brother."

"You can't talk to Mowrey. We are arresting him."

"I'll wait until he makes bail. He turns up dead, you'll know it was me getting payback." Ray caught my eye. "If I turn up dead, you'll know the sheriff and his henchmen murdered me."

Ike rose in a fluid motion and towered over Ray. "Dial it down. We abide by the law in this county, and if you make threats, you're likely to get yourself arrested."

Ray gestured to the ceiling. "Doesn't look like you've got more than one block of cells up there. Arrest me. I want a shot at Mowrey."

"You've worn out your welcome here, Starling. Cool off before you darken my doorstep again." Ike nodded to his deputies. "Escort this man outside."

When they left, Ike turned to me. "Sorry to drag you into that."

"No worries. I'm disappointed you talked him into a more reasonable state of mind, but that information about John's girlfriend Louise should prove useful."

"Or not. You never know which leads will pan out."

I gathered my stuff and rose. "You're pretty good at this."

"So are you. And I noticed you recorded the conversation."

"Wow. You're good."

"This can't go in the newspaper, Linds. Not yet at any rate. We have to build a solid case, and I can't have juicy details in the paper."

I sighed, knowing I would be sitting on this information. "Copy me on the police report. I'll print the boring, approved wording. I'm beginning to think you're sleeping with me to keep me from breaking your cases wide open."

"Not every sheriff has the opportunity to sleep with their newspaper editor. Most guys wish they were as lucky as me, but that's not why I'm sleeping with you."

"It isn't?"

"Nope. I'm sleeping with you because that's exactly where I want to be."

"No other newspaper editor would do?"

"No other woman would do."

I wrapped my arms around his neck. "Good answer, Ike Harper."

A knock sounded at his door. He groaned at the lousy timing and gave me a quick kiss on the forehead before breaking the embrace. "Come in," Ike said.

Deputy Sam Hicks leaned in with a grin. "Got Starling's soda can."

"Good job," Ike said. "Run his prints ASAP."

"On it boss."

"Raincheck?" Ike said when we were alone again.

"Long as it rains this evening, I'm fine with it." I used all my feminine wiles to sashay out of there.

The fresh air and sunshine cleared my head. I had bits and pieces of a story, but I couldn't print any of it. Not yet, at least.

Cousin Janey stopped her lime green Volkswagen in front of me. "We need to talk. Hop in."

Chapter 8

"Are you teasing me with a story I can't print?" I asked as I buckled my seat belt. "Because everyone else is."

"Nope. We're going for ice cream. Figured you could use some by now, and I'm way overdue."

Her "overdue" word choice lightened my mood. "You sound like a library book. But you're right. Ice cream would hit the spot."

"Good. That's the first sensible thing you've said all day. I can't believe you let a crazy woman follow you out of town. What if she were a mass murderer?"

"From my vast knowledge acquired from docudrama TV shows, serial killers are white males between twenty-something and forty-something. Deena Mowrey is a young woman."

"We don't know anything about her."

Janey wasn't easing over to the ice cream shop in the gas station. We were headed toward the highway, to my favorite ice cream sundae fast food restaurant.

"Ike's checking out all of them: Sonny, Deena, and Ray," I volunteered as we rolled past the used car place and turned on the spur.

"Did I miss something? Who the heck is Ray?"

"Ray is John Starling's little brother from Alabama. He thinks John was murdered, and you know what? He's right, but you can't tell anyone I told you so."

"My lips are sealed. Well, mostly sealed. Junior Curtis unseals them day and night."

I shot her a curious glance as we pulled in the parking lot. "How are y'all doing?"

Janey shoved the gear selector in park. "He wants a baby."

She burst into tears, which stunned me. Janey already had a six year old daughter named CeeCee by a no-good husband. Would she bear another child for a man she'd only been dating for a few months?

Due to the bucket seats, comforting her was awkward, but I did my best. "I'm sorry he upset you. How can I help?" I asked when she gathered herself.

"At lunch today he told me he wanted a baby. My baby."

She said baby. Twice. "What for?"

"Junior loves kids. He's good with them."

"I'll rephrase my question. Does he want any baby or your baby?"

"He wants us to be a family. Aunt Fay and Uncle Henry will have a conniption."

"Maybe not. I expected more flak when Ike and I bought the house from my parents, but the elders didn't mention we'd missed a step on the way to home ownership."

"Because they trust Ike to do the right thing. As far as they're concerned, Junior Curtis is Mr. Shady."

"How about a family dinner? Maybe they'd feel better if they got to know him. And they could pressure him in person to propose."

Janey reached into her handbag. "I haven't been entirely honest with you. He already proposed."

My jaw dropped at the size of the diamond ring she withdrew. It was a rock. "Oh, my gosh! This is wonderful, right? You're marrying him because y'all are so in love."

I heard air sucking through Janey's teeth as she grimaced. I couldn't imagine why she'd be unhappy about getting engaged. She was crazy about Junior. One look at them, and it was obvious they were a couple. I'd had reservations about Junior in the beginning but now that I'd gotten to know him, he was gentler and less scary, especially around Janey.

She eyed the ring like it could swallow her whole. "I enjoy his company, and his version of *you-know* is downright amazing, but he's all goopy-eyed around me. Like someone slipped him a love potion. What happens when he comes to his senses? I'm head over heels in love with him. If he walks away from me like Neil did, I'll die. Just curl up and die. I don't know what to do."

Unsure of what to say, I stated the obvious. "You took the ring."

"Junior is very persuasive. He wants me to wear it, but I can't until I tell the family."

"This isn't the dark ages. You don't need Uncle Henry or Aunt Fay's approval."

"Shows what you know. When I hit bottom before, they helped me so much. Gave me time to heal, paid my bills for a few months, and encouraged me to become a Realtor. My decision about Junior affects everyone in the family, even you."

I raised my hands in surrender. "You have my blessing. I've never seen two people more suited to one another."

"What about Ike?" Janey asked.

"What about him?"

"Y'all are as good as married. He's family now. What'll he think?"

"He'll be happy for you. Tell you what. Let's plan that family dinner at my house. I'll do a Low Country boil with lots of wild Georgia shrimp. You and Junior can make your announcement in front of everyone. That way you only have to do it once."

"You'd do that?"

"Yeah. Check with Junior and let me know what dates are good. I'll check with Ike. Speaking for myself, I'm thinking Sunday, but any day that suits you two is fine with me."

"Great. Thanks."

I opened my car door. "Let's get that ice cream now, my treat. I'm in the mood to celebrate."

"What are you celebrating?"

"That I didn't have a close encounter with a serial killer."

Chapter 9

Ike's sister kept Trent for the night, so Ike and I did a couple's riff on happy hour. After our sensual hunger was slaked, we cooked dinner, circling each other handily in the kitchen as we chopped, diced, and prepared chicken fajitas. A pot of rice steamed on the back burner.

"Feels like we've been doing this forever," I said, handing him the sliced red peppers.

He tossed them in the hot pan. "We're good, right?"

"Better than good. This feels righter than anything I've ever done. I had no idea living with someone would be like this."

"I always knew we'd be good together, but I let Annette distract me. I'm thankful you came home."

Some distraction. He'd gotten Annette pregnant in high school and married her the day after graduation. "Me too." I shared the news about Janey's engagement. "I should've asked you first, but I volunteered to host a family party here for her announcement. I thought it would be easy to do a Low Country Boil so that all the veggies and meat were cooked together. I apologize for making plans without your consent. If you're not okay with it, I'll let her know."

"Your family is welcome in our home, and I hope you feel the same about my family."

"I do." Heat steamed from my cheeks. Drat. The matrimonial phrase again. Why did I keep saying it? I cleared my throat. "Good. That's settled. Tell me about Sonny. Did he make bail?"

"His arraignment is tomorrow, but he won't be going anywhere."

"Because of the murder charge?"

177

"Got it in one."

"Did Crash contest the charge?" I persisted.

"Doesn't matter. The high-powered weapon used, the double tap, the gunpowder residue, and Sonny's statement seal the deal. Even if the judge wanted to be lenient, Mowrey is a flight risk. He's not from here, nor does he have deep ties to our community."

"Did you check out his former address in Florida?"

"It's an empty lot."

"Bummer. What about his prints? Get anything on them or Deena's?"

"Nothing yet. Sonny's pickup was purchased at Bill's Used Cars over by the spur. Paid cash. Another dead end."

"I wish I could help. Deena speaks with a Southern accent. If she's faking it, she's good."

"Even if they're Southern, that won't narrow the search parameters enough for a speedy result. That distinction covers the lower Atlantic Seaboard and all the Gulf states."

Something clicked in my head. "You said Sonny's car was purchased here. What about Deena's cherry red sports car?"

"Good point. I can follow up tomorrow."

I hurried to my computer at the kitchen table. "I downloaded my pictures from today. I took one of Deena leaning against her car. Let me see if I got the tag."

Ike set the pan on a cool burner and crossed over to stand behind me. My fingers trembled with excitement. Would my photograph provide the missing link for this case?

Finally, I located the image. Even though I zoomed in on the license plate, Deena blocked most of it. "Rats. I was hoping I had something for you."

"I can get the plate number from the tag office." He placed his hand on top of mine and moved the mouse. "Zoom in again."

"The dealer's name," I said as the metallic script writing came into focus. "You're a genius. It says Portside Imports. Wonder where that is."

We searched for the name online but came up with furniture stores. Adding "autos" to the search parameters netted us a promising lead in Florida.

"I'll call that dealership in the morning," Ike said, clicking back to the picture and zooming in on Deena's face. "Send me this, will ya?

I've never seen this pink-haired woman before. I want to copy the pic to my guys and ask if anyone's seen her."

I wrangled the computer back from him and emailed the photo. "Done." Another thought occurred to me. People with no past were that way for a reason. What if they were hiding themselves?

"You're doing it again," Ike said.

"Oh. Sorry. Just thinking about why people wouldn't have a past. What if Sonny and Deena are in Witness Protection? Will these probes put them in harms' way?"

"You're complicating things again, but I can reach out to the U.S. Marshalls and ask. That inquiry alone will put their faces and prints in more databases, but the likelihood of them being in the program are small. They would've reached out to their contact as soon as I brought Sonny in yesterday."

Rats. His logic trumped my guesses every time. I sighed. "You've felt it too, the gut sense something's not right with them. Sonny shot someone, so he's dangerous."

"He's also behind bars and not going anywhere," Ike said, turning back to the stove and spooning our dinner onto plates.

"Deena's a loose cannon. I don't trust her." I struggled to articulate my growing sense of urgency. "Can you send her picture to the deputies and contact the Marshall's Office tonight?"

Ike carried our plates to the dining room. "We're eating first. I'll zip back to the office to email those inquiries after dinner."

I followed with our iced tea. "You can use my computer."

"Best if I keep investigative queries on the office system. I don't want to do anything that might give the opposition the edge in a trial."

"You think Crash has a shot at getting Sonny off?"

"Crash is determined to make his mark on the world. All the trouble we got into as kids? Crash was the idea guy. If there's a way to spin this to his advantage, he'll do it."

"Sounds like you want him to win."

"You're mistaking insight for admiration. Crash has an advantage over other lawyers. He knows better than anyone exactly how I think."

"In that case, Deena made a smart move in hiring him."

"I'll say."

Chapter 10

I was standing beside Ike's office chair when he read his fingerprint search result. Deena's prints were in the system because she'd applied to be a foster parent six years ago. They belonged to a woman named Peggy Lou Gray. No criminal record was found. Further searches of her name revealed a former Mobile, Alabama, address, a concealed carry permit in Alabama, and her divorce record from a man named Lowell Gray.

"Another Alabama connection!" I whooped with joy. "We're getting somewhere. This can't be a coincidence."

"I'm not fond of coincidences myself," Ike muttered, clicking through screens. He pulled up the most recent driver's license for Ms. Gray. We leaned forward to study the photo. Her brown eyes were the same as Deena's, but the hair was a dark brown, the chin a little more pointed, and the nose more of a blade shape.

"No pink hair," I observed. "Peggy Lou looks nothing like Deena."

"Don't be so quick to rule it out. The height, weight, and eye color match," Ike said. "Meanwhile, I'll send the two images to a friend who has access to facial recognition software."

"You think this is the same woman? Seems more likely there's an error on the print match."

"Biometrics don't lie. The different aspects are cosmetic." He clicked a few more keys, opened a form, and typed, impressing me with his rapid-fire keyboarding skills.

"There," Ike said, leaning back in his chair, a satisfied look on his face. "I requested day shift to bring Deena in tomorrow for questioning."

"Good luck. She is scared to death of stepping foot in this building."

"Which means she's got secrets."

"If Deena is Peggy Lou's assumed name, Sonny might be an alias as well. Otherwise, there's no reason for them to be hiding."

"We've been running Sonny's prints through the system for over twenty-four hours. I added Mobile and Alabama to his keyword search. If he's there, I'll get a hit."

I mulled the case facts in my head. Sonny shot and killed John Starling with a high-powered rifle. Sonny's wife's fingerprints belonged to a woman named Peggy Lou Gray. Peggy Lou and John were both from Alabama. The victim's brother believed John was about to come into money. My cousin sold Sonny and Deena a house here, and they paid in cash. Uncle Henry said Sonny and Deena had minimal funds in the local bank.

"What about sending Sonny's picture and prints to the Mobile, Alabama, sheriff? Someone there might recognize him on sight."

"Mobile's a big city, but it's worth checking." Ike typed the email address of Mobile's Sheriff Joe Webster. A few minutes later, that email went out as well. "We've covered our bases. Ready to go home?"

"Yes."

In Ike's Jeep, he turned to me. "Anyone ever tell you that you have a brilliant mind? You should've gone into law enforcement."

"Don't think so. Chasing down bad guys isn't my thing. I'm in the right career as a journalist."

He considered that for a long moment as we rolled homeward, his headlights illuminating a narrow swath of River Road. "Ever think about writing murder mysteries?"

I stared at the darkness outside my window. I'd been lost before and hadn't known I was marking time. Coming home and connecting with Ike changed everything. What I'd found was too precious to lose chasing rainbows.

I placed my hand on his thigh. "I like my career. I tried on another life, and I didn't like it very much. This is who I am, and I'm content with my choices."

He grinned. "Good answer."

Chapter 11

After dropping Trent at school the next morning, Ike's sister brought my dog to the office. "We had a good night," Alice Ann said. "All Trent could talk about was the awesome meals at your house."

I stooped to give Bailey a hug, and she licked my face before waddling off to mooch treats from Ellen in the front office. "I assist Ike in the kitchen. He's the real chef. Trent is a good eater, so it's a good fit."

Alice Ann hugged me, released me, and hugged me again. "I'm so glad you and my brother are together. I've never seen Ike happier, and Trent is acting like a carefree young boy for a change. I'm over the moon you two are a couple. I mean a family. I mean . . ."

I didn't know where she was going with this, but since it sounded personal, I closed the door and lowered my voice. "It's okay, Alice Ann. I'm in love with your brother. I'm not using him as a meal ticket like Annette did. I won't chew him up and spit him out in small pieces."

"I get that, but Ike, he should marry you." Alice Ann wrung her hands. "I've told him that. Mama's told him that. Ike says he doesn't need a marriage license with you. He swears y'all are married in every other sense of the word."

"Don't gang up on him," I cautioned. Their well-meaning guilt trips could backfire. Ike hated feminine manipulation. "Thanks to his ex, he can't say the words 'I love you.' We nearly broke up because I wanted so badly to hear them. I understand him now. I froze inside when my brother died. Afterward, I went through the paces of life, not trusting anything or anyone. Coming home helped me see that people genuinely cared about me. Ike is on the same path of emotional recovery, but pushing him is wrong. I agreed to buy a house with him, to share his bed and his life, and to be a caring adult in his son's life. That's what he wanted from me, so that's what he's getting."

"He loves you," Alice Ann said, her arms stealing around my shoulders again for another quick hug. "He's been different since you returned. Different, good, I mean, but Mama raised us better than he's behaving. She wants and I want for y'all to have a happily ever after and for your home to be full of children."

The phone rang. I didn't pick up because my assistant would. "You and Jimmy could give her more grandchildren."

Alice Ann blushed. "Jimmy's coming around to the idea of getting hitched. We've been friends forever. Frankly, the romance for us is brand new."

"It looks good on you." I smiled and remembered I needed to speak to her about another matter. "To change the subject, Ike and I are hosting a family get together on Sunday evening at six. We're inviting both sides of our families."

"I'll tell Mama. We'll be there."

"Great." My office phone buzzed. "Excuse me. I need to pick up."

"I need to get to work. I'm late for my shift, and the boss appreciates punctuality."

Alice Ann left, and I answered the call. "He's trying to kill me," the female voice hissed in my ear.

"Who is this?" I focused keenly on this woman's voice.

"You know who it is. I can't go home. I can't show my face. I fear for my life."

It wasn't Cousin Janey or Aunt Fay. Not Ellen either because she was in the next room, and Alice Ann just left. It wasn't my mom or Trish, my father's lady friend.

Satisfied no one in my family was in harm's way, I risked a breath. "I don't know who you are, but if you're in danger, call 9-1-1."

Ellen stood in my doorway, questions in her eyes. I touched a finger to my lips and then switched the phone to speaker mode. My dog padded in and sat by my chair.

"I can't. The cops will kill me," the raspy voice continued. "Don't you see? I'm a fugitive. I can't turn to anyone in law enforcement, but I want to tell my story in the *Gazette*. That way, the world will know what they did to me. My story will be told."

My pulse kicked into high gear. A source wanted to give me an exclusive interview. Much as I'd love an exclusive story, meeting with a fugitive was risky. I needed to control where we met. "I'll clear my schedule. Come to the office now and talk."

"Nooo. Can't do that. Meet me elsewhere, and don't tell the cops."

That whiney tone sounded familiar. Was it Deena Mowrey? How cool if she wanted to share why she'd changed her name. "Why should I agree to those terms? I have to think of my safety."

"No one's safe in this world. Tell you what. Head north on the highway, and I'll text you my location."

"I'm not leaving without my staff knowing my whereabouts. Meet me here or in a public place."

The line went quiet. "Okay. We'll do it your way." The speaker paused. "Meet me at the Mid-County Diner. Come alone. If anyone accompanies you, I won't show."

"That restaurant isn't open this early."

"It will be today. Get here in ten minutes, or I'm leaving town without talking to you."

No way was I going without telling Ike. "I need more time. My camera is on the charger, and I have to reassemble it."

"No pictures. Come now or forget it."

Another protest rose in my throat, but the line went dead before I uttered a sound.

"Who was that?" Ellen said. "She said it was an emergency."

"I think it was Deena Mowrey, the wife of the man being held for the hunting accident turned homicide."

"You're not meeting her alone, are you?"

"I am."

"Ike won't like this," Ellen predicted.

Ike would have a cow, but this was my job. Reporters interviewed sources and wrote stories. I'd bargained for neutral territory and won. Things were moving fast, but I was thinking on my feet.

"I'll call Ike on the way to smooth things over, and I'll take my dog. We're meeting at the crossroads restaurant, for goodness sake. How dangerous could that be?"

Chapter 12

"I don't know if it's Deena," I told Ike as I sped across the county. "Let me get her story. I'll tape the interview on the phone. Then you can swoop in and arrest her."

"It must be Deena," Ike said. "Deputies went to her house this morning. No one was there, and the door was wide open. Her clothes and personal items were gone. Slow down and let me catch you."

"I have to go alone or she won't show."

"I don't like it."

"I'm doing my job. She wanted to meet me at an undisclosed location. I suggested my office. We compromised on the Mid-County Diner. Those restaurant gals will already be in the back prepping today's lunch. If Deena makes one false move, there'll be witnesses."

"We don't know enough about this woman. I can't guarantee your safety. I'm coming inside with you."

"I have Bailey."

"The dog that hides when there's trouble?" Ike groaned. "How reassuring."

"Bailey has good instincts. I'll follow her lead."

"Not good enough. We know this woman has a concealed carry permit. That means she has a gun. Are you carrying?"

"Of course not. Even if I owned a gun, I wouldn't carry it." Guns. I eased up on the gas. Was my life worth an unknown story by an anonymous caller? I'd been too swept up in the moment to even consider a gun might be involved. "I hear what you're saying, and you're right. I was blinded by the potential of an exclusive. I'll slow down, and I'm good with you sitting in on the interview."

"Great. I'm passing the old airport now, and I've also got a patrol car headed your way."

He was only a few miles behind me. "No sirens."

"Lady, you drive a hard bargain."

~*~

I'd never been to Mid-County Diner so early before, but the place looked dead. At noon, people trolled for parking spots, but I could park anywhere I wanted right now. No lights glowed in the windows of the building. I gulped and parked by the door.

No little red cars in sight. If Deena was here, she'd parked elsewhere. After double-checking that my phone and reporter pad were in my purse, I clipped Bailey's leash on her collar and stepped out of the car. Lois Lane had nothing on me. I'd get this story, even if I had an Ike shadow.

Bailey darted out of the car, headed straight for the bushes at the far end of the building. I bit back my annoyance while she watered the bushes, then I tried the door. It was locked. I knocked on the door. Nothing.

Where was my caller?

Not here, apparently.

I didn't like how exposed I felt, standing here, alone. The hair on the back of my neck prickled. Best to wait in the car until Ike arrived, I decided.

Everything happened at once. Bailey bolted to the right, yanking the leash from my hand, pulling me sideways and down. Something bit my arm. I heard a loud noise. The world spun and faded to black.

~*~

I awakened slowly, too tired to open my eyes. My mouth tasted like chemicals, and it was hard to swallow around my thick tongue. A hammer pounded in my head. I heard noises around me. Footsteps. Hushed voices. Felt a pressure and then no pressure on my right arm. Heard the footsteps retreat. So tired. I drifted off.

Mechanical beeps awakened me. Someone breathed loudly in the darkened room. I held my breath to listen and the noise stopped. What was going on? Why couldn't I remember anything? I tried to move, but my limbs felt like they were made of steel. A sharp jolt of pain lanced my thoughts.

I cried out. The beeps sounded louder, faster. Footsteps again.

Hurrying this time. A soft voice murmured something as I slid back into darkness.

~*~

I surfaced again. Heard the beeps. Felt the throb of pain in my left arm and the dull hammering in my head. Recognized my loud breathing and sensed deep shadows in the room. Something had awakened me. Pressure on my right hand. I gripped the lifeline.

"You're okay, Lindsey," a man said. "Someone took a shot at you, and you're in the hospital now. The doctor says you'll make a full recovery. The bullet grazed your arm, which is why it's in a sling. Bailey saved your life."

Bailey. That was my dog's name. I was Lindsey and I'd been shot. "Dad?"

"Shh. Don't try to talk," Dad said. "You hit your head when you fell and have a minor concussion. They said you might be dizzy for a few days, so take it easy, okay? Another fall and they'll keep you in here longer."

I was in the hospital. My dad held my right hand, my left arm was bent and secured to my chest. I'd taken a call from a whispering woman who wanted to give me her story. I'd driven out to meet her, but she wasn't there.

I cracked my eyes a bit. The room was spinning, but I gritted it out. "Day?"

"It's Saturday, dear," my dad said.

Saturday. I'd lost an entire day. "Where's Ike?"

Dad leaned over my face, smoothed my hair back with his other hand. "He's fine. Got a manhunt going for the shooter."

Why wasn't he here? I turned away from my dad as disappointment washed through me. Ike was doing his job. He was responsible for keeping everyone safe. I was at the hospital, getting help. I wasn't Ike's sole responsibility.

"I need water," I managed to say.

My dad brought a straw to my lips. The icy liquid felt amazing in my mouth. "Thanks."

"You're going to be fine. The fact that you're awake and speaking is a good sign."

"What about the newspaper?"

"Trish and I are helping Ellen pull the next edition together. It's like old times."

Old times. "Thanks, but don't get too comfortable as editor."

"The editor job is yours for as long as you want it. Trish and I have another cruise booked in three weeks."

A nurse entered, saw I was awake, and hurried away. Moments later, the room brimmed with people clad in colorful scrubs, and my father got the boot. I had to look at this little light and then that one. Questions came one after another, and I answered them all.

When the medical team started leaving, I grabbed the nearest doctor with my good arm. "I want to go home."

"Not today. We're keeping you under observation for another twenty-four hours."

"I'm throwing a party at my house tomorrow. I promised my cousin. I can't reschedule."

"Put someone else in charge of your party because even if you're home by tomorrow evening, you won't be in any state of mind for a party. You're in Intensive Care because of the shortage of hospital beds right now, so the visitation rules of one family member at a time are in effect. By the way, the sheriff is anxious to get your statement. He's called every hour."

Delight made me feel all warm and fuzzy, and the giddy sensation had nothing to do with the slowly spinning room. "He has?"

"Yes. He must think you have valuable information."

"Something like that," I said gruffly. "He's my boyfriend."

"Strange that your family omitted that information. Would you like him added to your approved list of visitors?"

My good hand fisted in the sheets. "Yes, I want to see him."

After the doctor left, Cousin Janey breezed in. "You look good for a woman who cheated death again," she said.

"Why didn't y'all let Ike in?" My voice came out sharp on purpose.

Janey's face twitched. "Aunt Fay said it was time to get his attention."

The throbbing in my head kicked up a notch. "About what?"

"About you two playing house without a marriage license."

Something boiled in my gut and it wasn't food. "That's none of her business."

"Don't shoot the messenger." Janey poked my chest with a finger. "That was a direct quote from you know who."

I closed my eyes, relieved my actions hadn't pushed Ike beyond the point of no return. "Poor Ike. Everyone's ganging up on him."

"Poor Ike my foot. Ike can take care of himself. Say, is there anything you need?"

"Clean clothes so I can go home."

"Not today."

"I'm still having your party tomorrow."

"Think again. We're delaying the party a week. Everyone already agreed."

"That's not fair to you."

"You weren't shot when you offered. It's okay."

I nodded, sagging deeper in the bed. "How's Trent?"

"He's in the waiting room with Alice Ann. May I send him in? Oh, and he's your nephew if anyone asks."

"I want to see him."

A few minutes later, Janey brought Trent to the door. He stood there, a look of terror on his pale face.

"Trent? Come in," I said, lifting my head like a turtle. For the first time, I wondered about my hair and face. Was there dried blood? "Sorry I don't look more like myself."

Trent eased into the room. "You don't look bad."

"Were you scared?" I asked, waving him close.

He nodded.

"Me too. I'm sorry you were upset. I wouldn't do anything to hurt you."

"I know. Daddy told me. He said he's gonna get the S.O.B. that shot you."

Ike wouldn't appreciate his son swearing, but I gave him a pass. "He will. Come closer, I won't break."

Trent stood beside me, his hands fisted, his teary eyes fierce. "I want Dad to shoot them back."

"Ike has to abide by the law, but he's good at being a cop."

Unexpectedly, Trent flung himself at me, hugging me and sobbing. One of his arms inadvertently hit my hurt arm, and I tried not to flinch. What was physical pain when someone's heart was breaking? I held him tight with my good arm and murmured words of comfort.

"I thought you were dead, Mama L. I thought I wouldn't have you anymore. I don't want you to go anywhere. I love you. Dad and I need you. Bailey needs you. You have to come back to us."

"I love you too." And in that moment, I knew I was walking out of this hospital tomorrow no matter what. My family needed me. I

189

untangled our limbs so I could look him in the eye. "I'll be home tomorrow, so make sure Bailey gets exercised in the morning."

He nodded, dark eyes gleaming. "Dad said Bailey saved you. That she pulled you away from the sniper's bullet."

"He's right. Bailey is a hero. We should do something special for her."

"I'll do it. I'll show Bailey how much she means to us."

"That's fine."

I glanced at the doorway. Ike filled it with his broad shoulders. How long had he been standing there listening to us?

"Dad! She's all right! Mama L's all right!" Trent darted across the room and hurled himself into Ike's arms.

"I see that," Ike said. "May I have a turn with her now?"

"Yes, but the doctor said don't tire her out. And no yelling."

As Ike set Trent down and watched him walk away, I noticed how pale Ike looked. His eyes, normally so warm and inviting, looked haunted. Even his stride as he came to me seemed off.

He bent to kiss me lightly on the lips, then he sat beside the bed, holding my good hand in his. "They kept me away from you, or else I wouldn't have left your side."

"I missed you," I said. "I'm sorry for everything. Did you find Deena?"

"She's gone to ground. I ordered roadblocks and put out an APB on her fancy car. I'll find her. You have my word on that."

"I never doubted it for a moment."

"Tell me what happened."

I reprised the story of the empty restaurant and how I'd decided to wait for him in the car. "Bailey lunged to the right, yanking me off my feet. I never saw Deena or anyone with a gun. I fell and woke up here."

"That's what I figured happened. We found a hunting blind catty corner to the restaurant. The location wasn't a random pick. She set you up. The bullet we dug out of the door matched the one that killed the bartender. Sonny wasn't our shooter. Not unless there are two sharpshooters in their family."

"Stranger things have happened," I offered.

Ike scowled. "Trent advised me to shoot her, and I wanted to take his advice."

I searched his tired face. "But you didn't. You love your job."

"When I saw you lying on the ground unconscious and your shirt stained with blood, I wanted to kill her with my bare hands."

His eyes burned into mine. "Saving you was more important than hunting her down. You're everything to me, Linds. I rode in the ambulance with you. I stayed with you in the ER until they kicked me out. Once you got patched up, your family and my mom arrived. They told the hospital you weren't married, and the hospital only allowed your dad and cousin to sit with you after that."

I gave his hand a squeeze. "I'm sorry. A few minutes ago, a doctor told me what they'd done. I immediately added you to my visitor list. No one can keep you out of my hospital room anymore."

"Good. Because I'm not leaving until we go home. How do you feel, Mama L?"

He'd heard Trent's new name for me and approved. "I have a killer headache and a sore arm, but my heart is feeling remarkably better."

Ike rose. "We'll rest quietly together. I haven't had a lick of sleep since Thursday night. Move over."

"You're too big."

He tried to lift the covers. "I'm just right, and I can't sleep without you."

I clung to the covers. "I haven't brushed my teeth, combed my hair, or bathed in a day."

"You look and smell great to me."

With that, he lifted me gently in his arms, sliding underneath me fully clothed, shoes and all. I nestled against him, content. The steady thumping of his heart and the comfort of his embrace allowed me to ignore my pain and drowse in his arms.

The floor nurse made him move the next time she checked my blood pressure, but he raised such a fuss, they wheeled in another hospital bed and set it up beside mine. Ike slept deeply, undisturbed by the noises here, but I couldn't stop thinking about Deena Mowrey.

She'd targeted me. She had drawn a bead on me and pulled the trigger. If not for Bailey, I'd be in the morgue. Deena's animosity toward me made no sense. I'd agreed to meet with her and listen to her story. For that, she'd decided to kill me?

Chapter 13

Seemed like I'd barely closed my eyes when a phone rang. Ike's low-pitched voice rumbled nearby. He sounded serious so I roused and took note of the washed-out walls. Where was I?

I pushed up a little higher on my pillow and a jolt of pain blasted from my left arm, taking my breath away. Oh, yeah. I was in the hospital because Deena Mowrey tried to kill me. I was lucky to be alive, though I wished she'd missed altogether.

It was light outside, so I took it to be Sunday morning. I wanted to go home. To sleep in my own bed. To wear clothes that didn't leave my backside exposed.

"That's interesting," Ike said, his voice strong and true. "He's definitely going nowhere anytime soon."

Something was happening with the case. To heck with the pain, I pushed to a sitting position, gritting my teeth as the world slowly spun to a standstill. The only way to get out of this bed was to get moving. Now that Ike had taken residence in my hospital room, I wanted privacy to go to the bathroom.

Whatever it took, I was walking to that bathroom. I traced the IV tube from my arm to the wheeled pole. Yeah, I could do this. Slide off the bed. Grab the pole on wheels. Trudge to the bathroom and do my business.

"I gotta go," Ike said. "Keep me posted."

He clicked off the call and padded around to face me. "Where do you think you're going?"

"Home. But first I have to make a pit stop in the bathroom."

"How can I help?"

Smart man. He knew the drill about getting out of here. "I need to do this by myself, but if disaster looms, I'd appreciate it if you kept me from doing a face plant. Once I show I can do this, I can make noises about going home today."

"Gotcha."

It wasn't easy, and I wanted to quit four times, but I made it there and back with my dignity intact. Ike tucked me in with a chaste kiss. His eyes brimmed with excitement.

"Tell me," I said.

"Had a break in the case. You were right about Sonny Mowrey being an alias. Deena is his ex-wife. His real name is Lowell Gray. Sonny and Deena Mowrey are really Lowell and Peggy Lou Gray."

"Imagine that."

Ike's grin nearly split his face. My heart leapt to see him so happy. I reached for his hand and interlaced our fingers. Warm and comfort pulsed from his touch.

His eyes twinkled. "There's more."

Of course there was more. He was a master at drawing out the suspense. "How much more?"

"Enough."

"I'm all ears."

"You won't believe this."

I groaned. "So help me God, Ike, if you don't tell me, I'll clobber you."

"That's my girl." He studied me with laughing eyes. "Seems we have a dead man in our jail."

Sonny was dead? "You think that's funny? What kind of man are you?"

Ike's expression sobered. "Death is never funny. As usual, you're thinking circles around me. Sonny's very alive. But his prints belong to a dead man."

"You're serious?"

"Absolutely."

This wasn't laying down kind of news. I propped up on one arm. "Dead? Like a zombie?"

"He'll wish he was a zombie by the time I'm finished with him," Ike said. "Dead like he faked his death. He has another wife in Mobile, Alabama."

"How?"

"The incident report says he drove his car into the Gulf of Mexico one night two years ago, and his body was never recovered."

"Why?"

"Not a hundred percent on that yet, but Deena cashed in an insurance policy, skipped town, and vanished. My guess is she joined Sonny, and they established their Sonny and Deena identities in Florida."

"It seems extreme. Why didn't Sonny divorce wife number two?"

"The insurance policy paid out five hundred grand. Defrauding an insurance company will land them in jail, even if they hadn't used humans for target practice."

I relaxed into my bed, tired by the exchange. "You're gonna arrest Deena."

"Damn straight I am." He reached for my covers again.

I swatted his hand, but he kept coming. "Ike, they'll make you move."

"They can try. You and I need to get something straight. Both of us are awake and alert, and I'm not going anywhere until I have my say."

"What's wrong?"

"You make me crazy." His laser-sharp gaze made my heart flutter. "When you got hurt, it took the starch right out of me. Promise me you won't do this again."

As much as his sideways declaration of caring meant, I couldn't give him what he wanted. "Promise I won't do my job? Interviewing people is what I do, same as you keep the peace and catch people who break the law. I didn't operate in a vacuum. I notified you, and I was waiting for you at the restaurant."

Ike squeezed his eyes shut. "I'm screwing this up." He look a long breath. "If I'm working a homicide, promise me I can accompany you on interviews related to the case."

"You want to be a reporter?"

He tensed. Was he taking my flip remark as criticism? I snuggled closer. "Ike, you can accompany me anytime you like. I was teasing you."

He took a breath. Then another. He carefully moved me until our gazes locked. I was surprised by the magnetic intensity in his.

"Good. Because I need you," Ike said. "I want to spend every day of my life with you."

My pulse raced, deafening me. Hopes and dreams tottered on the highest cliff imaginable. "Ike Harper, are you saying you love me?"

"Love doesn't encompass the depth of what I feel for you, Lindsey. I'm in *life* with you."

Stunned, I could only stare at him. His expression was so earnest, so breathtakingly poignant, that I couldn't move. This was a moment, a memory in the making. Energy flowed between us, vibrant and electrifying.

"I have one question for you," Ike said. "Are you in life with me?"

Time slowed to microseconds. Every nuance of his body was so intent on an answer that neither of us could function. Words failed me. I drew him in for a kiss. "Yes," I whispered. "I am in life with you."

He cradled me, mindful of my injury, his body trembling. I trembled too. For so long, I'd wanted him to admit he loved me, but this was more, something bone marrow deep.

I savored the intense feeling of belonging and reveled in living in the moment.

Chapter 14

It took forever to check out of the hospital. Between the forms, the doctor sign-off, and the wheelchair attendant availability, I was good and stuck until late afternoon. Ike lit out after our morning nap, sending my father and Trish to the hospital to keep me company and drive me home while he tried to round up Deena.

After being discharged, I expected to visit the police station, but I had to settle for being queen of my sofa. Thanks to the neighbors, I had enough food for a week. Ike's sister brought Trent home at dinner time. To my delight, Trent called me Mama L several more times. We were on our way to becoming a family.

The pain in my arm worsened after dinner. I debated forgoing the pain medication, but Trish told me I could cut back tomorrow. Her logic made sense, so I took two tablets.

When Ike arrived at bedtime, I could barely keep my eyes open, much less talk about the case with Ike. Between getting Trent tucked in bed, walking the dog, and herding me upstairs to our bed, Ike was too busy for a drawn out chat. Still, I gave it a try upstairs.

"How'd it go?" I asked, stifling another yawn as I watched him undress. "Did Sonny cave when you told him you knew his identity?"

Ike eased under the covers with me. "Sonny shrugged off the news. I couldn't get a handle on his reaction. I wish you'd been there."

"Me too. What about Deena?"

"Haven't found her yet. She's living on borrowed time. I requested more information about her from the cops in Mobile. They sent me a file on her. Deena Mowrey aka Peggy Lou Gray shoplifted as a kid, but nothing criminal showed up once she became an adult. Either she became a model citizen or she got better at stealing. Given the insurance fraud and her shooting at you, I'm banking on the latter being true."

"You'll get her."

He wrapped his arms around me. "You're my lucky charm for case solving."

I burrowed into his heat even though the room temperature was warm. Ike's scent soothed me, and my eyes closed immediately.

~*~

Monday morning's heavy clouds added a brooding, melancholy aspect to my thoughts. Without a hint of breeze, the dense air felt too thick to breathe. I wished it would rain so the moisture would have someplace to go.

Trent gave me a big hug before his father drove him to school. My dad and Trish did the breakfast dishes and headed to the newspaper to pull together the next edition. Which left me alone with my dog and feeling adrift in my own home.

I was too antsy to go to sleep, too unfocused to follow a TV program or read a book. Bailey followed me from room to room as I rattled around in my house, my left arm in a sling. I'd decided against prescription pain meds this morning, but I had dipped into the over-the-counter stuff. Consequently, the muted throb of pain idled in my mind like an outboard motor.

Case information eddied in my head. Sonny Mowrey was an alias. He faked his death and started over. Deena defrauded an insurance company. Bartender John Starling died in a hunting accident. What did those items have in common? The answer came up Deena every time.

If I was Deena, what would I do?

From the look of things, she'd set up Sonny as her patsy. He'd taken the fall for her with John's accidental shooting, but now she'd shot me. Had she found a new patsy? Ike's lawyer friend came to mind. He'd socialized with Deena in John's bar, and now he was Sonny's lawyer. If he knew bad things about her, he couldn't reveal them due to lawyer-client privilege.

I should warn Ike his friend might be in trouble. But before I fished my cell phone from my pocket, the doorbell chimed. Bailey barked and charged toward the door. She acted as if the hounds of hell were outside, not her usual M.O. when company called.

Between the knot in my stomach and my dog's unusual behavior, I feared whoever stood on my porch. Besides, I was wounded and fighting the urge to take another pain pill. I was vulnerable. No way would I answer the door. Friends and family knew I'd been injured. They wouldn't visit today.

Heart racing in my ears, I ducked into the downstairs bathroom, locked the door, and called Ike on his cell.

"Someone's here," I said in a terse whisper. "Bailey's going crazy. I'm hiding in the downstairs bathroom."

"Climb in the tub and keep your head down. I'll be there in two shakes," he said.

Chapter 15

Two shakes seemed like an eternity. Bailey barked nonstop at the front door. I huddled in the tub, banging the elbow of my bad arm and seeing stars. I cowered and shook, afraid to lift my head in case another bullet had my name on it.

A siren wailed. Ike was coming. The siren drowned out Bailey's barking, and then it stopped.

Heavy footsteps pounded on the front steps. "May I help you? Ike asked.

At Ike's approach, Bailey's bark changed to a whine. I'd heard every word as clear as a bell. Not much insulation in this old house. My thoughts raced. If Deena was out there, Ike would've arrested her. It must be someone else.

"I need to speak to Ms. McKay," a woman said. "I have information for her."

"Ms. McKay isn't receiving guests today. Move along, ma'am. This is private property."

"I must see her. I drove here from Mobile."

Mobile? I sat up to hear the conversation.

"Who are you?" Ike asked.

"Helen Gray of Mobile, Alabama. I'm Lowell's wife."

Lowell's wife. Not Deena, but the woman Sonny was married to when he faked his death. How did she even know me?

"Let's talk at the station," Ike said. "I'll make sure Ms. McKay gets your message."

"I vowed never to set foot inside a police station again. If you want my story, we'll talk here."

Neither spoke for a minute, but I imagined Ike staring at her, weighing his options.

"That's an unusual request, but this case has been unusual from the get-go," Ike said. "Wait here."

As I heard his key in the door and the clicks of Bailey's dancing claws on the wood floor, I scrambled out of the tub and unlocked the bathroom door.

Ike appeared, Bailey at his heels. "You okay?" he asked.

"Mostly." I hid my trembling hands inside the sling. "Sorry. I thought Deena came to finish what she started."

"Me too, but your visitor is Sonny's lawful wife, Helen. She's the woman he abandoned to run off with Deena, I mean Peggy Lou who became Deena. Helen won't go to the station with me. Are you up for company?"

"Yes."

He nodded. "You got that digital recorder handy?"

"My phone app works as a recorder. Are we interviewing her?"

"We are, though if you'd rather I question her on the front porch, that's fine with me."

The thought of sitting in the glider and purposefully moving around was more than my body could take. Fortunately, the warm weather gave me a better excuse. "In the air conditioning, please. I can't face the heat."

He searched my face. "You take pain meds this morning?"

I shook my head. "I don't want to get hooked on them."

"You're in pain."

"I'm functioning. Aren't you worried that woman will leave while we're talking?"

"I blocked her car with my vehicle." He pulled me close for a quick hug. "On the sofa you go. I'll call in her license plate to make sure she's who she says she is before I let her in."

Bailey stuck to me like flypaper as I strode to the sunporch sofa. She must be picking up on my anxiety. Fear made me stupid, but I was safe.

Ike left the door open when he went to the porch again. "She'll see you, but for my peace of mind, are you carrying any weapons in that handbag."

"See for yourself," Helen said.

A few minutes later he said, "A 38 special. Smith and Wesson. Never seen one with a pink handle before."

"It's a good gun," Helen said. "A woman can't be too careful these days. I never leave home without it."

"Lock your purse and gun in your car. You won't need them in the house."

"You're carrying."

"I'm the sheriff. If you want to enter my home, you'll lock this gun in your car."

"Point taken. I'll be right back."

A car door opened and closed. I prepped my phone and waited. What did this woman want with me? I didn't rise when she strolled inside. The arm sling spoke for itself.

Bailey barred her teeth, a low guttural sound emitting from her throat. I put my phone down, grabbed her collar, and got her settled.

"I'm Helen Gray, Ms. McKay," the woman said. "I want you to write a story about how Lowell and Peggy Lou done me wrong."

Helen Gray wore her years poorly. Her thin face had a haggard look, as if she ran too much and ate too little. Her androgynous hair style and clingy clothing on her narrow frame furthered the image of excessive training. She reminded me of someone, but I couldn't remember who.

"Please, sit down." In my head, I transposed the names she mentioned to Sonny and Deena. "Before we get started, have we met before? You look familiar to me."

"I get that a lot. I must have a lot of twins out there, but this is my first visit here."

"All right then. I'll hear you out, but this conversation will be recorded."

Helen perched on the wicker chair cattycorner to me, statue still. "Record away. Here's the deal. I met Lowell and Peggy Lou at the gun range about three years ago. Lowell wanted to shoot his new Glock, but Peggy Lou loved shooting and continued taking target practice lessons. That woman can shoot anything."

"And you?" Ike sat beside me, gun prominently displayed on his hip. "Are you also a good shot?"

"Not at all. Peggy Lou took top honors in the club's shooting demos."

I wasn't warming up to Helen Gray, but I couldn't put my finger

201

on why. She didn't give off a friendly vibe, but maybe my rattled nerves made me more suspicious than usual. It was good to have the recording to review later.

"What about Lowell?" Ike asked. "Did he continue his training?"

"No. Once he mastered his Glock, he was done. After that, he drove Peggy Lou to the demos. Poor bastard."

"Why do you say that?"

"Peggy Lou only saw Lowell as a meal ticket because he was selling the crap out of life insurance. She screwed the range instructor and anything else who looked her way while they were married. She didn't honor their vows."

"Did he confront her about the infidelity?" I asked, jumping into the fray.

"Lowell didn't complain. I felt sorry for him. One day at Deena's shooting demonstration, I asked if he'd like to do something fun with me and he said yes."

"To clarify," Ike said, "you began a relationship with him?"

"Yes. Lowell's got plenty under the hood and knows how to satisfy a woman. Peggy Lou had three more affairs before Lowell told her about us. Before Peggy Lou left him, she broke every dish in his house, including his great grandmother's Wedgwood platter. Lowell moved in with me, and when his divorce was final, we got married. I've never been so happy."

"But?" I asked, knowing there had to be more.

"But Peggy Lou skunked me. I never knew about Lowell's insurance policy or Lowell naming her as the beneficiary. Worse, he continued sleeping with his ex during our marriage. One day I woke up to learn Lowell's car was in the Gulf, and he was gone. I haunted the shore for weeks, searching for him, thinking he had amnesia. I visited every hospital and morgue, but I couldn't find him."

Sounded like Helen had a bad case of fatal attraction. If she couldn't have Lowell, nobody could have him. Especially not his ex-wife.

Helen stopped to scowl. "Six months after he died, my friend Marge told me Peggy Lou bought a fancy red sports car and dropped a load of cash at the spa where Marge works. A few days later, Peggy Lou left town for good. Mobile policemen visited me a few days ago saying Lowell was alive. Imagine that. After two years of thinking of him as dead, I had a miracle. Lowell was here in Georgia. Except he's in jail for shooting someone.

"Mark my words, Peggy Lou, or Deena as she calls herself now, rigged the evidence. She cashed his insurance policy, but I guarantee you she's trolling for a new Sugar Daddy to satisfy her urges."

Ike crossed his arms. "Quite a tale. Have any proof?"

"Proof? Peggy Lou stole my husband, and now she's thrown him away like garbage. I want her arrested so she can never see daylight, and I want to take Lowell home to Mobile with me, where he belongs."

"He confessed to shooting John Starling," Ike reminded her.

"He's protecting Peggy Lou. Despite everything she's done, he still cares for her. She's a bad egg, and he'll come around in time. But Deena isn't as smart as she thinks she is. I'll bet things didn't match up just right for the first shooting."

"Go on," Ike said.

Helen gave a ghost of a smile. "Like the missing weapon."

"You know where the murder weapon is?"

"Peggy Lou has it. At her house."

If Helen was to be believed, her rival was the mastermind and a sniper. A gum smacking, emotional, libido-driven woman didn't fit my idea of a mastermind or a sniper.

"I've had someone watching her house since Friday," Ike said. "No one's come or gone."

"Because she's holed up inside and her car is in the garage. That's the kind of survivalist Pablum her instructor parroted. If you can't clear an area before trouble starts, hunker down in plain sight."

Interesting. Deena had a secret hideout. I wanted to go over there right now and help the deputies find her. I needed to see Ike put handcuffs on her wrists.

"How do you know this?" Ike asked, leaning forward.

"Because I took the same course for a while, but it was pure propaganda about the end of the world so I quit. Peggy Lou spent weeks with those whack jobs, which suited me fine. Her absence gave me and Lowell more time together."

Ike settled into the sofa cushions. "Try again. We searched her place already."

"Part of the training was building a secret room in your home. Was there any room that seemed smaller than normal?"

I could almost see the gears turning in Ike's head as he retraced his steps through that house. He swore and rose. "Excuse me for a minute."

203

He went into the kitchen where I could still see him and made a call. I had no doubt that he was gathering his team to storm Deena and Sonny's place. I turned back to Helen, amused to see Bailey sitting up between us. I placed my hand on her collar again hoping she wouldn't bite Helen.

"You're a font of useful information," I began, marveling at her capacity for stillness. "What's the deal? Why are you helping the investigation?"

"Peggy Lou needs to pay for what she's done, to me and to Lowell. She's like the Pied Piper around men. Watch your guy around her. If her pattern holds, she'll shag her way out of trouble again."

"Again?"

Helen snorted. "Her police record from Mobile was clean, right?"

"It was."

"Peggy Lou stole things right and left. Sometimes she used her body to soften a mark, sometimes she used it for damage control when the cops came a-calling. Have the sheriff dig into her past. She always takes what she wants, but she's not taking my Lowell. Not this time. I'm getting him back."

"By defrauding the insurance company, he will be charged with a crime. He'll serve time for that."

"Not as much time as Peggy Lou does. And I'll be waiting for him when he gets out."

Ike returned. "Mrs. Gray, I'd like you to wait at the station."

"Can't." The woman stood and stretched like a cat. "I've got a meeting scheduled with Sonny's lawyer in five minutes at the fish camp."

"Don't leave town."

"Where would I go? You've got my husband. I want him back. And besides you ran my tag, so you can find me if I left town, but I'm not going anywhere. I'm in love with my husband. He means the world to me."

Ike glanced at me. From his expression, he was undecided about letting her go. I shrugged, unwilling to go to bat for a person I didn't know or like.

"Please don't make me go to your station." Helen's voice turned shrill. "I spent days sitting in one when Lowell went missing. Those were awful times. I'm getting heart palpitations thinking about it. Please, I'm begging you. Let me talk to the lawyer. I have to wrestle

Lowell from Peggy Lou's influence, and her hooks are in him deep."

"I'll allow you to go, but I'll escort you over there and post a deputy to make sure you don't leave town."

"Fine with me."

I pushed upright. "Stay put," Ike said. "I'll call you as soon as I know something."

"I'm coming with you."

"Not a good idea, Linds."

"The best idea ever," I retorted. "I want to see you take Deena down. She shot me. I need closure."

Helen honked her horn outside. "All right," Ike said. "But we do this my way."

Chapter 16

Just as Helen said, a rifle was in the trunk of Deena's red sports car. Ike bagged it into evidence and brought it to the Jeep. "Don't touch. And make sure no one else touches it either."

I waited and waited, my gaze fastened on the door, but no one came out. After half an hour, Ike returned. "I know where the secret room should be, but darn if we can figure out how to access it. I need fresh eyes. Can you help us?"

"You bet." I scrambled out of the vehicle, careful of my hurt arm.

"Stay close to me, and if I say get down, drop immediately."

"Have you been calling her name?"

"Both of her names, but we haven't heard so much as a peep."

He guided me into a study. I saw a desk and a bookshelf behind it, along with Alice Ann and Jimmy, his top deputies. They looked sheepish.

I cleared my throat. "In every movie I've ever seen with a secret room, someone's moved a book on the shelf and the entire case slides out of the way to reveal an opening."

"We have the same taste in movies," Alice Ann said. "I've moved every book on the shelf. Nothing."

Hmm. That made it harder. What else was in the room? A side table with a lamp. A few framed watercolors. A ceiling fan. And an air duct. "What about the vent? Did you look in there?"

"There's a small camera," Jimmy said. "You and Alice Ann do watch the same movies. This is déjà vu."

I lifted every painting, looking for something out of place. But the entire room was sterile. What was I missing? "The desk chair. Where is it?"

"Wasn't one," Alice Ann said.

I walked behind the desk. One of those clear protective mats covered the area rug under the desk and where a chair should be. "Can someone move this?"

Jimmy and Ike stepped forward and dragged the plastic out of the way.

"Grab a handful of that carpet where the chair should've been," I said.

Jimmy knelt and did so. Amazingly, a hunk of carpet about three by three came up in his hand. Underneath, the floorboards were cut in the same cubed shape.

"You did it!" Ike whooped and knelt down with Jimmy to lift the hatch. Below us, a built-in ladder descended.

Jimmy shined his flashlight into the darkness. "Found the missing chair."

I peered over the edge. The back of the small chair rested under the door handle. "How's that possible? If Deena's inside, someone locked her in there."

"I can think of one person who wanted us to find Deena," Ike said.

"I don't trust Helen," I muttered, but no one was listening. Ike climbed down the ladder and moved the chair. Jimmy and Alice Ann kept their flashlights trained on the area.

"We know you're in here, Deena," Ike said. "Show yourself and let me see your hands."

The latch snicked, and the door opened. A strong sewage odor wafted up to where I stood in the room. Deena stood in the gap, bedraggled and dirty.

"Water," she said.

Ike stepped to the side of the short tunnel. "Come up nice and slow. My deputies will assist you."

Deena climbed the ladder, pale and droopy. She collapsed on the floor. Ike followed her, checked her for weapons, and cuffed her hands in front of her. She didn't protest, wouldn't look at any of us. Alice Ann brought water and helped her bring it to her mouth. When she tried to down the whole thing, Alice Ann said, "A little at a time or it will come back up."

"Damn him. Sonny said he'd connect the plumbing down there,

but he didn't. Only one twelve-pack of water down there. I could've died in that hellhole."

"Hold that thought," Ike said. "We'll get your statement at the Sheriff's Office."

"I won't talk unless Lindsey's there. I watched you through the vent cam. If not for her, I'd still be trapped below."

"I'm calling the shots," Ike said, "but I'm happy to have Lindsey sit in on the interview." He nodded to Alice Ann and Jimmy. "Transport her in your car. Lindsey and I will follow."

~*~

"What shall we call you?" I asked after sitting down beside Ike in the interview room. "Peggy Lou Gray or Deena Mowrey?"

The woman shrugged. Gone was the beach bunny look she'd sported before. Her pink hair hung in clumps. She seemed smaller, more hunched over after spending four days locked in the bolt hole. Her fingers and toes were bare, and she'd been processed and Mirandized. "Call me whatever you like."

"Okay then, Deena. You defrauded an insurance company. According to our confidential source, you killed the bartender and nearly killed me. What's your story?"

"I was framed. I'm innocent."

"You know how many people sit in that chair and say that?" Ike asked.

"No, you don't understand," Deena insisted. "I didn't shoot anyone. Helen is the crack shot, not me."

I glanced at Ike and back to Deena. I'd planned to gloat when the bars locked behind Deena. Now I wasn't so sure it would play out that way. Had we been conned by these women? "That's not what we heard."

"It's the truth. Helen and Sonny, I mean Lowell, were into that survivalist mindset. Sonny built the safe room in our house. I was glad to have a hideout, especially during the search, but then I got trapped inside. Helen snuck in my house, jammed the lock, and trapped me."

"Go on."

"John Starling said Helen paid him to spy on us. He was Helen's boyfriend in Mobile, but he became my boyfriend a few weeks ago."

"You're a married woman."

"We only pretended to be married this time around. No biggee. Sonny and I have an open relationship."

"What does that mean?"

"We slept around, or at least I did. I don't know who Sonny slept with. Didn't care."

"Supposing for one second you're right, how do we catch Helen?"

"You won't. She took that survivalist BS seriously."

"I have Helen under surveillance," Ike said.

"Check again. She's long gone."

Ike took my arm and we rose. "We'll see about that."

In the hall, he hugged me. "Good work. Sure you don't want to be a cop?"

"I'm sure."

He phoned his deputy on Helen's stakeout. "She's still at the restaurant?" Ike asked. "Check inside."

I used the restroom and grabbed a soda while we waited for a return call. My arm didn't hurt at all.

Ike answered his cell on the first ring. His face darkened as he listened. "Impound the car and check the motels and other restaurants."

He hung up and faced me, his shoulders bent. "She's gone. I thought I had her."

My empty stomach wasn't happy with this news. "Someone's been a step ahead of us this whole time. What if Deena's right? Helen could be thinking circles around us."

"Not on my watch." Ike ordered road blocks on the roads out of town before he glanced my way again. "Ready to talk to Deena again?"

"Not yet. Who do you believe?"

"None of 'em. Deena, Sonny, and Helen are liars."

"One of them is a killer," I said. "The others are lying, for sure, but how do we sift through the lies?"

"Interrogation 101. We keep them talking until their story cracks."

"I may not be up for that."

"Until Helen is under lock and key, you won't be alone, and I can't spare anyone right now to guard you. If you get tired while we're questioning Deena, come in here and rest."

I didn't much like it, but I understood. "Okay."

We opened the door and found Deena asleep face forward on the table. "Wake up," Ike said in a stern voice.

Deena pushed up from the table. "I was right, wasn't I?"

"How'd you know what Helen would do?" I asked.

"She's a planner. Not a spontaneous bone in her body. Way back in the beginning when we first met Helen, she saw how easy I had it being married to Sonny. At one time I thought I could contribute financially to our marriage by being a foster parent, but Sonny said I didn't have to work. Helen saw he was a good provider, and she wanted him. She wrecked our lives one step at a time. I was so mad when I found out that I went crazy breaking dishes."

Helen had mentioned the same thing about the dishes. Either it was true or they were in this together. "How'd she give the officer the slip?"

"She could've had a disguise planted there and walked out. She could've hired or stolen a boat. Helen is very good with details, like the lock on our safe room door. She knew how to defeat it. But she doesn't know everything."

"I'm all ears. Please continue."

"I figured out how to get Sonny back. He didn't like being bossed around, and that's all she ever did was boss people around. I told him if he faked his death, he'd never see her again."

"But she found you. How?"

"One of Helen's friends recognized Sonny at a convenience store out by the interstate where he went to get a six-pack. Marge called Helen on the spot. According to John, Helen made several trips here to see him before she framed me."

"Does Marge have a last name?"

"Marge Nash."

"We'll check with Marge, but you were in possession of a rifle that uses the same ammo that killed John and wounded me."

Deena's cuffed hands waved in the air. "I didn't shoot anyone. Helen did."

"Are your prints on the rifle?" Ike asked.

Deena groaned. "Yes. I hefted it on my shoulder as soon as I saw it."

"How'd that happen?" I asked.

"Helen tricked me. She left an anonymous tip on my phone to check the trunk of my car for a gift from a secret admirer. I couldn't resist picking up the rifle."

"That fingerprint evidence will send you to prison."

"That's why you have to do something. Helen planned everything. And there's more."

Ike and I waited in silence.

Deena's eyes brimmed with tears. Her lips quivered. "That bitch stole my money."

~*~

"We have a solid case against Deena," Ike said with some heat. We'd questioned Deena until Ike and I were fried. Deena had gone into a cell and we'd retreated to Ike's office for ham sandwiches, courtesy of Alice Ann.

"She's lying, but her story could be true," I asserted. "Deena sounded pissed about the missing money."

Ike laughed. "That was the only thing I believed coming out of her mouth."

I allowed the silence to settle around us before I spoke. "What about Marge Nash?"

"The Mobile cops will question her, and I'll call the gun club back and ask about Helen's shooting ability."

"You could ask Sonny to tell you the truth."

Ike nodded. "Thought of that one myself. Wait here while I get the other inquiries going and move Sonny."

Absently, I touched my temple with my good hand. "Sure."

"Is this too much for you?" Ike asked.

"I'm fine. Just habit to rub there." I paced the office until he returned. This was a love triangle gone wrong, that much was certain.

When I entered the interview room with Ike, Sonny's head reared back. "Hell. I was right. The bitch *is* here."

Ike slid into the chair beside me. "Who's here?"

His gaze went from my face to my sling and back to Ike. "Sorry about your girlfriend." Sonny hung his head. "You can't force me go back to her."

"Tell us about your wife," I said.

"She's a cancer," Sonny muttered.

"Who?" Ike prompted.

"Helen." Sonny sounded rattlesnake mean. "I hate her."

"Helen's your legal wife, not Deena," Ike said.

"Deena may be an alley cat, but she's devoted to me. Helen thought she owned me. When I realized my mistake, I told Helen I wanted a divorce. She said she'd kill me and Deena if I left her. Faking my death was the only way to get away from her, but she found us anyway."

"Have any proof?" Ike continued.

Since Sonny was talking just fine, I focused on listening. Sometimes you could tell as much from what a person didn't say.

"Yeah, that bartender guy, Starling. Deena got him to open up to her. Helen paid him to move here and spy on us, but he felt bad about it. He said he'd go to the cops with me, if I wanted. That's why we were pretending to be hunting. To think of a plan. But Helen shot him."

"Why didn't you tell me that before?"

"Because I'm safer in here, and once you figured out our identities, Deena would be safe in jail too. That was my plan."

"Your plan worked. You and Deena are in jail."

"And Helen's out there laughing her head off. She got her revenge. I bet she even sicced Ray Ray on you. He drove over here from Mobile and raised sand, right?"

"He did."

"Helen can move mountains, whether they want to move or not."

"Ray also told us about a woman named Louise that John was friendly with." Ike fixed him with a pointed glance. "You know who that is?"

Sonny's face flamed. "Deena's real name is Peggy Louise, Peggy Lou for short, but her mom called her Louise. Deena must've been messing with John to use that name with him."

"Did either of you know John when you lived in Alabama?"

"Nope. We met him here, at the bar, because Helen sent him here to spy on us."

We cycled through the questions twice more, but Sonny's story tracked every time. Ike had me wait in his office again while he moved the prisoner back to his cell.

"Well?" I asked when he returned. "You believe him?"

"Maybe, but we need proof."

"What about the other information you were checking out?"

"Let me access my messages." He checked voice mail first. "Gun club called. Helen was the crack shot, not Peggy Lou. According to the gun club, the instructor was disappointed in Peggy Lou's performance. Helen was accurate and precise."

The information energized me. "She could've framed Deena, Ike. Helen could be our shooter. Deena had no reason to shoot the bartender. Whereas, if the bartender crossed Helen, she would've had a motive."

"All we've got is conjecture."

Bailey disliked Helen on sight. My dog had good instincts. "What about Helen's friend Marge?"

Ike scanned his emails again. "She told Mobile deputies she'd passed through Danville around Valentine's Day. She didn't admit to recognizing anyone."

Helen's friend had been here. That was a fact. "What if Helen took both shots? After she shot me, she could've tipped Deena off, knowing she'd hide in the secret room. Helen waited until shift change and snuck inside Deena's place to plant the weapon and lock Deena in the bolt hole. That explains everything. If Helen's the mastermind behind this, and I believe she is, the pieces fall into place."

"You're brilliant. I'll put out an APB on Helen as a person of interest in our homicide. I wish I had a current photo of her. Nobody ever looks like their driver's license picture."

I dug through my purse for my phone, paged through a few screens, and flashed an image at Ike. "How'd you get that?" he asked.

I grinned for all I was worth. "While I was setting up my phone to record our chat this morning. Thought it would be good to have a picture of Helen for the paper."

"Send it to me. I'll put this photo in everyone's hands from here to Mobile. Helen Gray is a person of interest in a homicide. She's armed and dangerous."

"Now what?"

"Now we let the long arm of justice do its job."

"I don't want to look over my shoulder for the rest of my life. We need to find Helen."

"We'll get her tonight."

Chapter 17

Ike arranged for Alice Ann and Trent to stay at his mother's place overnight. Trent was excited about going to grandma's, Alice Ann less excited about keeping watch all night.

"What makes you think Helen will come tonight?" I asked as we got ready for bed. After today's roller coaster highs and lows, I could sleep for a week. My arm throbbed, but I didn't care. Catching Helen trumped taking a pain pill.

"Both Deena and Helen identified you as being smart. Helen's scheme is falling apart. We've got Sonny and Deena, and Helen is stuck in the county. She would've gone to ground as soon as she left the fish camp restaurant."

"You're paying a ton of overtime to keep those roadblocks staffed overnight."

"We can afford it. Applying pressure is something I understand well. Helen won't get away. My gut tells me she'll come tonight."

"We should've kept Bailey here for an early warning system."

"Trent needs Bailey. She won't let anyone sneak into my Mom's. I won't let anyone get to us. Now lay down and leave room for me. You hog the bed."

"I do not, Ike Harper, and you have some nerve calling me out when you steal all the covers."

"That's so you'll turn to me for warmth." He tapped his temple with a finger. "See? I'm smart, too. Like a fox."

"Lucky me. I've got a thing for foxes." I snuggled close, drowsing in the heat and comfort of his arms. The line from a hymn flitted through my head: *I once was lost but now I'm found.* And what I'd found was pretty darn amazing.

~*~

"Lindsey, hon, wake up," Ike whispered in my ear.

"What?" I spiraled out of a deep sleep to find him vibrating with urgency.

"Someone's in the house."

"You sure?"

"Certain. Remember the plan?"

"I got it." Pure adrenaline sluiced through my veins. The plan. While Ike went downstairs to neutralize the threat, I was supposed to hide in our bathroom. I touched his chest to make sure he wore his bulletproof vest. It was there.

I padded to the bathroom as requested. Once he left, I made a new plan and grabbed the aluminum bat from under our bed. I tiptoed down the hall to the moonlit stairs. Slowly, I descended to the ground floor, avoiding the steps that creaked.

I snuck behind Ike's recliner, crouched, and listened.

Suddenly I saw a flash of light in the kitchen, heard a startling kapow, and smelled sulfur. I ducked as recognition clicked. *That was a gun!* A thud followed. Someone got hit.

Please let Ike be safe.

If Ike shot the intruder, he'd have given the all-clear whistle. No whistle sounded. Which meant things were not good. My breath seemed air-hose loud. I tried to think positive. It didn't work.

Helen shot Ike.

He'd gone down.

Panic curled around my thoughts. I felt sick to my stomach. Ike had to be all right. He'd worn the vest.

But it was dark in the kitchen. How would she even know where to aim? What-ifs multiplied like bunnies in my thoughts. *She could've shot him in the arm or the head.*

I stuffed a fist in my mouth to hold the anguish inside. I had to be strong, for both of us. With Ike down, it was up to me to hold the line. If I didn't stop Helen, she'd get away with multiple murders.

She will kill you if you don't stop her.

A bat was no match for a handgun. Ike's gun safe was in our bedroom closet, upstairs, not that I knew how to shoot any of them. The only thing I had going for me was the element of surprise. She didn't expect me to be downstairs.

I had one chance to best her. One chance to knock her down with the bat. She was in my home, on my turf. Home field advantage counted for a lot in sports and during a home invasion.

A tiny beam pierced the darkness. Helen must have a flashlight. She'd quickly discover the bedrooms were upstairs. Blood rushed in my ears. Seconds dragged like hours.

The light neared. She'd turn for the steps, that's when I'd move. My ears hurt from listening so hard. Finally, I heard a rustle of fabric. The floorboard near the steps creaked. A sharp intake of breath sounded. The light winked out.

Go!

I launched, baseball bat raised like a hammer. Estimating where she had to be, I swung with all my might. Hit something solid. The bat fell from my hand.

I rammed my body into the intruder's.

We fell onto the steps, me on top, the intruder underneath. Someone screamed. The room lights flashed on. Ike towered over us, handgun pointed at the intruder's head.

The wiry person beneath me squirmed, bucked, and yelled. I held fast, determined to secure Helen.

Ike made a chopping motion. Something clattered to the floor. I glanced down. A pink gun. Ike kicked it out of the way, did something to his gun, and pulled me up.

"Shoot her if she moves," he said, thrusting his handgun in my hand and kneeling on Helen.

His weapon felt heavy and dangerous. If I moved wrong, I could accidentally shoot Ike. I poured all my attention into aiming at Helen. My hands trembled more than I liked.

Ike cuffed Helen and called to report the intrusion. "Help's on the way." He rose, secured Helen's weapon, and pried his gun from my hand. "Thought you were waiting in the bathroom."

"Couldn't. Not with your life at risk." I noted the gash on his head, the torn fabric of his vest. "You're okay?"

"Feels like I took a fastball to the ribs, but the vest protected me. Because I was moving, the impact knocked me down. I nicked my head on the counter. Took me a second to regroup, but you had things well in hand. Thanks for the backup, partner."

I basked in his praise. "Did you really expect me to shoot her?"

His lips twitched until a fleeting smile surfaced. "Not possible with the safety on."

~*~

"You people are making a big mistake," Helen said to Ike after he'd gotten her situated in the interview room. She jangled the handcuff attaching her wrist to a ring in the table.

"Tell us about John Starling," Ike prompted.

I sat beside him. He'd made me leave my phone in the office for this interview. It was going on four in the morning, and tomorrow was nearly here. Helen wouldn't have many good tomorrows. She'd spend her life in jail if she was lucky, get the death penalty if she wasn't.

An odd look came over Helen. Her gaunt skin turned orangey red like she'd been parboiled. "I don't know any John Starling."

"John Starling of Mobile, Alabama. The man you slept with instead of pining away for your allegedly dead husband. That John Starling. We know you know him. We have surveillance footage of the two of you at a restaurant here."

We had no such thing, unless Ike found it and didn't tell me. He must be bluffing. I crossed my fingers that Helen believed him.

"That's a lie. We always ate at John's place."

Gotcha.

Helen wasn't as smart as she thought.

"Was John your boyfriend?" Ike asked

"John was … a diversion. He wasn't Lowell by any means. But he helped me."

"With what?"

"Getting my revenge on Peggy Lou. She stole my man."

From what I'd seen of Sonny – or Lowell as she knew him – he was a wuss. Nothing going personality-wise. I didn't understand why these two women thought he was such hot stuff. Since Helen used Sonny and Deena's real names, it followed that Ike would do the same for the interview.

"Did you sacrifice John to frame Peggy Lou?" Ike asked

Helen surveyed us as if we were underlings. "John said he'd help me."

"He agreed to die for you?"

"I accepted his offer of help."

I schooled my features to hide my disgust. Shooting him with a sharpshooter rifle. Not even facing him with her deception. What a coward.

"But Lowell took the blame," Ike continued. "Your plan backfired, didn't it?"

"He tried to save John. When that didn't work, he fired both rifles, called the cops, and stayed in jail."

"Why did you spare Lowell?"

"He's mine, that's why."

"And Peggy Lou?"

"That bitch. I wish her hair would fall out, and her new boobs would explode."

I hoped my eyes didn't pop out of my head. Helen's nasty and spiteful voice took me back to adolescence. I'd run across my share of mean girls, but Helen was in a league of her own. She had the emotional maturity of a teen and the shooting skills of a survivalist. Clearly, she did not play well with others.

"Did you plan to kill her?" Ike prompted. "Is that why you locked her up out of sight?"

"She put herself in that hidey hole. I had no intention of going back for her. If you didn't find her, her death wasn't on me."

"She couldn't get out of there – because of you."

"No one will believe it."

Ike whipped out a flash drive. "Think again. Lowell had cameras all over that house. We have you cold."

Helen tried to jerk her hand free again. When that didn't work, she burst into tears. If Ike was bluffing, he got her good. If he had the video, Helen was doomed. I felt no sympathy for her. She'd shot me and killed a man. She'd shot Ike with lethal intent and tried to kill me a second time, but neither of us were easy to kill.

"You failed, Helen," I said, my voice quivering. "Lowell and Peggy Lou are free of you." Time for me to try a white lie of my own. "And we know it was you on the call directing me to the restaurant. Voice recognition software is amazing. Plus, we learned you have the marksmanship to pull off that sniper shot. Peggy Lou did not."

"You should be dead," Helen fumed. "If not for that stupid dog, you'd be gone, and Peggy Lou would've been declared the killer. You ruined everything."

Ike's phone buzzed. He glanced at the text and smiled. "Give it up, Helen. We found the money in your car."

Helen pounded on the table with her free fist. "That's my money.

They stole it from me."

"It's the insurance company's money, and they want it back."

She jerked against the restraint and started screaming. "It's my money. Nobody else can have it. It's mine."

"You won't need any money where you're going," Ike said, rising. He motioned me to follow. "We're done here."

Ike and I beat a hasty retreat. The crowd of deputies emerged from the viewing room and clapped Ike on the back. He accepted their praise and held me close. I couldn't stop trembling. "It's over," Ike murmured in my ear. "She'll never hurt you again."

Chapter 18

By the time Sunday evening rolled around, I felt nearly a hundred percent. No more headaches and only a twinge in my arm if I moved the wrong way and pulled the stitches. Our family get together was well attended and Ike wowed everyone with his cooking.

My entire family surrounded me, bellies full of Low Country Boil and elated by Cousin Janey's engagement announcement. Even Junior Curtis, Janey's beau, was beaming. I was thrilled for both of them. Janey looked so radiant, Junior looked like he'd won the lottery.

"Janey's getting the man of her dreams," I whispered to Ike when we had a moment alone. I leaned in to him, tired, but in a good way. As his arms held me close, his scent filled my head and all was right in my world. I wanted this day to never end. I'd never thought to feel so connected to my family and friends.

Ike released me and then caught my shoulders as I stepped away. His eyes locked with mine. Something burned deep in those eyes. Intent, maybe. Whatever he was about to say mattered a great deal to him.

"What about the man of your dreams?" he asked in a loud voice.

I couldn't breathe. The silence rang. It clanged. It echoed. I couldn't fathom the meaning of his question.

Me, the person who excelled at reading between the lines. I had nothing. Not even conjecture. We were together. He knew it, and I knew it. Why would he pose this personal question in front of our entire families?

Finally, I found my breath and my voice. "Ike? What's going on?"

"Son," Ike said over his shoulder, "it's time."

Trent walked up to me, solemnly holding Bailey's leash. My dog wore a brand new red collar, and something sparkly was tied to it with a pink ribbon. I dared not hope or dream. I couldn't fathom where this was going. My nerves scattered to the four corners of the earth.

"Ike?"

He bent down on one knee beside Trent and Bailey and snagged my hand. "Would you do me the honor of marrying us?"

What on earth? A marriage proposal? I tugged on his arm, my cheeks flaming. "You don't have to do this. I know how you feel about marriage."

"This is important. We're in *life* together, Linds. I want to make this official. On the books, so that everyone knows you're mine and I'm yours. So I'm never excluded from your hospital room again, nor you from mine. What do you say?"

Through teary eyes, I glanced at him. "Yes." My voice cracked and came out breathy. I cleared my throat and tried again. "My answer is yes."

Trent untied the ribbon on the collar and handed Ike something. A ring. The narrow band was white gold with twisted strands supporting the stone. The diamond flashed and sparkled as it slid on my finger.

A perfect fit, just like Ike.

"You like?" Ike asked.

I pulled him into a one-armed embrace. "I love it, and I love you and Trent and Bailey."

Trent jumped up and down and Bailey barked. "We're getting married," Trent boomed. Ike kissed me while our family cheered. Junior Curtis came up afterward and clapped him on the back. "Welcome to the family, dude."

"I got here first," Ike said, holding me like I was a precious gem.

"This isn't a competition," I said.

"It sure isn't," Janey said. "We've been talking to Ike about a double wedding. You in?"

I eyed the crowd. "Everyone knew he would propose tonight?"

"They did. It's the worst kept secret in town," Janey added. She leaned in. "But I might beat you in the baby race. We've been trying ever since Junior proposed."

My head swirled again, and heat radiated from my core. Engagements. Marriage. Ike and I had never talked about having children. It was scary and terrifying and wonderful.

"Double wedding, yes or no?" Ike asked.

"Yes," I somehow managed.

"Good. That's settled."

Alice Ann circulated with champagne for the adults, sparkling cider for the kids. Ike cinched one hand around my waist as we toasted our happiness.

He must've noticed I was overwhelmed because he whispered in my ear. "It'll be okay. I promise. Don't you trust me?"

"I do."

Ike flashed a mischievous grin. "That's my girl."

--The End--

About the Author

Southern author Maggie Toussaint writes mystery, suspense, and dystopian fiction. Her work won the Silver Falchion Award for best mystery, the Readers' Choice Award, and the EPIC Award. Under her name and her pen name of Rigel Carson, she's published sixteen novels as well as several short stories and novellas. The next book in her paranormal mystery series, *Confound It*, releases June 2018. Maggie serves as Chapter President for Southeast Mystery Writers of America and as Vice-President for Low Country Sisters In Crime.

Connect with Maggie at the following sites:

Email   maggie@maggietoussaint.com

Website   https://www.maggietoussaint.com

Blog   http://www.mudpiesandmagnolias.blogspot.com

Facebook   http://www.facebook.com/MaggieToussaintAuthor

Pinterest   http://www.pinterest.com/MaggieToussaint

Twitter   http://www.twitter.com/MaggieToussaint

Newsletter sign up at my website.

More Books by Maggie Toussaint

Thanks for reading my Lindsey & Ike Romantic Mystery novella series. I hope you'll try my other series and standalone books.

Cleopatra Jones Mystery series
In for a Penny, book 1
On the Nickel, book 2
Dime If I Know, book 3
No Quarter (novella), book 4

Dreamwalker Mystery series
Gone and Done It, book 1
Bubba Done It, book 2
Doggone It, book 3
Dadgummit, book 4
Confound It, Book 5

Lindsey & Ike Romantic Mystery Novella series
"Really, Truly Dead," novella 1
"Turtle Tribbles," novella 2
"Dead Men Tell No Tales," novella 3

Single Title Mysteries
Death, Island Style
Murder in the Buff

Mossy Bog Romantic Suspense series
Muddy Waters, book 1
Hot Water, book 2
Rough Waters, book 3

Single Title Romantic Suspense
House of Lies
No Second Chance
Seeing Red

The Guardian of Earth series
G-1 (writing as Rigel Carson), book 1
G-2 (writing as Rigel Carson), book 2
G-3 (writing as Rigel Carson), book 3

Short Stories
"High Noon at Dollar Central"

Cookbook
KP Authors Cook Their Books